For Jurgen and Irene Diederichsen
Friends in fair and foul weather

MONKSHOOD

MONKSHOOD

Hugh McLeave

ROBERT HALE · LONDON

© Hugh McLeave 2007
First published in Great Britain 2007

ISBN 978-0-7090-8426-6

Robert Hale Limited
Clerkenwell House
Clerkenwell Green
London EC1R 0HT

www.halebooks.com

2 4 6 8 10 9 7 5 3 1

Typeset in 10½/14pt Century Schoolbook
Printed and bound in Great Britain by
Biddles Limited, King's Lynn

chapter one

On guard is the position of readiness for offence and defence. The fencer salutes her opponent by raising her weapon, striking down as she puts on her mask, moves the right foot forward, bends her knees and remains poised for action.

It was the last thing Aileen expected to see in the prison, but there they were, three dogs cavorting round Calum Weir on the lawn in front of the sports field while he fed them titbits from his pocket. In her astonishment she broke stride and the assistant governor halted beside her, wondering if she had suddenly taken fright at the sight of the double murderer she had come to interview and wanted to call off the meeting.

'No, it's the dogs that threw me,' she got out, pointing to the three terriers, a Welsh Terrier, a Yorkie and a West Highland.

He shrugged and flashed badly capped teeth at her. 'Calum has that effect on all animals, human and otherwise. He just has to look at them. There's nothing we can do about it – they chose him as their friend, and even that traitor of a Welsh Terrier who belongs to me wouldn't think twice of dropping my wife and me for him. Like us, the dogs trust him.'

That astonished her, too, their attitude to a man serving a life sentence. However, she had already guessed they must have faith in Calum Weir, for they had not even bothered to search her or her handbag when they let her in through the front door or in the admin building.

As they approached, the Welsh Terrier turned and snapped at the whisky dog and the Yorkie started yapping. Weir picked up the big terrier, one-handed, by the loose flesh on the back of its neck, cupped his other hand over its ear and whispered something which set it howling like a banshee. Abruptly he dropped it and it slunk away.

Ogilvie, the assistant governor, introduced them and ordered Weir gently to look after her. He glanced at his watch, murmuring that he would give them half an hour more than the sixty regulation minutes and would then come and fetch her. They watched him cross the field and disappear into a cell block.

'Time – that's what life's all about,' Weir murmured almost to himself, then turned to look her up and down. Even in the few seconds he scrutinized her, she realized the truth of what Ogilvie had said. Nobody had ever looked at her with that hard intensity.

'So, you're the Aileen Seaton who's been badgering me to talk to her,' he said. 'If they'd told me you were young and well set up as well as bright I might have given in sooner.'

'Oh, I'm not so young or so bright. And as for my set-up, that depends on who's looking, don't they say?'

'Ay, you're right.' She caught Weir looking at her with a question in his expression. 'But I gave in because I wondered what you'd look like.'

'What do you mean?'

'Well, I had seen you before, but not so as I would recognize you.'

'You mean fencing?'

'I used to watch it on the box, but you don't get much of an idea of anybody wearing all that kit and a face guard as well.'

'It's seven years since I hung up my foil, so I've changed a bit,' Aileen said.

'Not as much as me in that time.'

Aileen had, in fact, fenced for Scotland several times when she was at university and afterwards when reading law; she had represented the country in one Olympic Games, and had won several trophies at the sport. Although she had stopped competitive fencing, she still kept her hand in at the local association and carried a foil and an épée and her fencing gear in the back of her Rover.

She thanked him for agreeing to the visit. She did not confess that she'd come here in trepidation, wondering how she would react to a man guilty of a horrible double murder, who had spent five years behind bars; she wondered, too, if she could meet him without being overawed by someone who had done so much and written so many books.

While she was explaining, not very eloquently, some of her reasons for writing to him to ask for this interview, she was trying to size him up, trying to compare the man before her, not only with the dozens of pictures on his book jackets and in the newspaper files but with the stories and biographies he had written and the account of his trial.

'Well, what do you think?' he said, cutting across her small-talk. 'Do I look anything like me?'

His question tilted her, for she felt he had grasped the thought in her mind. In fact, she discovered to her embarrassment she had been staring at him as though mesmerized. She had started by trying to remember which of his grey-blue eyes was made of coloured glass. She knew he had lost an eye and part of his cheek-bone when he got in the way of a stray bullet during a riot on an assignment in the Yemen.

But the eyes were so well matched and the flesh round its socket had been so well sculpted it took her several seconds to decide it was the left eye; and that only because the skin round the good eye puckered while the plastic surgery skin had remained smooth. Also, half his eyebrow had never grown back.

Without being aware, she must have been gazing at his face, trying to decipher why, in a curious way, it looked so much more interesting than the photographs and descriptions she had seen in the newspaper archives. She knew his nose had changed, having been broken in his youth when he boxed as a sparring partner for young professionals in Brady's Gym.

'Well, what do you think?'

He was still eyeing her and it was unsettling, that intuitive look and that right eye, which might have detected that morning's run in her right stocking without her turning round. She hesitated in case she said something out of turn.

'Yes, you do look like you,' she said, finally. Then to deflect another question, she pointed to the dog. 'What happened to him? What did you say that set him howling?'

'His name's Rory. The whisky dog's Meg and the Yorkie's Sami. They're the head warder's and the governor's. For Rory, I have a different threat each time, but he always believes me.' Weir bent down to run his hand over the rough Welsh Terrier coat. 'When he plays up, I warn him he's heading for the vivisection room or cancer research or, worse still, a lab study into what makes dogs devour WowWow or the other tinned crap which pays for much of the cultural crap they feed us humans on the telly.'

Weir said all this in a dry, matter-of-fact tone which might have sounded cynical or tongue in cheek, but didn't.

'Rory knows you wouldn't do any of those things?'

'He doesn't know that. Dogs don't tell lies and don't expect us to give them anything but what passes for our truth.'

'Then he'll be unhappy.'

'He's an outsize ego, he's a nuisance and he gives me a guilt complex. He's pissed on my leg several times, to make it his territory and exclude Meg and Sami, he's always sniffing round me to see if I've been with another dog he doesn't know or having whisky or chocolate without cutting him in on it.'

'What about her?' she said, indicating the whisky dog. Meg was sitting on her rump, front paws planted firmly on the grass, head tilted quizzically to one side, eyes intently following Weir's every gesture.

'Ah, her! I've yet to hear her bark. Either she knows too much or knows nothing, and she's too bright ever to tell you which.' Weir bent down to fondle her and a wet tongue lapped his hand. 'She's a good listener and not a bad critic. She never utters when I read her my latest rubbish or give her my views on everything from warnings about the addictive adjuncts to dog food to the empiric philosophers and the reasoning behind Kant's demolition of Descartes' proof of God's existence.'

'And you think she understands all this philosophy?'

'Who's to say she doesn't?'

Weir gave her that lop-sided grin then pointed to the Yorkie.

'Now Sami, he takes each moment as it comes and enjoys things. He lets tomorrow take care of itself and he'll never learn that life's a serious business, thank God. He'd love to come and share my cell if I'd let him.'

'Wouldn't he think he was a prisoner?'

'Dogs don't bother about concepts like liberty or guilt. They value love and companionship.' He stroked Sami's muzzle and moustaches. 'Sami thinks man's greatest invention is chocolate and he doesn't give a damn how much whisky I have. I wish I was like him.'

'Whisky?' she queried. 'Can they smuggle you in whisky to one of Her Majesty's prisons?'

'Here, you can get anything if you have the money and the contacts. But even here they have a job getting me the Macallan.'

'Is that the whisky you like drinking?'

'Ay.' He nodded. 'Oh, not for its taste though it's about the best there is ... just for its anaesthetic, hallucinatory, mood-elevating and problem-dissolving properties. And one other reason, it helped to kill Kingsley Amis and anything that did that can't be too bad, don't you think?'

'Do writers always make back-biting remarks about other writers?' she said, and could have bitten her tongue. She had forgotten that Ross Kanaday, whom Weir had been convicted of murdering, was also a writer and a rival of the man at whom she was throwing the question.

'Not all of them,' he replied, looking at her with a wry smile. 'Not those who share a publisher, or those that expect a rave notice in return. But I expect the law game's the same.'

He had a low voice with a Scottish burr but he phrased his talk like a writer who realized the weight and meaning and placement of words. She had to admit his conversation slightly wrong-footed her. When he saw she did not rise to his back-biting comments about Macallan whisky, Kingsley Amis, writers and the law, he shrugged then called the dogs to heel. It was time for their afternoon walk and would she like to join them and have a look at Creeburn, the finest open prison in the Southern Uplands with a view of Sassenach country, the auld enemy, across the Solway Firth? She nodded and fell into step with him.

They were ice-breaking, both of them. To keep off the subject that had brought her here. But when she caught him looking at her, his eye had a twinkle and he seemed to be amused by something. It was difficult to believe she was walking in prison grounds with a man who was serving a life sentence for murdering his wife and her lover, killing them with such deliberate brutality that their faces were unrecognizable.

While they walked, she cast a glance round the prison buildings, the high walls, the fences. Several of the prisoners were wandering round, half a dozen were working in the kitchen garden and about the same number in the flower garden on the edge of the prison grounds. Behind a high grille, two teams had started playing serious football and Weir commented that a visiting team had come in from another open prison in England. 'They arrive to Scotland to learn the game at its source,' he said with that grin that creased the flesh round his good eye and gave his face a quizzical look.

She felt she had to thank him for letting her visit him. He shrugged. 'I got fed up not answering your calls and tearing up your letters. But let's be frank, I don't want to make a habit of it. Once is enough.'

'Was that the only reason – that I was badgering you?'

'Maybe ay, and maybe och ay,' he said, then went silent, leaving her wondering what else might have persuaded him to break his silence and invite her to visit him.

From that remark and other hints, Aileen observed Weir's tone had changed and she realized how warily she'd have to tread to keep this man's confidence. From her own colleagues in the law practice and from people who had known Weir, she had learned that he never had more than one or two visits a year – and those he granted reluctantly.

'How long have you been here?'

'In stir, as they say. Five years – four years, eleven months and five days to be precise. Here, in this home from home, four years.'

'It's a long time out of one life.'

'Time's a man-made thing, just something we use to measure the little bitty run we're given. At one time I counted my life by the second hand of my quartz watch. Here, I go by the slant of the sun on yonder hills and take the days as they come.'

'But it's long, a life sentence....'

Weir was bending to stroke the muzzle and throat of the Welsh terrier and did not look up. He said, softly: 'Well, we all do a life sentence one way or another. I'm doing quite a bit of mine here, that's all.'

Observing the way he looked at the dog and fondled him, she remembered this man had shot his own dog, Appin, when he murdered his wife and her lover. Would the Weir she was watching caress Rory really have done that? As she looked, he picked up a stick at his feet and threw it, backhanded, for the three dogs to run and retrieve. Sami, the Yorkie, snatched the stick from under the nose of the Welsh Terrier and hared off with it until the bigger dog bowled him over with a paw, seized the stick and brought it back. Weir had a tug-of-war with him to recover and toss the stick. He called over his shoulder:

'Anyway, it's not so bad here ... a big advance on Barlinnie with its Glasgow yobs, its sadistic screws, its perverts, its junkies, its stinking food. And this is paradise compared with that hell-hole psychiatric prison they put me in at first. You've heard about the man they asked why he was banging his head against the wall. Because, he said, it's great when you stop. That's how I felt getting away from the sick-tricyclists' prison and hearing Barlinnie's wooden portcullis slam behind me. Just watching those criminal loonies wandering round the grounds of the madhouse was enough to make you join them.' He looked at her with that lop-sided grin. 'You've seen Jackson Pollock action paintings, a crazy, unfathomable skein of coloured drips. Well, that's the pattern those demented characters were tracing on the lawns when they weren't trying to rape, strangle or knife each other or me.'

Weir spoke like a book, but then she knew he had educated himself largely through books that he read in the reading room of the Mitchell Library or borrowed. He never had money to acquire them. He was a writer who knew how to choose and arrange words to fit his perceptions.

Aileen put time and space between her last and her next question, realizing Weir was talking about the time in his psychiatric prison that he had hoarded the tranquillizers and sleeping pills the doctors had prescribed and how he had swallowed a good fistful to kill himself. Had he not been a top-security risk and under strict surveillance every fifteen minutes, they would never have caught him in time to pump the drugs out of his system and connect him to a dialysis machine and wrench him out of his death coma.

'But you'd rather be on the other side of those walls and that barbed wire, wouldn't you?'

For a fraction of a second he hesitated. But it was enough to encourage her; to make her feel the weeks of her own time she had spent on him, and the coaxing she had done to get herself here, were not wasted.

'No, I can manage without that lot out there in the wider zoo.' He pointed beyond the wall bordering the country road. 'I consider I'm lucky. Fifty years ago I'd have taken the eight o'clock walk and the long drop in Barlinnie or Peterhead. Here, I have my own room, three meals a day and no worries. I can even do a bit of scribbling and daubing when the screws are looking the other way.' He looked fondly at the three dogs. 'What would Rory, Meg and Sami do without me – and more to the point, what would I do without them? I promised them we'd go out together when our time came.'

Aileen glanced at him, wondering if Weir was talking tongue in cheek, but his face had a serious set and his voice no tinge of irony. She wondered if she had not come on a fool's errand.

They walked to the cell block where Weir was serving his time. Inside the building, they met several men who hailed him. As they passed one of these prisoners, he suddenly turned and let go at her with a two-tone whistle. A few moments later, another stopped them and nudged him and said, 'Hey, Cal, who's the popsie?'

'See?' Weir said, grinning at her. 'That's three beholders with beauty in their eye, who agree about you.'

She let his remark go, but nevertheless felt flattered. He pointed out the common room where the prisoners watched TV and the odd film. Then the library where he worked for several hours a day, cataloguing and issuing books to the prisoners. It impressed her that these modern cells had toilets with a shower for every half dozen. There was a gym where prisoners could exercise and play basketball and volleyball.

Weir's own cell had a window looking out over the open area and the sports ground; it had several books on shelves, pencils and paper and a transistor radio. To her surprise, she saw he had a laptop computer on a side table. 'It's to keep a catalogue of the library books but I also do a bit of quiet, illicit scribbling on the side,' he said, then hoisted his shoulders. 'It's a drug like coke – anyway, writers are like kings, popes and Egyptian donkeys, they live and die in harness.'

Weir explained that he also did a lot of paperwork for prisoners who had complaints to make about the service, who wanted to apply for parole, who had litigation with the director of the Prison Service, who wanted to contact the ombudsman. He also helped quite a few prisoners with their personal problems.

'No ashtray,' she commented.

'No. I used to smoke, but in Barlinnie the snout barons and the screws wanted too much in cash or favours for their wares so I gave up. It doesn't bother me.'

She pointed to the bookshelves. 'You don't have any of your own books, then?'

He shook his head. 'A book's like some illness you catch – whooping cough, measles, flu. You throw it off and once it's out of your system you don't want it back. That's how I feel about my books.'

'You haven't asked why I've come.'

'I was waiting for you to tell me.'

'I had the idea of writing your life or doing a book on the Weir case.'

Weir shook his head slowly, stopped, looked at her hard with that curious flecked eye then laughed. 'My life's not worth a damn and not worth wasting your time on. It hadn't much of a beginning, the middle bit wound up here – and what do you have for an end?'

'But the books and poems and your newspaper work....'

'Nobody's interested, apart from the people who've read about the murders.'

'All right, take the murders. How would you react if I said I thought you weren't guilty of murdering your wife and her lover?'

'Everybody in this prison thinks he's innocent and for the governor everybody here is guilty as charged.'

'What would you say if I applied for a retrial on new evidence?'

'I would say you were wasting your time, and mine.'

'And if I went ahead....'

'They would stage a rerun of the first trial and out of bloody-mindedness perhaps stick me with a few more years than the twenty I'm doing now.'

He held his cell door open for her, then locked it behind them as though to close off that line of conversation. They walked in silence down the long corridor enfilading the cells on either side. Now, she realized it smelled of disinfectant, stale air, the odour of male bodies and some sort of stew emanating from the prison kitchen.

Ogilvie, the assistant governor, was waiting outside for them. But before he collected her, she had time to whisper to Weir:

'Did you hear on your transistor Dan Meney had died in an accident?'

'Ay, I did.'

His voice had dropped to the point where the three words were almost inaudible.

Aileen had the impression that Calum Weir had some secret that he would divulge to no one, some reason for making every excuse to avoid a retrial of his case and to remain in that prison until the end of his term or even the end of his life.

As she drove back to Glasgow she could remember his face vividly and replay everything he had said in that low, burring voice. She could recall minutely how his reddish-fair hair sprouted from his temples and grew thick on the root phalanges of his fingers; she could see that good eye of his and wonder why the prosthetist who had done it so brilliantly had not added the final touch of placing those myriad tiny flecks in the blue iris, like the sighted eye; she could remember the deep cleft in his upper lip and the tracery of blood vessels round his bad eye. Remembrance of the dogs cavorting round him gave her a warm feeling. She could understand their attitude to him.

For she felt the same way. Why had her mind's eye filled with so much detail about Calum Weir? Why did she know his face, his hands, his gestures and his voice so much clearer than she had ever known her husband's even after six years of marriage?

Was it because what he had written had impressed her, or just his presence? She did not know. But one thing she did know – somehow she would secure Calum Weir's release from prison. Even if he was as guilty as Brutus or Bluebeard she would fight to free him.

It was naïve and visceral, it was primitive and irrational, but somehow she felt that fate had made that appointment just over two weeks ago with a man called Dan Meney.

Perhaps even more stupid and illogical, she felt her own fate and that of Calum Weir were bound together. And somehow she had to free him not only from his physical prison, but the prison of his own making.

Weir stood watching her walk to her car in the compound the other side of the high wire fence. It fascinated him how she still moved like the champion fencer, quickly, precisely; she had the fluid, natural grace of a cat. He stifled the question in his mind about how it would be to make love to her. A futile thought for someone who had a double murder on his sheet and owed society at least another seven years with good conduct.

But he could not remember when he'd experienced the same yearning about a woman. Not for more than five years. What was it about her? That relaxed, loose-jointed way she carried herself? Or the way her fair hair was sculpted to the oval shape of her face and head with blonde streaks in it? Was it the toss or tilt of her head? Or some gesture?

Weir could not put his finger on it. He knew he wanted to see her again, even though he realized how dangerous that might be for him. And for her.

He waited until she had turned her Rover round and made for the car park entrance. As she looked and spotted him, she lowered the window, waved then made a V with two fingers. He raised a hand in response. He waited until she had disappeared over the hill in the direction of Dumfries and the Glasgow road before walking back to his cell.

Why hadn't she told him about Dan Meney until just before she was leaving? And more to the point, what had that drunken junkie told her? Why did this woman seem so sure he was innocent when he did not know himself whether he had murdered the blue-blooded bitch he'd married and that hack, Kanaday, latest in the long line of those she was having it off with?

For he had no recollection of what had happened in those thirty minutes after he found his wife and Kanaday in his bedroom. He remembered some things, like the call that had brought him to the mansion in Langside; he could still see himself parking the car outside the front portico and the rain beating on the windscreen; he recalled wondering where Joseph the manservant was when no one answered the door; he dimly recollected mounting to the bedroom on the first floor and seeing them in bed.

He remembered his rage and he remembered one thought: he meant to kill them.

Then nothing.

For months those thirty amnesiac minutes had tortured him as he ransacked his brain to try and come up with something from that void; he tried word association; he challenged it with questions, knowing that the brain only answers the questions you pose it and worries over unanswered questions until it finds the answer. Or drives you mad. His dialogue with himself ran something like this:

Did I run back to the car and get my Beretta pistol and the jack handle? Did I come and shoot them then bludgeon them to death and after that mutilate their faces with a broken champagne bottle?

Which one did I shoot first – my whore of a wife or that shabby lover she took?

Did I announce I was going to shoot them?

Were they scared? Did they say anything before they died?

Why can't I remember emptying the whole magazine into them?

What did I do after I shot them?

They say I bludgeoned them over the head with the jack handle twenty-seven times then broke the empty champagne bottle over the marble mantelpiece and thrust the ragged and razor-sharp ends into their faces until they were unrecognizable.

Surely that I should have remembered.

But his brain had not resolved all those questions; and the fact he remembered nothing preyed on his mind to the point that he convinced himself and people around him, including his lawyer, that he was going mad. They needed no further proof when he had hoarded the sedatives in the psychiatric prison and swallowed enough to kill himself.

He and his defence lawyers might have pleaded diminished responsibility, but he had a horror of withering his life away in a prison for the criminally insane. He confessed to the crime and was given a life sentence, which meant twenty years.

And when they finally released him from the psychiatric hospital and the Glasgow prison and transferred him to the open prison in the southern counties, Weir came to terms with himself. He admitted his guilt. He had suffered some form of brainstorm and brutally and sadistically murdered his wife and her lover.

And now this young woman lawyer was trying to open those cerebral wounds that he thought had scarred over.

When she had written to him asking to come and visit him to talk about the book she was writing about the Weir case, he decided not to answer her letters. However, her references to the case and the trial triggered memories that he thought had vanished. He began to dream strange surrealistic dreams and nightmares which woke him in the dark, shivering. Sometimes in dreams he would see those mashed and bloody faces before the police handcuffed him and let him from that grisly bedroom in Creggan House.

He would also wake with names in his mind that meant nothing to him – although he was aware that the brain never invented memories. They were there, perhaps repressed, perhaps dormant, perhaps just waiting for the right moment to outcrop.

Who was the German, Helmuth Wolfgarten, for instance? A name that had erupted in his dreams several times. He scoured his mind; he hunted through what papers he had, he tried it on the books he had read; he keyed it into his notebook computer. Nothing. If it had existed and was attached to some experience, it now seemed lost in the darker catacombs of the mind.

Yet, he knew that this name signified something. If it didn't why did it appear in flaring red block letters, or patterned in reds, blues, yellows? It was shouting something at him.

Another recurrent dream was seeing Lorna, his murdered wife, looking as she had when he fell for her – beautiful. She was dressed like a bride in white and carrying a bouquet of flowers, clusters of yellow and blue flowers, their colours mingling and glowing against Lorna's breast. Then she offered them to him. And as he put out a hand to accept them they turned to dust, which enveloped and choked both him and his wife.

He had yet another dream so full of horror he dreaded going to bed and having to confront it. It had birds that blinded him, dogs that tore out his heart and devoured it in front of him while a dark human silhouette forced him to drink from a chalice in which something like dead fingers were sizzling. They were poisoned.

They frightened Weir, those dreams, made him feel he was really going mad. They must mean something, those nightmares; yet they defied any attempt to compare them with his memory and baffled his intuitive ability to solve puzzles.

That evening when he had given Sami, Rory and Meg their walk and was back in his cell, he wrote to Aileen Seaton at the address she had given him. He told her to drop any idea of doing a book either on the Weir case or on himself. She should disregard whatever Dan Meney might have told her. Although he could not stop her from writing either his life or the story of the case, he could not give her any co-operation or agree to any more visits.

He decided to wait a day before giving the letter to Ogilvie, the assistant governor, to post.

But two days later he found the letter in his table drawer. Was his subconscious mind, or fate, dictating that he should not post the letter but tear it up? He had the urge to do just that. Then he thought: Why cut himself off from the only person he had met in five years who was interesting, intelligent and pretty? Why not let her go ahead and write her book? Who knew? She might find something like the truth about the case. And help him to find himself.

When he reflected, she had already disturbed the tranquil routine he had built up here, had made him realize there was a world beyond these walls. But she might reopen all his old wounds. And what if her truths proved too much for him to bear?

He handed the letter to the head warder asking him to put it through the prison post.

chapter two

In the March, the fencer pushes one foot forward, then brings the rear foot level thus resuming her position before the March.

Aileen had never heard of Dan Meney until one day two months before meeting Calum Weir in prison. That day she had gone to Brodick on the Isle of Arran to take evidence in a negligence suit she was conducting for a patient against one of the clinics on the island in the Firth of Clyde. She had meant to catch the return boat just after noon, but was delayed by an abrasive, argumentative clinic administrator. Then, halfway across the firth, there was another hold-up when the *Glen Sannox* had to heave to and pick up three people in a dinghy that had broken its mast and was drifting. Was this one of many other days she had known when inanimate things seemed to conspire against her with dumb hostility? What else could happen? Aileen had the bizarre feeling something or someone was pulling the strings.

Although it was six o'clock when she recovered her Rover in the car park at Ardrossan and she still had twenty miles to drive to Glasgow, it seemed such a lovely evening, she decided to take the country road across the Dalry Hills. At that hour the long evening sunlight and the sea mirrored in the blue sky had thrown that rolling landscape into relief. Its green hills stippled with woods, its farmhouses and hamlets, even the Ayrshire cattle, looked to be painted in stark colours with a palette knife. It was beautiful, breathtaking. She drove slowly, savouring the view and refusing to hasten after the Rover's long shadow thrown by the evening sun.

She had just emerged from the high bank beyond the first small reservoir when she noticed a car approaching and travelling fast along the Dalry Road between the hedges. Even half a mile away, on the hill the other side of the reservoir, she could see it wobble, then shimmy from one side of the road to the other.

To Aileen, the car looked out of control and she eased her foot off the accelerator to watch it slewing from one side of the country road to the other. Was the driver drunk, or ill? She wondered if he would take the straight road to West Kilbride or turn left and come towards her.

As she observed the car, it suddenly veered left, struck something, overturned and plunged over the bank into the Munnoch Reservoir. It all happened in less than a minute. But curiously, she seemed to perceive the whole event in slow motion, as though time was standing still. However, on reflection she imagined her own mind might have seized up with the horror of the scene.

When she realized what had happened, Aileen pulled herself together and accelerated to where the car had left the road. She ran the Rover on to the grass verge and left it there. Slithering down the bank, she kicked off her shoes and felt her way into the water towards where the car had sunk. Her stockinged feet buried themselves in the silt and mud of the reservoir and she had to pull them out and advance step by step until she reached the car.

Somehow it had righted itself and was sitting tilted to the driver's side. But she could see it was still sinking. In a few minutes, the car might slip down the muddy bank into the deeper part of the reservoir.

With the water up to her waist and her feet giving under her, Aileen managed to grasp the rear wheel of the car and steady herself. She groped along the body to the door handle on the driver's side. It took all her strength to lever the door open against the pressure of water, then hold it open. As the door gave, the figure behind the wheel slid down his seat and collapsed on her. His head and face were covered with blood and she saw he had smashed his head against the windscreen, breaking the glass. He was groaning in agony. Only his seatbelt prevented him from falling out of the car into the water.

Aileen reached across the unconscious figure and unclipped his seatbelt, holding him by his jacket collar as she did. As she released the belt, the man floated out. She grasped him under the armpits and inched her way backwards up the slope until she reached the bank. Pulling him on to the bank, she stretched him out then ran back to her car to find her mobile phone and dial the police and ambulance services in Largs and Ardrossan to tell them what had happened and ask them to send help urgently.

In her car boot she found a blanket and draped this over the inert figure. Those head injuries looked lethal and the man showed little sign of regaining consciousness. Dipping the dish-cloth from her picnic basket in the water, she began sponging his face and head. Blood was still welling from his scalp and fore-head. She had a flask of whisky in the car and went to fetch this, thinking it might pull him round if she could feed it to him.

When she returned he had opened his eyes. They were wide and unfocused. For some reason, she noted he had little black flecks orbiting the pupils, which were dilated. He was staring at her. His eyes had fear in them.

'Where am I at and who're you?' he said in a hoarse whisper.

'My name's Seaton ... Aileen Seaton ... I'm a lawyer. You've had an accident.'

For a long moment, he thought about that statement, still fixing her with that frightened stare.

'Ay, an accident ...' he croaked. 'An accident, that's it ... an accident.'

'You'll be all right,' she said. 'An ambulance is on the way.' She uncorked the whisky bottle and held it to his lips, but he clamped his mouth shut as though refusing the liquor.

'Never mind that ... now hear what ah say ... my name's Meney ... Dan Meney. Now listen to me....' He paused and sucked in a deep breath and moaned with the pain it provoked. Those strange eyes with their wide pupils and orbiting flecks told her he was in shock and felt scared. She had to bend over him to catch what he said. It came in slow phrases. 'Should hae done it a long time ago.... Life's a bastard, is it no'?.... Meant to do myself in.... I didn't hae the guts.... Listen, lady ... something I've got to say ... afore ah go ... something serious, like.... You ever hear tell o' Calum Weir?'

'A writer, isn't he?'

'Ay ... himself ... a great man ... a champion writer....' Once more he drew breath, slowly, painfully, then grimaced and paused while his bloodshot eyes peered at her. 'Calum ... great man ... great buddy ... he's in jail for murder ... never did it....'

'You mean he's innocent.'

'Ay ... others did it.'

'Who are the others?'

'See Ca ... he'll maybe know ... but he'll no' tell you ... but get him ... to tell you.' Again, he sucked in breath and paused. 'And lady ... tell Cal to forgive me ... Dan Meney ... for whit I did.'

Meney had shut his eyes and when she nudged him several times, he did not respond.

From the hill road, Aileen heard one siren then another. A few minutes later a police car and an ambulance appeared on the hill road. In the time it took her to swallow a mouthful of whisky and brace herself, they had pulled up beside her car. She described what had happened to the police sergeant and constable while the ambulance men manoeuvred their stretcher over the reservoir wall and began to examine Meney before they moved him.

'Did he tell you how the accident happened?' the sergeant asked, notebook in hand.

Aileen described what she had seen, and said Meney was too badly injured to explain how the car had pitched into the reservoir.

'Did he say anything at all?'

There, Aileen hesitated. She had anticipated that question and had wondered what to reply. As a lawyer, she realized the value of such a confession from a man who had intended to take his life and probably knew he was dying and meant to atone for something.

'No, he didn't say anything that I could understand. He was in a great deal of pain and I had a job to get him out of the car.'

He wrote her name, address and designation in his book. 'It was a courageous thing you did, Miss Seaton. I hope he'll thank you for it – if he survives, that is.'

As they carried him up the bank, she overheard an ambulance man talking to the police. Chilling phrases. 'Pretty sure his cord's crushed. No feeling in his legs.... His head's taken a beating and his ticker's not too good.... Looks like his ribs have caved in. I just hope we get him to casualty.'

'Yeah, and you can just hope there's somebody there can cope,' his mate put in.

Meney was still unconscious when they levered him into the ambulance. They drove to the road junction, turned round and made for Largs with their siren going full blast. Aileen felt it would do no good to accompany them; she sat on the bank taking sips of whisky, watching the ambulance and police car until they had disappeared over the horizon rim and made towards the coast. That white, blood-grimed face still haunted her. That, and the fear of death in those intense blue eyes with their constellations of tiny flecks.

And the croaking confession.

All the beauty and pleasure had leaked out of the day. Still dazed and confused with everything that had happened in the last hour, she rose to make her way back to the car. It was then she noticed she had left her mobile phone just by the spot to which she had dragged Meney. Water running from his clothes had soaked the leather case of the instrument, though she hoped it had not ruined it.

When she had recovered the phone and brought it back to the car she suddenly began to shiver violently and realized her clothes were sopping wet from her chest down, including her nylon stockings and shoes. In the rush and excitement of saving Meney from drowning, calling the police and giving them an account of what had happened, she'd been oblivious of the chill breeze and her wet clothing. Now she felt cold to the marrow. Rummaging in the canvas holdall where she kept her old competition sword and foil, she found the tracksuit and trainers she wore for jogging and a towel. She stripped naked, rubbed her body dry with the towel and climbed into the tracksuit and trainers. But she went on shivering as she recalled Meney's moribund face and heard the echo of that whispered confession.

Still bewildered she drove back to Glasgow, her mind filled with the image of Meney's face and the faraway sound of his voice telling her a man was serving a life sentence for a crime he had not committed.

chapter three

In the running attack or flèche, the back foot is thrust forward and the fencer continues forward on a run. At the end of an attack, she goes back to her alert position.

When Aileen let herself into her flat, she immediately rang the Largs hospital and asked if Meney had survived. Eventually, she spoke to the casualty officer who had treated him and who told her there was never any hope of saving him. His head and spinal injuries were too severe. All they could do was sedate him and make him as comfortable as possible. He had died half an hour after admission.

'Did he recover consciousness?' Aileen asked. 'Did he manage to say anything?'

'No,' the casualty officer said. 'He never even opened his eyes.'

Aileen poured herself a large tot of whisky and gulped half of it neat before diluting the rest with water and sitting down to think about everything that had happened. She had taken the purest, most honest form of confession – not only from a dying man but one who had evidently chosen to end his life. Why her? How did they come to meet, almost collide, on that lonely road at that hour? Chance? Coincidence? She was no more superstitious than most people, but that day she had met so many strange omens.

She had missed her boat. They'd had to pick up the yacht crew. Her car had stalled. And on a whim she had decided to take the tortuous hill road through Dalry, Kilbirnie and Johnstone to Glasgow. Those curious incidents troubled her, yet somehow they comforted her. She often had doubts about justice when she argued cases where the accused walked free and the innocent were imprisoned or fined. But when something like this happened, she wondered whether there wasn't a higher hand correcting human errors of judgment.

Yet however those things had happened, they left her with a problem. What did she do? Meney had never recovered consciousness so she assumed he had confessed to her alone. She could ignore the confession and leave the matter there. Justice had delivered its verdict on this writer, Calum Weir. Who was she to question its truth?

Only there was her own conscience and her professional ethic. And there were personal reasons why this matter troubled her. Aileen had given up criminal law practice when she saw the sword and the scales of justice being tipped either for or against the accused. Either by the police pushing their investigations too far or not far enough. Or by smart lawyers leading witnesses and the jury by the nose. And by partial or incompetent judges.

She also had a personal reason. Her own father had suffered from a miscarriage of justice that had devastated the whole family. A general practitioner, he had been accused and found guilty of medical negligence. He had been the duty doctor one weekend in his small West of Scotland community and because of car trouble he was three-quarters of an hour late reaching the bedside of an asthmatic child he had never seen before.

When the child died from severe status asthmaticus, the parents sued him for negligence and malpractice. They hired a smart lawyer and won their case before a dim-witted judge. That case and its stigma had all but broken her father; it had driven her young brother, Roddy, to drugs and divided her family. And those events, together with her own dubious experience of criminal law, had driven her into civil law, where the margin of judicial error was much smaller and less wounding.

However, her own feelings did not mean she could leave the matter of Meney's confession there; with what amounted to his last breath, this man had bequeathed her his confession and if she did not act on it, his dying eyes and croaking whisper would surface in her conscience for ever. She would always wonder whether this writer, Weir, was serving a prison sentence for some crime he had not committed.

But how to act? By rights she should report what had happened to the procurator fiscal in Glasgow and let him make inquiries which might lead to a retrial of the case against Weir. But reason whispered that her report would finish like so many others in the dusty files of the procurator's office. Justice did not like admitting its own errors, let alone redressing them, and would do everything to avoid blaming itself and to spare itself of stigma at the hands of the media.

Aileen had to confess to herself that she was caught up in this incident of Meney's death. It was like a gauntlet thrown down which she had to pick up, the sort of challenge she loved when she was fencing in competition. Civil law was anything but exciting, and here was the chance perhaps to redeem someone who was wrongfully decaying in prison, someone of value.

She tried to remember what she knew about the writer. Like most other people, she had read about the Weir case five or six years ago. In fact, a member of her old law firm had handled the writer's defence. She knew that Weir as an author did not figure much in the Top Ten or on station kiosks and supermarket shelves, although he had a reputation as an original writer. But if he had never written a line, that gruesome murder of his wife and her lover would still have made the tallest of tall headlines throughout the kingdom, and beyond.

Aileen went through to her study in the four-roomed flat she had inherited from her husband when they divorced; there, she lit her laptop and spent ten minutes describing every instant from the moment she noticed Meney's car slithering and swerving towards the reservoir. Having printed the document, she consulted her computer diary for the next day and found she had the afternoon free from appointments, and no court appearances.

She put Weir's name into Google and the search engine came up with a dozen books he had written and a short biography of the writer. He was thirty-nine, born in a Maryhill slum and orphaned as a child; he had written an autobiographical novel about his upbringing which had sold several million copies in paperback, half a dozen other novels sited in and around Glasgow and several non-fiction books.

Aileen remembered reading Weir's autobiographical novel at the time it was published. It brought into graphic and sometimes crude prose the mean streets and mean streaks of Glasgow with its razor gangs, its townies, keelies and junkies; it led you by the hand into the city's sordid tenements. Nobody who hadn't lived those experiences could have literally flung them on the page in such raw and emotive scenes. That book, *Some City Slum City*, had brought him offers from newspapers like the *Daily Record* and the *Express* to write features and cover big events. He became something of a name in Scottish journalism but opted out for months or even years to write the books he thought important.

Weir had married twice. His first wife was Liz Maxwell, a prominent journalist in the city. From all accounts it was more a series of pitched battles and sexual forays elsewhere than a marriage. He divorced Maxwell to marry Lady Lorna Innesfall, the woman he had been convicted of murdering. She, too, seemed a bit of a handful. Weir's web entry gave several pages about the murders and Weir's trial in the High Court.

Her printer was coughing out all this material when she heard a curious beep on her mobile phone. She pressed the main button and said hello.

'That you, Dan ... where you at?' said a thick voice with a guttural Glasgow accent.

'Who do you want?' Aileen said.

'Dan ... Dan Meney. What's up? You got his mobile? Can I speak to him?'

Aileen thought quickly. 'Yes, I've got his mobile but Dan's not here. You'll have to ring back.'

When the instrument went dead, she gazed at it. Almost exactly like her own, but obviously not. Where was hers? She took the lift to the basement car park under the flats and opened her car. There, between the seats, lay her own mobile phone, which she must have dropped in her panic after ringing the ambulance.

So, she had picked up Meney's mobile phone at the scene by mistake. What should she do about it? Meney was dead, but he must have some next of kin. When she had sorted things out she would look for his wife or son and hand over the phone.

Another thought hit her. Meney was dead and someone had rung him, not knowing about his accident and death. Other people might ring and wonder who was using his mobile. Aileen broke open the back of the phone, removed the SIM card and immobilized the instrument. She taped the card with its tiny electronic chip on to a square of paper, folding this and placing it in her wallet.

She sipped the whisky remaining in her glass. That call troubled her. It reinforced her curious feeling that somehow something or someone was drawing her into the case of Calum Weir and she wondered why. What did she have to do with the case of a writer who had murdered his wife and her lover five or six years ago? Bits and pieces of the trial in the High Court of Justice came back to mind and she recalled that it was an open and shut case with hardly any courtroom dialectic and even less drama over the few days it lasted. Weir, it seemed, had resigned himself to being found guilty.

A question still burned in her mind: Why me?

However, next day during her lunch hour she went to the Mitchell Library and looked up Calum Weir in a couple of literary reference books and *Who's Who*. His half-dozen novels were all set in Scotland, four of them in his native Glasgow among the slum tenements of districts like Bridgeton, Shettlestone and Maryhill as well as the new council estate where he had lived his childhood and adolescence. She copied his titles into a notebook then went in search of them in the bookshop in Renfield Street.

They had two of his novels in paperback, and something that astonished her – a biographical essay on the poet and historian, Drummond of Hawthornden, friend of Ben Jonson. There was also a short collection of poems and his essays on Burns and James Hogg, the Ettrick Shepherd. She bought them all.

His novels followed the pattern of his autobiographical story, *Some City Slum City*. They had been written by someone who had known at first hand Glasgow gangland violence, shot through with the despair and hopelessness of the slum boy, with the struggle to survive, with the drug and sex scenes. They were so powerful, she felt they might have been burned into metal with an arc-welding torch. Some of those scenes of razor-gangs seared so deeply into her mind she wondered how he had borne to write of such blood and lust and if she could continue reading.

But she had another surprise. One of the novels had been set in the Highlands in the Stuart country of Appin. It was a love story without a trace of violence, and it had a lyrical quality. Almost poetic. Those descriptions of the rugged Highland land-scapes proved that Weir knew and loved nature. Aileen also read some of his lyrical and love poems, which owed something to the French symbolists. He had also written essays on Burns, Scott and the Lake Poets.

Several days later, when she had finished reading the novels and essays, she obtained the transcript of the Weir murder case from the High Court records. If she could believe the man who had written those novels could commit murder, she could not envisage him committing the murders for which he had been condemned. Not the man who had written that insightful and poignant essay on Robert Burns and his study of Walter Scott as a poet and novelist. Not the man who had written a poem with lines like this:

You could never know that true love cannot lie;
And it can betray unspoken lies.
When you swore you loved me and would love me always,
Your green eyes said otherwise
You said your lips burned at the touch of mine,
They were bloodless, white.
You forgot that love wounds never scar over, they bleed for ever
In the affected heart,
And they kill as surely as a poison dart

Aileen had rung Ben Alison, a newspaperman she knew on the *Express*, to pull copies of what their library had on Dan Meney. When they arrived in the next day's post, she saw that Meney had several convictions for assault, most of them pub or street brawls. For these assaults he had done two prison terms of a month and two months. He had also done six months for a serious assault on his first wife and two prison terms of three and six months for burglary.

What intrigued Aileen was the fact that his last prison terms he served in Barlinnie and she confirmed that Weir had been in the notorious Glasgow prison at the same time. Was that where he had met Weir? What was their connection? How did Meney know Weir was not guilty of the murders? Did he himself know who committed the crime?

She rang a friend in the procurator fiscal's office in Ayr asking her to look up the autopsy record on Meney. From this, it seemed when Meney's car somersaulted into the reservoir he had imbibed enough drink and injected himself with enough heroin to knock over an elephant. So, it looked as though they might bring in a verdict of accidental death at the inquest.

Meney had made a dying confession, but something had stopped him from revealing everything he knew about the Calum Weir case. Instead, he had only allowed himself to declare Weir himself might be persuaded to tell her who he thought had killed his wife and her lover.

When she had let these facts crystallize in her mind, she found where Calum Weir was serving his sentence and wrote to him asking if she could come and visit him. She said nothing about how she had become involved in the death of his friend, Dan Meney, but merely mentioned she was interested in writing about his case. She gave him the barest details about herself.

It took three letters and a wait of two months before she received a short note from Weir saying he would see her, although as far as he was concerned his case was closed.

But her first visit left Aileen feeling that Meney might be right. Weir might be innocent. She also had the conviction that Weir wasn't sure himself of his innocence; he might have had murder in his heart when he came on the scene in the bedroom. But what if someone who hated him had laid a trap for him, committed the murders and pinned the blame on him?

Why was he so reticent about the circumstances of the case? She had to find out for her own peace of mind.

And for another reason: she found Weir fascinating, both as a man and a writer.

chapter four

The feint is a simulated attack to deceive the opponent and lure him into making an attack.

Robert George Geddes took his feet off his desk as she entered his office. He smiled then rasped a 'Ciao bambina' through his cigarette smoke. Aileen knew the greeting was Geddes's way of convincing himself he was still at the cutting edge socially, still sharp, still virile. Four years before, Aileen had worked as a partner for this law firm of Blanes and Grimmond, doing first criminal then civil cases; she only hoped Geddes had forgotten making a big play for her and being spurned. Judging by his scuffed shoes and soup-stained tie and that sallow face, he was still in his bachelor flat importing whatever women he could pick up in Brymes or some other Glasgow bar for one-night stands.

She caught him gazing at her with too much interest.

'Aileen, you look great, great. You look like you did in your fencing days … you look like … let me see … like a rare, rare orchid.' He took both her hands in his then kissed her first on one cheek then the other. He drew back and grinned at her. 'That's it, a rare orchid, beautiful and fragile and hard to cultivate.'

His tobacco breath enveloped her, and she noticed that voice of his had even more of a husky rasp than she remembered. She had observed it coerce or bamboozle witnesses and juries in criminal trials; she knew that to more women than not, it sounded exciting, even passionate. That sexy rasp came, Aileen knew, from chain-smoking the strongest cigarettes, which had furred his vocal cords, which had left a yellow tint on the fingers of both hands, and formed a pyramid in his ashtray even during his few hours in the office that morning.

'They lose their bloom quickly, orchids,' she said.

He shrugged that objection aside. 'For the real orchid-lover that doesn't matter. It's here for ever.' He tapped his right temple.

Aileen looked at him. Geddes was fiftyish and had rugged good looks, a thatch of red hair, greying at the temples and pale grey eyes with nothing behind them that she could discern. His dead-fish stare had always given her the creeps. That, and his mindless banter and obsessive philandering.

She also knew he had been dried out in several private clinics when threatened with liver cirrhosis. They told how, even as a student reading law at Glasgow, he would go on drinking binges for a week or more. But always a canny man, he stuck an enve-lope bearing his address in his lapel pocket. In it was enough money to pay his taxi and a decent tip from anywhere in the city.

'Bob, you know why I'm here,' she said.

He looked at the folder full of papers she was carrying then his eye fastened on the bound copy of the trial transcript. 'Ay, and I don't think I can help,' he muttered.

Geddes had handled Calum Weir's defence. Reluctantly, he took the papers she handed him, the computerized notes she had made and the questions they raised. She noted his fingers tremble slightly. Was it nerves, or was he still feeding his current stomach ulcer neat whisky? Aileen pulled herself up, telling herself to stop looking for faults, being hypercritical and remember this man was still one of the most brilliant advocates at the Scottish bar. He was looking, dubiously, at the folder as though undecided whether to open it and start reading.

Aileen decided for him. 'It'll save you reading all that if I can tell you about it?' she said, retrieving the papers. Observing him hesitate then look at his three briefs with their red ribbons undone and the pages scattered on his desk, she added, 'What about giving me ten minutes over a drink in the Grosvenor?' That bait, she knew, would stifle his arguments.

'Ten minutes, then.' He stubbed out his cigarette. 'But no more.'

In the hotel bar, she ordered him a double Bowmore, his favourite whisky, and told him about Dan Meney and her own research, which had left her with doubts about Weir's guilt. A second whisky steadied him and he listened intently and even had her repeat what the dying Meney had confessed.

'Tell me, Bob, in your view was Weir guilty?'

'Is Auld Nick guilty?' Geddes gulped half the third whisky as though it was the hair of the dog that had bit him the previous night. 'He more or less confessed.'

'Less than more, or more than less?' she asked.

'All right, so he didn't spell it out completely either in writing or in court. But silence is tantamount to a confession. And he clammed up about everything.'

'Then why didn't you plead diminished responsibility? After all, the shock of seeing his wife in bed with another man might have disturbed him mentally to the point that he didn't know what he was doing at the moment he shot them. And then clubbing them with a jack handle and disfiguring them with a broken champagne bottle shows the sort of frenzy he was in.'

'We thought of diminished responsibility, but Calum didn't fancy spending most of his life caged in a loony bin with inmates hell-bent on killing each other. You know that even when he went into a psychiatric ward for a report on his mental state he tried to do himself in and came out almost suicidal.'

Geddes flicked a finger at the barman, obviously an old friend who knew the code, and another double Bowmore materialized. Half of it went straight down, for Geddes evidently wasn't much interested in its bouquet, only in its spirit content. His voice formed patterns in his cigarette smoke. 'Look Aileen, you're a wonderful girl and you're a good counsel with a fine civil practice. Leave Calum Weir where he is and forget him. He's done almost half his time with good conduct, and if he keeps his nose clean he'll be out in another seven years.'

'But if he's innocent.'

'He's as guilty as Jack the Ripper and Barbe Bleue rolled into one.'

'Who were *they* and did they do it?'

'Aileen, cut the Glasgow humour, will you?' Through the whisky slur, his voice had taken on a hard rasp. Working with Geddes, she had noticed that when he was focused on something, or worried, he had this funny tic of rolling his next cigarette through his fingers before lighting it, rather like a conjurer palming a card or a coin. He was doing that now. 'Look, Aileen, I'm serious. The Weir case was tricky and involved a lot of quaint characters. Take my advice and steer clear of it, and keep your distance from Weir.' He added, almost with a tinge of envy, 'He has a way with women.'

Aileen let the comment pass. She said, 'Bob, tell me something – among the quaint characters involved in the Weir case, would you be meaning somebody like Superintendent Frank Jennings?'

'What do you know about him?'

'Only that he's a friend of yours. He's your partner at Killermont golf course, isn't he?'

'That doesn't mean a thing.'

'But don't they say he writes a neat confession, he likes fat, buff envelopes and has friends in both high and low places?'

'That's hearsay, and defamatory to boot,' Geddes snapped. 'Jennings didn't write Weir's confession. The man himself did that by the way he defended himself.'

'And he seemed to have gone out of his way to leave his imprint everywhere,' Aileen said.

'What does that mean?'

'The broken champagne bottle in the faces of the victims. That could have been lifted out of his book, *Some City Slum City*.'

'You've just proved my point. Who else but a gangland type would have done that?'

'Somebody who had it in for Weir and wanted to set him up for the crime.' She fixed those opaque eyes of his before putting the next question. 'What about his old slumland friend and rival, Johnnie Marr?'

'You mean Sir John Marr?' Geddes said pointedly.

'All right, Sir John Iverson Marr, Knight Bachelor of Braehead.'

That had let a glimmer of light into those cold eyes. 'I see you've been doing your homework,' Geddes said. 'What about Johnnie Marr?'

'You know all about the great man? He played a part in the story, didn't he?'

He was rolling that cigarette through his fingers again and Aileen noticed he had a variation on the tic, transferring it to his left hand and then back to his right. Almost as though his mind was following some circular argument. Marr, the man she had mentioned, had been brought up much like Weir, though in a different district. But he had gone on to become a rich man through drug-pushing, betting shops and other rackets before consolidating his fortune and reputation as a property developer. Geddes had either lost the script or needed the adrenalin kick of nicotine, for he had finally lit the cigarette and dragged the burning tip a good half-inch down the tube to fill both lungs with smoke while he was thinking.

'If you're talking about Marr's friendship with Weir's first wife, Liz, that meant nothing. It didn't even figure in the case.'

'Don't she and Weir's first companion, Kirstie, stand to collect from what Weir would have inherited from his second wife had she died naturally?'

'She didn't die naturally, she died very unnaturally.' Geddes consumed another half-inch of cigarette to get that retort out.

'Who gets her money, then?'

'Ask the probate office. Her next of kin as far as I know.'

'Did you know her?'

'Only from seeing her dead and listening to the police and other trial witnesses.'

Geddes drank the dregs of his Bowmore, looked at his watch and murmured that he had a client in his waiting room and had to leave.

But Aileen did not mean to let him go like that. She had saved one of her more important questions for him. 'Why didn't you ask Frank Jennings on the witness stand why he hadn't bothered to trace the mobile phone call which brought Weir back to the house at Langside?'

'What was the point? Weir took the call and acted on it.'

'Did Weir tell you who called him?'

'Of course he did.'

'Well, who was it?'

For a moment Geddes hesitated, then said, 'It was Dan Meney.'

'Was he sure? Half of Glasgow speaks like Dan Meney and I don't know that I'd recognize a voice like his over a bad mobile phone connection.'

'Who said the connection was bad?'

'Weir did – indirectly – when he said it took him three tries to get through to Creggan House to find out what was going on. Then he gave up because it was permanently engaged. He was in some sort of blind spot in the satellite network.'

'That's your construction.'

'But you didn't follow through and find out if somebody hadn't taken the phone off the hook, did you?'

'It wouldn't have made a blind bit of difference.'

'Like the fact everybody failed to trace the call or calls. Like really discovering what happened in that half-hour in the middle bedroom at Creggan House.'

'It happened the way it is there,' he snapped, pointing his glowing cigarette at the trial transcript.

'Maybe for people who didn't want to look any further,' Aileen said.

'What does that mean?'

'Question for question – why have you never visited your client, Calum Weir?'

'He didn't want to see anybody, including me.'

'Why? Because he didn't think the trial was your finest hour?'

'That's an insult and if you air it I'll have you before the Bar Council and a libel jury.'

'You're very touchy these days, Bob,' Aileen said, though she noticed her feint did nothing to deflect or disarm him.

Aileen had left a mobile phone on the table between them. Now she pushed it across the table to Geddes, murmuring that when she pulled Dan Meney out of the lake in Ayrshire that evening and the ambulance had left with him, she discovered his mobile phone in the car when she searched for his name and address.

Geddes gazed at the instrument, his eyes suddenly alive. He picked it up and pressed the on-off button to light up the screen. His hands really were shaking as he thumbed the main button. When he saw the message on the screen, 'Insert SIM card', he turned to Aileen.

'Where's the chip?' he said.

'I don't know,' Aileen lied.

'You mean it wasn't there when you found the phone? You mean this thing didn't work?'

'That's right, and I asked myself why.' Geddes's eyes were riveted on her face as she went on. 'Know what I think? Meney had planned to commit suicide and he had removed and thrown away the memory chip to prevent anybody going over his list of phone contacts. What do you think, Bob?'

Geddes didn't believe a word of her explanation. He fixed her with the High Court look he gave bad or awkward witnesses. 'You should have handed this in to the police,' he said.

'I wondered if I should let his widow do that. I'll be seeing her in a couple of days and I'll give it to her then.'

'I'd do that if I were you,' Geddes said. But she could see that the story of the missing chip had rocked him. He lifted his glass, realized it was empty, banged it down and rose. He turned to look at her and said, 'Aileen, take a bit of advice from me – don't let your imagination run away with you, and don't let your fancy notions about Weir involve you in any attempt to reopen his case. It was open and shut, so leave it that way.' He stubbed out his cigarette and with a curt nod, he stepped quickly across the bar and downstairs.

Aileen sat there until he had disappeared then took out a notebook and jotted down her impressions of the meeting. Geddes intrigued her. He evidently did not wish to talk about Weir and the murders. She wondered why and what he was hiding.

For he was hiding something important.

Geddes did not go straight back to his chambers, but stopped at a pub just off George Square and ordered himself a double Bowmore, cursing Aileen Seaton while he gulped half of it neat.

He was well over his quota for this hour of the day; he had three briefs to prepare and was due in court that afternoon. But he had to clear his lines and had chosen this pub because it had a callbox in the toilet alcove. What he had to say he did not trust committing either to his office line or his mobile. Anyway, secretaries had big ears.

He took the rest of his Bowmore into the phone box and dialled Frank Jennings's personal number in police headquarters. When Jennings answered, Geddes told him to find the nearest callbox and ring him from there.

Within five minutes Jennings had come through. 'Where's the death or the fire, Bob?' he said with a lift to his voice.

'Somebody might be lighting the fire under you, and even our friend Marr.'

'So, we have a real problem, have we?' His voice had dropped half an octave.

'I think we have. You remember Calum Weir?'

'Who could forget that unforgettable bastard.'

'I wish I could and we all could. But Weir's found somebody who wants to reopen his case and prove he's innocent.'

'Somebody we know?'

'Nobody you know. A lawyer who used to work with me called Aileen Seaton. She's a good lawyer and she's a pretty determined woman who's just put me through the hoops about how I handled the trial. She may have a go at you, which is why I'm warning you.'

For a moment the line went silent but Geddes could hear the rasp of Jennings's plastic lighter and then the deep inhalation of smoke before he answered. God, he wheezes worse than me, Geddes thought.

'What has she got ... do you know?'

'She's got something, but she keeps her cards close to her chest. But I know she's seen Weir in Creeburn Open Prison and got something out of him, which is more than anybody's done before.' Geddes involuntarily dropped his voice. 'Is there anything he might have told her that we don't know?'

'Not that I know of. Anyway, do we have anything to hide?' Jennings asked.

'I don't know. You'd know that better than me. We didn't look all that hard and we wrapped up the case pretty quickly. And if you remember, Weir didn't have much of a say.'

'But it was an open and shut case. There he was with his two victims in a locked house. What more did we want?'

'Well, to paraphrase the words of the general confession, it's not only what we did that matters, it's what we left undone.'

'That's lawyer gabble.'

'All right, then, get an earful of this. You may remember a layabout and junkie and jailbird called Meney, Dan Meney. He did odd jobs for Weir and spent a lot of his time in stir, some of it in a cell with Weir. You should know he also did a few special errands for Johnnie Marr. Meney was the man who was supposed to have called Weir back to Creggan House that night.'

'So – what about this hophead?'

'Frank, your eye isn't what it was. Three weeks ago you should have spotted that Meney thought his car could swim through a loch down Largs way. If he hadn't done himself in that way he'd be dead anyway for he'd enough heroin in him to kill two people. And you may ask yourself and your friends where he got that.'

'For Chris' sake, Bob, give me a headline – what has this Meney got to do with your lawyer woman?'

'She pulled him out of the loch. And just before he died he told her Calum Weir didn't murder his wife and her boyfriend. He might even have given her a few clues about who set Weir up. And for Aileen Seaton that kind of dying confession means something. So she's following it up, and she's the sort of dame who won't stop at anything but the truth.'

'Well, she won't get far.'

Something in the tone of that remark made Geddes wonder what Superintendent Jennings had in mind. 'What do you mean by that, Frank?' he asked.

'I mean she's not going to find anything to reopen the case, that's all.'

'Well, don't tangle with Aileen unless you have to. If you'd seen her fence or cross-examine trial witnesses you'd know she's a tough competitor.'

'Oh! She's the champion fencer, is she?'

'Then you've heard of her.'

'Wait a minute.' Geddes heard the lighter ratchet as Jennings lit another cigarette and thought. 'Didn't her old man get into trouble with the General Medical Council a few years back?'

'It wasn't a GMC case, it was a court case. And Aileen defended him against a trumped-up negligence charge.'

'And she lost, didn't she?'

'She lost because justice was having a day off that day. So don't underestimate her.'

'I suppose I'd better tell Johnnie.'

'When you do, tell him to keep his head down and wait to see what happens.'

Jennings suggested meeting that evening at their golf club on the outskirts of the city, but Geddes pleaded his heavy workload. He had decided to keep his own profile low. A canny lawyer, he did not want to be seen with a policeman who might become involved on the prosecution side in any appeal that he might have to make for Weir, or if the case were retried.

chapter five

A fencer is covered when the position of her sword hand and sword prevent her opponent from making a thrust.

Creggan House in Langside was just as she had imagined it from reading the press reports and the trial transcript. On that grey day under low clouds and a chill breeze, it lived up to its billing as the scene of the crime. After five years it still lay empty although several dozen people had looked at it either as a prospective house or business office, or perhaps out of curiosity. Some of the serious clients had obviously desisted because of the crime; others might have been deterred by the legal wrangling over the estate of Lady Innesfall.

Aileen had done her homework and had even talked and manoeuvred the main estate agent handling the property to let her have plans and borrow the keys over a weekend.

In case someone spotted her car she had come by bus. Now, she walked beyond a crescent of private houses to gaze at the empty house where it had all happened. It was one of those three-storey mansion houses with a touch of Scottish baronial. It sat well back from the road at the end of a drive in about three acres of ground. A wall about two metres high surrounded the house; there were two wrought-iron gates, a wide double gate at the front and a smaller single gate at the rear. Both were locked. Its two dormer windows meant it had one or two attic rooms; on each corner of the roof they had stuck a turret, with wrought-iron railings round all four.

So this house with its gothic atmosphere was where Weir had

lived with his second wife and where he had murdered both her and her lover.

For several minutes Aileen stood looking at the house and its overgrown front gardens; she was trying to match the sight to what she had read of the house and the crime in the newspapers of the time. In the past weeks, she had waded through piles of cuttings about the case in the Herald Library and had the Law Association Library copy the full trial transcript for her. That script she knew by heart, so often had she read it searching for this or that question which would unlock some of the truth of what had happened in those frenzied minutes in that upstairs bedroom.

It had been drizzling that September night just after seven when Weir drove up to the heavy iron gate and opened it with the remote control. He then parked his car by the pillars at the front door and sounded the horn. He was surprised there were no servants to greet him for they must have heard his car and the alarm when the gate was opened. But he assumed Lorna had changed their routine or given them the night off.

He drove his car to the garage at the side of the house but left it outside as there were three cars already there, his wife's Jaguar, her Rover and the Escort that the staff used.

He had gone directly to the bedroom.

She could heard Geddes's court-room voice: 'Can you describe what happened when you entered the bedroom and saw your wife and her lover naked in bed in the act of making love?'

'I was astonished.'

'Just astonished?'

'No, I was enraged that she should have got somebody to call and say she was ill when all she wanted to do was humiliate me by seeing her having sex with someone I disliked and despised.'

'So, what did you do then?'

'I didn't have time to do anything. When I entered the room there was a loud bang and a blinding flash which stunned me. I remember something like a blow to my heart and I fell to the floor. After that I remember nothing more.'

'So you contend there must have been someone waiting for

you to trap you – the person who called you and said your wife was ill and needed your help?'

'It's the only explanation.'

'And why do you think this person knocked you unconscious?'

'He or she meant to kill my wife and Kanaday and make it look as though I had done it.'

But his testimony did not impress the jury, for the prosecutor, the Lord Advocate, demolished the idea that someone with Machiavellian cunning had plotted to murder Lady Innesfall and her lover and incriminate Weir. For him this was the simple act of vengeance committed by a man both enraged and outraged at the way his wife had betrayed him with a hated rival.

Walking round to the back garden, Aileen looked at the seals on the iron gate and even on the tool shed against the wall bounding the road.

When she had been standing at the front of the mansion, she had already noticed a curtain flutter at the window of the last house in the crescent, the one nearest the mansion. Now, as she returned, someone was standing by the front gate of the house. An elderly woman dressed in a long black frock and two strands of pearls round her neck. She had a silk Paisley shawl over her shoulders.

'You're not thinking of buying the place, are you?' she said in a soft, susurrating voice that Aileen placed north of the Highland Line.

'Yes, I had thought about it,' Aileen replied, tongue in cheek, but thinking the old lady had given her a ready-made alibi for her visit. 'You must be Mrs Donald.'

'McDonald,' the woman said. 'If you're thinking of living in that house, you should know what happened there ... dreadful business.' Like many Highlanders she doubled up on some of her Ss and sounded them like escaping steam.

'I'm aware of that,' Aileen said. 'They explained some of it at the estate agents office and it doesn't bother me.'

'You wouldn't be having the keys, now would you?' Mrs McDonald asked, her little button eyes alive with excitement.

'Yes, they trusted me with them.' She smiled at the woman, who was looking at the keys in Aileen's hand, wide-eyed. 'Were you living here when the crime took place?'

'Ay, I wass all that.' She came closer to whisper, 'They even made me give evidence.'

That didn't take much persuading, Aileen thought; she remembered reading about Mrs McDonald in the press reports of the crime and her evidence in the transcript covered several pages. She had seen Weir arriving in his car just before the crime; she described hearing shots and even counting them, then the screams of the victims. Her evidence had done much to convict Weir.

But reading and analyzing Geddes's defence in the transcript left Aileen with the impression that it did not carry his usual conviction. He did not seem to think he could win the case.

'Have many people seen the house? I mean prospective buyers?'

'One or two – from the agent's office in Glasgow.' Mrs McDonald paused then looked up at Aileen. 'I know the house ... and I was wondering....'

'If you could come with me, do you mean?'

'Ay, I do. You are Mrs...?'

'Miss Caralan,' Aileen said, lying with a straight face and thinking she had told so many lies at the estate agent's and elsewhere in her inquiries that she was developing a flair for it.

She opened the main gate and they walked up the drive while Mrs McDonald explained how the house had been built by a ship-owner who had hardly moved in when his wife died, so he could not bear to live there. She said, 'Some houses are lucky – but not this one.' Another millionaire who had made his pile out of mining coal occupied the house for eight years before he went bankrupt and sold to a couple who ran a private school.

'And how did the Weirs come to live here?' Aileen asked.

'As I understand it, Lady Lorna's father, the Marquis of Laureston, acquired it. You know, they say it was for one of his mistresses. Lady Lorna had it renovated and redecorated when she married that villain who murdered her.'

Aileen opened the door and they entered. Inside it felt cold and damp; the place smelled musty and the air was stale. But even empty and unlived in, the hall impressed her with its size and circular shape. It was lit from a dome in the roof, though now the light was murky. Around the walls there were half a dozen bronze figures on plinths and several paintings of hunting scenes that nobody had bothered to remove. A wooden staircase with a wrought-iron handrail curved upwards to connect the ground floor to the upstairs rooms.

'I suppose you would like to be seeing where it happened,' Mrs McDonald whispered.

Yes, you old ghoul, Aileen thought to herself. But out loud, she said, 'No, let's have a look first at the rooms on the ground floor and the servants' quarters.'

All four rooms were empty, except for one which had the wooden frames and the mattresses of two twin beds. They looked at the derelict kitchen complex with its larder and washroom. Nothing seemed to have been touched in five years and the electric oven, washing machine and fitted cupboards were layered in dust and grime.

'I'm hoping they are not assking you too high a price for the house,' Mrs McDonald said. From the moment they had entered, her voice had dropped to a whisper as though she thought they might be overheard. 'It would be costing a lot of money to put all these rooms back in order.' She smiled winningly at Aileen. 'But then I expect you have a husband and a family to help with that sort of thing.'

Aileen did not rise to the bait and left the lady guessing; she shut and locked the kitchen and closed the doors of the rooms then moved back to the entrance and climbed the stairs. She was trying to imagine Calum Weir coming in through the massive oak front door and pausing to look round for the manservant or the maid before climbing these stairs.

Mrs McDonald followed her. 'The main bedroom ... where those terrible things happened ... is to the left. It gives on to the front garden of the house,' she said.

Aileen stopped on the landing and waited by the window for

the other woman to reach her. She pointed to Mrs McDonald's house. 'That's your house over there. So, you must have seen the bedroom window from where you stood on the night of the crime. Did you notice if there was a light in that room when the murderer came back?'

Mrs McDonald shook her head, hesitated, then said, 'But you see, these windows have inside shutters and they were closed, I think.'

You think, you old blether! Could you hear and count the shots through these shutters? Could you hear screams? Just how much of what you told the court was Highland fantasy?

Before she ventured into the main bedroom, Aileen looked in the other rooms.

A dog basket lay in the corner of one of the rooms and it suddenly struck Aileen that no one at the trial had asked this woman about Weir's collie, Appin. He had been shot through the head, but no one had thought to ask why Weir, a dog lover, should shoot his dog.

'From your window overlooking the wall round the mansion you would have seen this man, Weir, come and go from time to time,' she said.

'Ay – from time to time.'

'On the occasions when you noticed him return to the house by car did anyone come to greet him?'

She thought for a moment, then said, 'Ay, Appin was always halfway down the drive as soon as he heard the car.'

'You'd hear him bark, is that it?'

She nodded. 'That bark of hiss got on my nerves at times. Yappin, I called him.'

'Did you see or hear Appin the night of the murder when his master came back?'

Mrs McDonald crossed her arms to pull her shawl closer round her thin body and stared at Aileen, a puzzled look in her grey-blue eyes. 'Now come to think of it, I didna hear him that night.' She put a finger to her right temple. 'Ah, but it was teeming of rain that night, was it no'?'

'Had you heard him that night before Weir came back?'

Mrs McDonald nodded. 'The manservant, Joseph, let him out round about six before he drove off in his car with the maid. They had the night off that night.'

'You didn't see or hear Appin after that, then?'

'No, and I thought it funny seeing the murderer's car and no' hearing the dog.'

'The last you saw of the dog was before the rain started. Did you have a clear view of the gate and driveway when the rain started?'

'Of course I did. I saw him open the gate as he approached, then drive up to the house.' Mrs McDonald bridled. 'You wouldna be saying I'm telling lies, now would you?'

'No, of course not. I suppose you saw him come back to the car and open the door and lift the boot and take things back to the house?'

'That I did.'

Mrs McDonald was impatient to show Aileen the bedroom where everything had happened, and to look again at the crime scene herself. For her part, Aileen did not mean to indulge this busybody any more than she must. She opened the door and they both entered the square, high-ceilinged room. It had two tall windows, both with inside shutters. Underfoot were polished floorboards, but no carpet. They had left the double bed with its sprung frame where it must have been that night. But no mattresses. (They would be blood-soaked, Aileen thought.) That, with two bedside tables and a massive wardrobe in carved mahogany, were the only furniture in the room. There was a small chandelier hanging from the centre of the ceiling and two lights on brass stands on the bedside tables.

'He fired the shots from the door,' Mrs McDonald was saying, though Aileen was listening with only half an ear. She would have liked time without distraction to look in the wardrobe, the bedside tables and cast an eye over the walls with their patterned wallpaper. She noticed one of the chandelier lobes was missing and wondered why.

'They found him lying on the floor,' Mrs McDonald was saying. 'He still had the gun in his hand....'

'And I suppose he had the champagne bottle he used to mutilate their faces in his other hand,' Aileen said. But to herself.

'You heard all the shots, did you?'

'Ay, every one of them.'

'There were twelve, weren't there?'

'That's what I told them in court.'

She might have picked holes in those answers, but there was no point in offending this Highland lady further. Instead, she said, 'You phoned the police when you heard all the shots. How long did it take you to get through?'

'Not sso long. A matter of minutes.'

'And how long did it take the police to get here?'

'About quarter of an hour, I would say.'

Aileen asked a few harmless questions about the layout of the house, which she had already studied on the plan, then thanked her for her help. As the lady took her leave and walked through her small garden to her front door, Aileen wondered if she should have asked her to let her look at the grounds of Creggan House from her gable window.

For she was sure Mrs McDonald had neither seen nor heard half of what she had affirmed, now or at the trial.

She returned the keys the next day. But before handing them back she had them copied. She told the estate agent she was interested in the house but would like to look at it again, perhaps in a few days or weeks. That visit had given her an idea of what had happened; but she meant to go round that bedroom and other parts of the house to look at certain things that she was sure Jennings had not spotted.

Back in her flat she found Weir's letter advising her to drop her idea of writing his life or an account of the Weir case; he told her that he did not wish to have her visit him or to collaborate with her in any way.

She put the note in the file she was compiling on Weir and decided to ignore everything he had written.

chapter six

*An attack may be simple or composed. If it follows one or more feints
or a beat or deflection of the opponent's blade, it is composed.*

Aileen had begun to realize that Weir might have a mental
block or even have had a complete blackout about what
had really happened the night of the crime at Creggan
House. He did not feel ready or able to confess what he knew
about that half-hour when they say he went berserk. Even with
his co-operation, she might not get much help from him about
the crime. So, she was on her own and this meant making the
rounds of everyone involved with the writer and the crime and
fitting the pieces together and hoping she would solve the
mystery.

Her obvious departure point was the family or friends of the
man who had already confessed: Dan Meney. His confession was
paramount. For she was positive Meney knew he was dying when
he made it; moreover, she was almost certain he had deliberately
driven his car over the reservoir bank and meant to kill himself.
It was as though his last thought before he went over the bank
was about Calum Weir. Aileen had the strong suspicion that
Meney felt guilty about some wrong he had done his friend, Weir,
and suicide might be his way of atoning.

She had to see Meney's wife or companion.

With some difficulty she traced Meney's last address to one of
the new Glasgow housing estates north of the Maryhill suburb.
As she knew the area, Aileen decided not to trust leaving her car
where it might be stolen or vandalized; she took a bus and

walked through the rain to the part of the estate where a woman told her Meney had lived.

'Is his wife still there?' she asked.

'Ay, but she's no' his wife,' the woman said with a sideways look.

This estate was a rough blend of high-rise blocks and new council houses, one of which Meney had rented. At least from the outside, it looked less rundown than most of the houses and flats. Many even had their windows boarded up and most had been daubed with garish graffiti, mostly four-letter words or crude sexual drawings. It was typical of so many of these housing complexes where crime flourished, from petty theft through drug-pushing to gang warfare and even murder.

A woman half-opened the door to answer her knock and peered at her. Aileen found herself staring at a face she should have been able to place but for the moment it fazed her. A fine-boned white face framed in a mass of jet-black curly hair. Dark blue eyes, bright, interrogative. A pretty face. Aileen smiled at it and it smiled back. From the laughter lines round the eyes and mouth, Aileen put the woman at around forty. A shabby, flimsy print frock did nothing for her figure which was still good. Maybe a bit fleshy round the waist and hips. She stood erect and ran her eyes over Aileen. Younger, she must have been very attractive, in fact beautiful. Aileen wondered how she came to be living in a sordid slum with a junkie like Meney.

She had decided to keep quiet about Weir, merely saying she had come to talk about how she had discovered Dan Meney drowning and dying and wondered if he had survived and what had happened to him. She caught the woman gazing past her at the window and fluttering curtains of the house next door before she opened the door wider and gestured her to enter. Aileen followed her along a corridor and into a living room where a single-bar electric fire was burning. Aileen could see Meney and his companion had little to live on: lino on the floor, cheap armchairs, a sofa, a sideboard, gate-legged table and another pine-wood table supporting a small-screen TV set with an indoor aerial.

'So you were with Dan when he died?' she said. Her burring accent and flat intonation was back-street Glaswegian with the harder edges buffed off.

Aileen shook her head, explaining what had happened at the reservoir and how she had pulled Meney out and fetched the police and an ambulance. She understood he had survived until he reached the hospital. While she talked, she took Meney's mobile phone from her handbag and put it on the table, saying she had found it after the accident. She said nothing about keeping the SIM card, and Meney's companion hardly glanced at the instrument.

'Dan didna suffer, did he?' she asked, and when Aileen shook her head she added, 'He died in Largs hospital. The police came and drove me down to identify him. It was in the *Morning Record* – you didna see it?'

Aileen shook her head. Her glance went to the mantelpiece and several photos there in cheap frames. One of them she recognized as this woman with Meney; but beside it was another of her in a much younger version. She and Weir were standing smiling at each other, their arms intertwined.

With a start, she realized she was looking at Kirstie Gilchrist, Weir's first companion and perhaps his first love. Kirstie, she knew from her study of the cuttings and reading Weir's autobiographical novel, had grown up with the writer; they lived in the same row of tenement houses in Maryhill and they had met at the local school but had really got to know each other when they started going to the 'jigging' at the Locarno Ballroom and the Barrowlands in the Gallowgate.

'Is that Calum Weir, the writer?' she asked.

'Ay, that's Cal,' Kirstie said. She rose and took the framed photo from the mantelpiece, smiled at it then shook her head as though reminiscing as she passed it to Aileen. 'Cal and I were very close when we were younger.' She looked at Aileen, a smile crinkling her eyes. 'That was in the papers, too. But you've probably read about Cal and the murders.'

'Yes, I did follow the story – but I didn't know you and he were....'

'Living together ... we lived with each other for years. We even had a son who's now eighteen,' Kirstie said. 'Calum wanted to marry me. He asked me dozens of times, but I always said no.'

'You said no. Why was that?'

'I didna think I was good enough for him, it was as simple as that.' She shrugged. 'I loved Cal, and it was kinda hard saying no. But he knows I did it for him.'

She took the picture back and looked at it then gazed at the electric fire for a long moment before turning to face Aileen. 'Even that far back I knew Cal was a genius and he was going places and I didna have what it took to go with him.' She shook her head, shrugged and flicked a dark tress off her right eye. 'Course, nobody knew then he'd finish up where he is now.'

'What was he like to live with?'

'Like nobody I ever met before or since.' Those curious dark blue eyes followed the whorling cigarette smoke upwards and Kirstie gave a short sigh. 'Cal was … well, Cal was unique. You know he was an orphan?' When Aileen shook her head, Kirstie said, 'Cal kept that to himsel', but his old man walked out when he was just turned three and his mother died a year later.' Kirstie made a hand-to-mouth gesture to signify either she had taken an overdose of pills or died of drink. 'They wanted to put Cal in a city orphanage but he was tipped off and they never found him. And the police and social workers did their damnedest to get him. He hid out for six weeks in an empty flat in the housing estate on what he could scrounge until they stopped looking and then a widow woman called Agnes Weir took him in, next door to us, and brought him up.'

'So Weir's not his real name?' Aileen exclaimed. 'Nobody seems to know that.'

Kirstie made to say something but suddenly stopped and looked suspiciously at Aileen. 'You're no' from the newspapers, are you? I mean, you're not going to write this?'

Aileen shook her head. She produced a card listing her professional qualifications, saying she was only interested in writing Calum Weir's story and trying to prove his innocence. Now that she had spoken to Kirstie, she had decided she must disclose to her what Dan Meney had confessed just before he died.

'How did you get together, you and Cal?'

'We lived a few doors from each other and went to the local school. I was a couple of years older than Cal, but that didna matter. We'd go to the picture house together.' Kirstie smiled. 'That's where young folk got to know each other ... in the dark, and you often came out not knowing what the picture was.' She chuckled. 'Then, we both liked the jigging on Saturday nights. Cal was a champion dancer – you should have seen him jiving and jitterbugging.' Kirstie smiled at the recollection then added, 'But then, Cal was good at everything.'

'Everything?'

'Ay, everything. He could talk like a book on anything you mentioned, he could hold his own with his teachers on poetry or history, and if anybody whistled a tune he'd pick it up and play it straight off on the piano or a melodeon.'

'But didn't he have a reputation for getting into fights?'

'Only with Glasgow toughs and keelies who were jealous of him and needled him.'

'Would that have included Johnnie Marr?'

At that question, Kirstie narrowed her eyes and looked at Aileen pensively before saying, 'What do you know about Cal and Johnnie Marr?'

'They used to know each other as boys. Didn't they used to swim together in the Kelvin and the canal locks?'

'Ay – and they used to fecht like wild cats.'

'What about?' From the odd, oblique look Kirstie shot her, Aileen had a sudden flash of intuition. 'They fought about you, didn't they?'

Kirstie nodded. 'Johnnie thought he could bribe me with everything from Macallan ice-creams to seats at Green's picture house, and when I wouldn't play, he tried beating up Cal to frighten him off.'

Kirstie's eyes shone and her face lit up at the recollection. 'And Cal, who was half a head smaller, gave him the tanking of his life. Johnnie never came back to Maryhill after that.'

Aileen seized the chance to put the question that she had come to ask. 'Do you think he's guilty of murdering his wife and her boyfriend?'

Kirstie reached a hand over to the sideboard, pulled a drawer open and rummaged, one-handed, for a packet of Marlboro and a plastic lighter. That small ritual and the fact that she did not light up straight away made Aileen think she was giving herself time to put her answer together, or perhaps trying to break the tobacco habit. Aileen noticed, too, the fingers rolling the cigarette nervously looked rough and the nails had no varnish.

'It was kinda hard to believe Cal did all they said.' She shrugged. 'I wasn't there, but I did go to the trial and all the evidence was against him.'

'But you didn't really believe the evidence. Why?'

'Because I lived with him for two years and he had the best nature of anybody I've ever met. Not like Dan and others. Cal and I never had any rows. He might ha'e shot them, but he'd never have done what they say he did with the wine bottle.'

'But the brawling that landed him in jail?'

'Cal was always being provoked,' Kirstie said with a toss of her head. 'You know what Scotsmen are when they've had a dram or two. They'd heard about Cal as a newspaperman then a writer and thought they'd take his scalp. They didna know how well he could fight.'

'But did you know Dan Meney thought he was innocent?'

When Kirstie shook her head, Aileen described what had happened the afternoon she tried to save Dan Meney's life. As she described how the car had suddenly veered as though it had been deliberately driven over the bank, Kirstie suddenly lit the cigarette and dragged deeply on it.

'Do you think maybe he wanted to do awa' with himsel'?' she whispered.

'I wondered,' Aileen said. 'Especially after he insisted on telling me when he knew he was dying that Calum Weir was innocent. But it was probably an accident,' she added for Kirstie's peace of mind.

'How would Dan know Cal was innocent?' Kirstie said.

'They were in Barlinnie at the same time and maybe Weir let something drop about the murders.'

Kirstie shook her head. 'No, it's no' that. Dan would have told me. He did odd jobs and a bit of gardening for Cal at that big house they had Langside way. But he wasna that close to him. Anyway, I think Cal told everything he knew at the trial.'

At Aileen's prompting, she said she had known Meney for several years before he went into prison; but they had only lived together after he came out. Neither of them had visited Weir in prison, for he had refused all visits. Kirstie had written him several letters asking if she could go and see him. He only answered the first – with a no. She was amazed that he had consented to see Aileen, and wondered why.

'Maybe he just wants to talk to somebody,' Aileen suggested.

'Cal doesn't need anybody to talk to,' Kirstie said. 'We used to go days without him saying a word – especially when he was thinking about some book or poem he was writing in his head.' She ran a hand through her mass of dark, curly hair then massaged the nape of her neck. 'It's something you've said or done that's made him see you. Cal never does anything without thinking hard.'

They were interrupted by the sound of someone heavy-footed groping downstairs. Aileen saw the door open to frame a bleary-eyed youth that Aileen would have put at about twenty. He was naked except for underpants so skimpy they revealed more than they hid. On his tousled hair sat a baseball cap, its skip down the nape of his neck. Don't say he sleeps in that? Aileen thought. He did not even look at Kirstie or Aileen, or perhaps was too sleepy or doped to notice them as he blundered across the living room to the kitchen which led off it. They could hear him running water and putting a kettle on the gas stove.

'That's Jamie, my son,' Kirstie said, shaking her head and smiling as though to excuse him. 'He's a night-bird and this is his breakfast time.'

'You say Jamie's *your* son. You mean he isn't Meney's son?'

'No, he's Cal's son. Cal acknowledged him officially when he was born, but I had him christened under my own name. He's Jamie Gilchrist.'

'I'm Weir's bastard,' came the shout from the kitchen.

Kirstie shrugged her shoulders.

'Did you know Liz, the first wife?' Aileen said, loud enough for Jamie to hear. When Kirstie nodded, Aileen asked what she thought of her.

'Liz was all right. But Cal always said she thought anything he could do she could do better. She could write better and fight better ... she could out-drink and out-think him ... she was a better news reporter and got bigger headlines and by-lines ... she could earn bigger money....'

From the way she reeled it off, Aileen assumed Kirstie was quoting from some comment Weir had made about Liz Maxwell. As she stopped to refresh her memory, a shout came from the kitchen.

'She could fuck better than him as well, she said. And she proved it. She was a whore, a real copper-arsed whore.'

'Is he right?'

Kirstie smiled and nodded.

As though he realized they were discussing him, Jamie came into the living room; he had found a pair of jeans and a T-shirt somewhere but he was still barefoot. He asked Kirstie if she had a light for his cigarette and she threw him a plastic lighter. Aileen noted how the flame trembled as he applied it to his cigarette; when his mother introduced them, she noted the flickering eyes and the twitching head and thought, a junkie who needs his morning fix.

Aileen felt sorry for him. She knew that if she had a close look at his arms she'd find the usual syringe spotting along the veins where he had mainlined himself. Maybe he was lucky and still had a few veins that hadn't collapsed on those arms, meaning that heroin had not taken him over completely and he still had a chance to break loose from the drug.

But looking at him, she doubted that he had the will. He would run out of arm veins and start on his ankles, his legs, his thighs. Until he had nowhere left to put the needle. And that meant the end.

She might know nothing about Jamie, but she did know he would do anything to get his daily heroin fix. He'd betray his best friend, he'd lie and steal, he'd get up to every form of skulduggery and racket, he'd beat up and rob his mother.

Yes, and to satisfy his craving he'd even commit murder.

She had seen it all before. In her own young brother, Rory.

'Glad to meet you, Jamie,' she said.

'Yeah,' he mumbled, though his eyes gave the lie to the word and said, unspoken, 'What the hell are you doing here?'

So Weir had acknowledged his paternity. That meant this boy stood to inherit something from the writer's literary estate and probably some of the money that would have gone to Weir had he not foregone it as a murderer who could not benefit by his crime.

When Aileen had taken her leave and disappeared, Jamie went into the kitchen and returned to the sitting room carrying two mugs of tea and chewing on a toasted sandwich running with butter and jam. He handed one of the mugs to Kirstie.

'What'd her ladyship want?' he mumbled as he collapsed in one of the armchairs without bothering to remove the old newspapers and magazine on it.

'She's been to see Weir in prison and has an idea he's innocent.'

'That's the best giggle I've had this morning.'

'Afternoon,' Kirstie said, pointedly.

'Who gave her that notion?'

'Dan.' Kirstie shrugged. 'It was her pulled Dan out of the water and it seems like he told her Weir didn't do the murders. She brought back his mobile.'

'What's she gonna do – try and prove he's innocent?'

'Ay – and she thinks Cal was set up by somebody.'

'Who?'

'Oh, somebody who knew all about him and knew he hated Lady Innesfall and Kanaday enough to murder them.'

'That could mean you and me and the first bitch he got hitched with ... and Marr....' He looked at her, took a bite of his sandwich and swigged some tea. 'Who else?' he said.

'I'd never thought about it but Dan might've had something to do with it,' Kirstie said, a worried look on her face.

'Dan hardly had enough up here—' he tapped his forehead '— to put a bet on a horse and you think he could've done those murders. That's crazy.'

'I said something to do with it.' Kirstie went to the window and looked down the housing estate. She could make out the figure of Aileen disappearing round the corner towards the bus stop. 'All I know is Dan didn't sleep for a week after those murders, and he went off his sleep when the trial started in the High Court.'

'That means fuck all.'

Jamie eyed the mobile phone lying on the table where Aileen had placed it. Picking it up, he pressed the main button, then stared at the message which told him to insert the SIM card. He removed the back of the phone and shook his head.

'What are you looking for?' Kirstie asked.

'No chip in this phone,' Jamie said, then in a musing voice, he added, 'Dan wouldna have taken the chip out. So somebody else must have it.' He turned to his mother. 'Did that dame say anything about the phone not working?'

Kirstie shook her head, wondering why Jamie seemed so worked up about a mobile phone that Dan hardly ever used.

chapter seven

The glide is a sliding thrust which secures an opening by forcing aside the opposing blade.

A few evenings later, when she had finished in her office and looked in her postbox at the flat, there was a note from Weir in his own hand asking her to visit him if she had time. It did not surprise her that he had changed his mind about seeing her, and perhaps co-operating with her. On her first visit he had given the impression that he was still anxious to recover his memory of what happened the night of the crime. Indeed, Aileen thought that his amnesia had probably perturbed him to the point where he had tried to commit suicide.

Perhaps this move meant he had remembered something that could be presented as new evidence for a retrial.

Yet when she arrived at the prison all he seemed to want to do was talk. She wondered if he knew she'd seen Kirstie. Something he let drop hinted that Kirstie had perhaps phoned him to tell him about their meeting and the sort of questions she had asked.

Now the prison official and staff trusted her enough to allow her to interview Weir in his cell. He was waiting for her and took her hand in both of his, holding it for a few seconds and looking at her in a way that almost embarrassed her.

Aileen had to remember she was still there on the pretext of writing a book on the Weir case. But they had hardly started to discuss her ideas for the book when Weir was called into the corridor to see one of the prisoners. As she waited, Aileen flipped open a block of drawing paper and found to her surprise portraits in pencil and charcoal and some watercolours. With the faces were several landscapes, which she recognized as bits of the Uplands country around the prison. Weir could certainly draw and some of his pen-and-ink and watercolour sketches had caught the heather-clad hills, the woods, farm buildings and hamlets which he could see from the prison grounds.

Weir returned to see her looking at the drawings.

'They help me fill up the days,' he murmured.

'But they're good, both the landscapes and the portraits. Are there people here who let you sketch them?'

'Nothing they like better, most of them. Quite a few of the inmates here think they're celebrities and posterity should be aware of them and their wrongdoings.' He shook his head and pointed to the sketchbook. 'But these aren't the Mug Alley types you meet here. Most of them are done from memory. I like to look at people, try to size them up then put my idea of them on paper. And I sometimes make fifty tries before I come up with my perception of a face or a shape.'

Aileen turned over several pages, thinking that Weir might have made a living as a painter. His faces looked as though they had been flung headlong on the page; they had vitality and he had also seized the main characteristics of a face and emphasized these. She stopped at one sketch of a head and shoulders which were done in vivid slabs of watercolour. Streaks of colour, reds and blues, covered the face like veins and capillaries. Weir had jammed the face and head and hunched shoulders together and given the man's features a grim set.

'Who's this?'

'Surely you've seen something like that face before?'

Aileen nodded, dubiously, then said, 'But if it's the face that I might have seen in photographs, you've altered it and given the impression it's of somebody you don't much care for.'

'That's one way of putting it.' Weir looked at her. 'It's Johnnie Marr,' he said.

'Is that what he really looks like?'

'It's what he should look like,' Weir said, then added, casually, 'I wondered if you had seen him?'

'No, not personally, though I've read about him. And I intend to see him because I think he knows something about who really committed the murders.'

'He might at that,' Weir murmured, then shut the sketchbook as though to blot out the image of Marr. He looked at her. 'But take my tip and keep well away from him – he's poison.'

'I don't give a damn – if he knows some part of the truth?'

'That word again – truth!' Weir formed a zero with a thumb and forefinger. 'The whole truth and nothing but the truth is just a courtroom slogan. In my case nobody's ever going to come up with the real facts. So forget that unattainable commodity, truth.'

'Unattainable!'

'Ay, it is. It doesn't exist outside maths and they don't exist outside the human skull.'

'Before he got rich and became Sir John Iverson Marr and was just Johnnie Marr, you were both friends.'

'Until I realized friendship was a one-way ticket for Johnnie Marr.'

'What happened between you?'

'It's a long and pointless story.'

'It started with Kirstie Gilchrist, didn't it?'

'Ay, and maybe even before that.'

As though to parry the question on her lips, he pointed through the cell window and said the day was fine and every fine day in this part of Scotland in spring was a bonus. Why not take the dogs for their walk?

As they made their way over the courtyard towards the kitchen gardens, Weir nodded towards a big barrel-bellied man with a square, shaven head jammed tight on his shoulders, who was shambling towards them. His massive chest seemed about to burst his prison denims. 'Listen, if you're searching for that will-o'-the-wisp commodity, the whole truth, or even if you're looking for appeal-court work, there's your man.' They both fell silent as the man approached. When he passed with that rolling, shambling gait, he skewered Aileen with the glare in his dark eyes and the scowl on his jowly face.

'Don't blame him for the hate signals,' Weir said. 'All women are his enemies. His name's Roderick Briggs and he's doing twelve years for raping a prick-teaser who was wearing skin-tight, button-up jeans at the time with a leather belt which she might even have padlocked and who already put away two men that she accused of raping her.' Weir shrugged. 'Briggs was unlucky to meet one of these women who play the rape game. But there's a good dozen like him who've been stitched up by the police and the prosecutor for one crime or another that they didn't commit.'

'Do you include yourself?'

He shrugged then turned to smile at her. 'If I am, who am I to gripe? I've met some of the most fascinating people in here, and heard their stories that make fiction taste like yesterday's cold tatties.'

They were walking through the prison gardens towards the sports complex when they heard two dogs barking. Sami, the Yorkie, and Meg, the whisky dog, were racing towards them, and Sami threw himself into Weir's arms and licked his face while the other dog yapped at her jealously. From a distance Rory looked on with a jaundiced eye.

'Sami had another friend here whose name was Tammy. He was inside doing five years for serial bigamy and has just left.'

'A serial bigamist.'

'And a drunk, to boot. Tammy was a sexual Hercules with four wives, and he kept them all going at the same time – until he was caught trying to get off with a fifth. Want to know how?' When Aileen nodded he went on. 'He was at this party and had several too many and saw this stunning creature across the room. He went over and started to chat her up, telling her she had a voice like Tate and Lyle's syrup, eyes to take the shine off sapphires, a nose like Cleopatra's and a ripe cherry of a mouth that turned him on. He was starting on her breasts and working downwards and she seemed to be listening, enraptured and asking for more. Tammy felt he was home and dry and he'd hooked his fifth until he voiced his only sincere thought.

'He said, "You won't believe this, but you remind me of a beautiful woman I once knew."'

'"And so I should, you great bastard,"' she came back. "I was married to you for four years before you went out for a pint and a packet of fags and scarpered." And that was how Tammy got five years for her and his other four wives.' Weir turned and grinned at her. 'His rest-cure in here probably saved his bacon.'

Aileen never knew whether Weir had a compulsion to talk because he rarely saw visitors, or whether all his digressions were intended to keep her off the main object of her visits – to persuade him to talk about the murders and to have the case reopened. Or maybe he wanted to know what she had discovered since the last visit. But she had to admit to herself that she found his conversation so gripping she did not want to stop him talking.

A ball flew over the sports compound fence. Sami and Meg both ran after it, and the Yorkie brought it back and laid it at Weir's feet. He punted it back to the prisoners playing five-a-side football. He pointed to a spindly young man with dark, tousled hair and said, 'Now he's another interesting tale. Looks happy, doesn't he? He was a chartered surveyor and he's in here for bank robbery. Only he didn't do it. He confessed to a bank robbery which he didn't do. He did it to get rid of his wife, who was driving him up the wall.'

'And did he? I mean, get rid of his wife?'

'Ay, he did – in a way nobody would believe if I wrote the story as fiction. The real bank robber turned up to visit the phoney robber, to find out why somebody would confess to *his* crime. He met the fake prisoner's wife during visiting hours, they took to each other and are now living it up on the stolen money. So, Charlie's divorced, he's on his own and happy and he'll be out in six months, a free man.'

Aileen found Weir the most fascinating man she had ever met. Listening to him gave her a sense of inferiority, even illiteracy. Kirstie was right; he could expound on almost anything and everything with assurance but without any pretension. Literature, music, even science. But he never initiated a subject and never pontificated. As though he seemed scared of boring people.

Several times during that walk, Aileen had to remind herself she was in the company of a double murderer, and she was trying to unravel the mystery of that murky night at Creggan House when Weir ran amok and shot and mutilated his wife and lover.

Either that, or someone who hated Weir or hated one or both victims laid a trap for him, committed the crime, then left him to be indicted then convicted for the double murder.

They were walking through the beds of leeks and beans and potatoes and tomatoes that Weir had planted to supply the prison kitchen with some of its fresh vegetables. Sami and Megi were frisking round them.

Beside them, in several beds, he had also planted shrubs and plants like veronicas and berberis, as well as annuals. He caught and held her attention as he spoke about his pleasure at growing belladonna, delphiniums and trollius, which were budding and would soon flower. Next time she came she might see their gentian-blue and yellow flowers mingling. He had also laid out a herb garden with thyme, rosemary, marjoram, sage, mint and other aromatic plants.

'With this, the library and your other work, you have a full-time job here,' she remarked.

'It's my way of living – and when you think of it living's a full-time job,' he said, and she could sense the pathos in that statement.

Sami and Rory were working together like navvies, their front paws throwing up dirt and grass as they scrabbled at the roots of several plants with tall stems, spiky leaves and indigo flowers. Weir was still talking to her but turned and spotted the dogs. He stopped talking and bounded to their side. Picking up Sami, he threw him unceremoniously to one side then heaved the Welsh terrier away from the hole they had dug. Meg, the whisky dog, had obvious memories of this forbidden game for she kept her distance while the others slunk away.

Aileen saw the two dogs had exposed the tuberous, tapering roots of that clump of spiky plants. Weir bent down to examine the roots then shovelled the earth and grass around the roots with his hands and tamped this firmly with his right foot. He turned to the watching dogs. Sami he lifted and held, one-handed, by the scruff of his neck while he shook a fist at him then shouted at him never to do that again. He repeated the operation with Rory, who looked frightened by what he whispered in his ear.

'What was all that about?' Aileen said.

'That,' Weir said, pointing to the plants, 'is aconite.' Then he added without a smile, 'If the governor and the screws knew anything about gardening it wouldn't be here.'

'It's poisonous, isn't it?'

'It is all that – deadly poisonous but beautiful like many poisonous things.'

It was something about the way he made the remark that set her wondering why he grew it. Had he meant to poison himself with it as he had tried with barbiturates? She did not dare ask, but followed Weir as he walked briskly away through the herb bed and between the flowers and vegetables. He seemed still lost in thought.

Aileen caught up with him and broke the silence. 'As a journalist and novelist you must have made quite a lot of enemies,' she said.

'Like every writer who's honest enough to print what he thinks.'

'So, how many people thought you were a poison pen?'

'Well, for a start the whole Talmudic race and its God when I hinted that Anne Frank didn't write much of her diary. They like to keep the holocaust industry going.' Weir grinned. 'Then I expressed the same sort of doubts about Christy Brown's book, *Down All the Days.*'

'Who wrote that, then?'

'I suspect not Christy's left foot, but some writer manqué of a priest who was trying to prove the point that there's a divine miracle even in the most crippled among us.' He stooped to break off and open a pea pod to check how ripe it was. 'And you can chuck in the Frenchman, Bauby, who wrote a book with his left eyelash. I don't buy that, either.'

'Calum, you're a cynical iconoclast,' she said.

'Ay, I am that. It's my trade. And in a lonely place like writing and in a confined space like a life sentence, you get that way and stray off the straight and narrow.'

'Well, since everybody else has an opinion, who do you think wrote Shakespeare?'

'I believe Shakespeare was a team job with his actors, friends and the audience all chipping in. I'm certain they gave him some of his best lines. And why all the Italian plays? Nobody's ever gone back to the source material. In my view a lot of it was pinched from Italian renaissance writers though nobody knows how, where or which. Maybe some Italian got off a boat with a load of manuscripts. We'll probably never know. For, perhaps like the Elizabethans, the Italians didn't put much on paper, for everybody was mind-stealing and plagiarism was a profession in those days.'

'These days, too,' she put in. 'Don't you know something about that?'

He broke stride and looked at her. 'So you've read about that bastard Kanaday pirating and hijacking a lot of my stuff.'

'It was mentioned in the trial as one of your reasons for killing him – and firing six shots into him and only five into your wife.'

'I see you have a tombstone sense of humour,' Weir said, then grinned at her. 'But it's like mine, a bit grisly.' He looked at her and said, 'But as far as motive goes, a lot of people had that. And everybody has murderous impulses. If you doubt it go and ask Tolstoy, who did a moonlight flit from home at eighty-two and died in a railway station. Motive? Ask the Countess Tolstoy.'

'Calum, keep to the point. Do you remember anything of that night between going into the bedroom and your arrest?' she said.

'No, hardly anything.'

'But there must be some trace of those lost thirty-odd minutes,' she said. 'They can't all be lost. I sometimes wonder if you want to remember them.'

'I do and I don't.' Weir stopped abruptly by the high fence bounding the prison perimeter. 'And do you want to know why I don't? I'm scared, Aileen Seaton … I'm scared,' he said. 'That's why.'

It was the first time he had used her given name and, for that matter, her surname. And she could see from the tense clench of his features he was speaking the truth. He looked worried, even distressed, as he stood there in the lavender and rosemary bed he had planted.

'You mean you're scared you'll remember you killed them – or scared you'll remember enough to realize who killed them?'

'Meaning myself in both cases?'

'Meaning yourself – or somebody very close to you. If you're scared you might have done it or they might have done it, that's why your mind's blocked.' She looked at him square in the face. 'You're scared you'll discover you did murder them, and you'll never be able to trust yourself again outside of this prison.'

Weir stared at her as though he had discovered she was reading his mind. 'I have nightmares that make me scared to go to sleep,' he said.

'What sort of nightmares? About what happened that night?'

He shook his head. 'No, they're horror films … I don't want even to describe them. I wake up sweating and shivering with bizarre names and pictures running through my head but not making sense.'

'Is there one image or dream that repeats as though it's challenging you to try to decipher it?'

'How did you know that?'

'Oh, I was married to a psychiatrist and neurologist who knew what was happening in everybody else's brain, though not his own – or mine.' Aileen shrugged. 'But some of his table and pillow talk rubbed off on me.'

'I never know whether they're dreams or something that's happened to me.'

Aileen looked at him. 'I think they're dreams, but deep down your brain is trying to tell you something … only you have to decipher the something. They're like Salvador Dali paintings, they're surrealist, all mixed up. But there's always some connection with the brain that inspires them. When you wake up, jot down what you remember of them and we'll try and make sense of them.'

'I'll try, but my mind's full of half-finished sentences.'

She wondered if he was punning about his own half-finished sentence here, but she left the thought unexpressed. Instead she put another question:

'How would you like them to let you out for a week or a fortnight in my care? They trust you here and I think I can swing it for you with the prison board.'

'What, me? An old lag! Where would I go? Where would I stay?'

And he went on to raise every objection. After five years he'd become institutionalized. Outside the prison he'd be an alien. He had his routine where one day borrowed another. What would this prison do for a librarian? Where would they get another man to scribe letters for the illiterate? What would Meg and Sami and Rory do?

She realized that beneath the banter he was serious and even seemed afraid of leaving the prison.

'Calum, this place can get along without you. And you'd have to stay with me since I'd be vouching for you.'

'Can you trust me, a double murderer?'

'I have the same trust in you as Sami, Meg and Rory.'

'They weren't at the trial.'

'Then they're unbiased – like me.' She took his hand in both of hers. His hand felt cold and brittle. 'But even if I had doubts about your innocence, I would still make the offer to stand surety for you.'

'What will your flat neighbours say?'

'I'll go the rounds and tell them all about you, and if they don't like it they can stuff their dislikes.' She looked at him as he threw the boomerang he had made for the dogs. Normally, he laughed at Sami's discomfiture when the stick came back thus denying him his function to retrieve it. But now Weir looked serious as though turned in on himself.

'I don't know,' he muttered.

'Calum, we can have a weekend with my parents. My father's a local doctor and my mother was a local schoolteacher. She already knew about you and she's read most of your books. I've told them all about you. I had to bite my tongue in case I flat-tered you.'

'So what did you tell them?'

'I told them I'd fallen in love with a one-eyed writer doing life for a double murder and also holding the Scottish literature record for the number of four-letter oaths in a single page.'

'If that's not flattery I don't know what is.'

'It did impress then – almost knocked them over.'

'And they're still not scared I'll murder them in their beds?'

'They're not even scared that you might rape their daughter.' Aileen looked at him. 'Or that she might let him.'

'Aileen, I haven't had a woman in five years, but I'm not at the point where I would want one who didn't want me.'

'I want you.'

'Even with all the women I've had?'

'I've met Kirstie and I've heard all about Liz. Tell me about the others.'

Weir looked at her, shaking his head. 'You're an odd girl,' he said. 'I've never met anybody as honest or as … frank.' He picked up Sami and stroked his head. 'Kirstie and I were as close as anybody. You know she turned me down.'

'She told me.'

'Liz and I had a thing that began and ended with sex. We were never intimate as lovers are and we never gave everything of ourselves.' He shrugged his shoulders, then grinned. 'There was a German girl called Ulrika who could turn me on just with her voice. Her glottis was honey-coated and she had the most exciting uvular R I've ever met. Even reciting her shopping or laundry list would get me going. They sounded like Brahms and Schumann Lieder. Her sex talk was great, too. And she had the best hand with Hungarian goulash I've ever met.'

'You should have recorded her shopping lists and her recipe. But you can tell me more when they give you leave from here, or a parole. Calum, you'll think about the parole, won't you?'

'Ay, I will.'

'And try to remember those dreams?'

'I'll try.'

As she walked through the courtyard to her car, Aileen wondered what he would decide about coming out for several weeks' leave, or on parole. She didn't have to wonder why she had asked him. She wanted Calum Weir to make love to her. And it didn't matter a damn to her whether or not he was a double murderer. If he was, he had cause.

She meant to free him from this prison and from the prison he had created around himself.

chapter eight

Parries are defensive actions that protect a fencer from attack. Direct parries meet the attacking blade and deflect or beat it away from the target.

Aileen did not look forward to confronting Calum Weir's first wife, the formidable Elizabeth Rowan Maxwell. This woman journalist had fallen for Calum Weir, had taken him under her wing and buffed his rough edges off. She had inducted him into hard-grafting, hard-hitting, hard-drinking Glasgow journalism where reporters fought physically to scoop each other and some newspapers boasted of their heavy mob almost as though they were an offshoot of the old razor-boys.

Calum had told her that pretty well everything he knew about newspaper work he had learned from Liz Maxwell. She first impressed him when she gave him a lift in her Jaguar, which had a car radio tuned to two of the police frequencies. At times, they got to the crime scene ahead of the CID and had to hide until the detectives had discovered what crime had summoned them. Then, the pair could emerge, their notebooks poised. It was Liz who taught him to screw out the light bulbs and remove the handset diaphragms in phone boxes to stymie the opposition. Ay, he said, and she taught me how to screw other things as well. Herself first.

Liz did something much more important for Calum; she helped him form his writing style by dunning into him advice on how to keep his stories brief and bright, to use short Anglo-Saxon verbs and nouns and few adjectives in simple sentences. That way his words could carry the heaviest emotional as well as literary traffic and make an immediate impact even on the simplest mind. That way the words also fitted the compressed tabloid news columns. Liz, he said, was good with short words; she could string together four-letter words like an Irish navvy and handle herself just as well if it came to a fight.

Aileen had arranged to meet Liz Maxwell in a restaurant off Buchanan Street. However, when she got there at lunchtime on Friday the head waiter told her that Miss Maxwell had been called into the *Daily News* office a short walk away. Would Miss Seaton care to join her there? Aileen walked to the newspaper office overlooking the Clyde, where a porter escorted her to the editorial floor, a huge room with twenty or thirty desks, each with its desktop computer.

Liz was sitting before one of these computers. She had a phone handset wedged between her ear and her left shoulder, was holding a conversation with someone and at the same time typing line after line two-handed on the computer screen with impressive speed. She took one hand off to flap it at a seat beside her.

Aileen sat down and tried not to eavesdrop on the interview Liz was conducting with some local celebrity who was appearing in a TV series. But even listening to a truncated version of that ruthless cross-examination convinced her Liz would have made a brilliant criminal lawyer. She wrung everything out of that TV star – from his bank balance to the names of his covert boyfriends.

Liz finished her call and spent quarter of an hour editing what she had already put on the screen. Aileen spectated, envying this woman her prowess with a computer, her ability to shunt text here and there around the screen, and her absolute assurance. When Liz had printed the result and handed it to a messenger for the features editor, she turned to Aileen.

'Sorry about all that crap. I do a bitchy piece about the latest character they've immortalized for a week by cathode or flash-bulb exposure and they brought me in to decant a bit more vitriol and four-letter words into this word-spinner.' She thumbed at the computer, which she switched off, then plunged into a handbag to produce a cigarette and a lighter. She lit up and drew the fumes in deep.

Aileen didn't know whether Liz was just living up to her legend when she took a flat silver hip flask out of her bag, screwed its cap off and filled this miniature silver tumbler with whisky, which she drank neat.

'Sorry to bring you into this word-mill, but I didn't want you to sit on your jack in the restaurant for half an hour. Looking at you, half a dozen characters might've tried to pick you up. Let's go.'

As she fell into step with Liz Maxwell and walked through the editorial floor, Aileen could credit some of the tales she had heard about her. Liz was tall with spiky blonde hair cropped close to her head and face; she had blue eyes and fair skin though used heavy make-up to cover the exploded capillaries over her cheekbones and disguise the evidence of high living and hard drinking.

She had learned quite a bit about Liz Dalziel alias Maxwell alias Weir alias Maxwell once more. A surgeon's daughter, she came from Kelvinside, light years socially distant from Weir's Maryhill and Shettleston. From home it was a short walk to Glasgow University where she studied history and modern languages. She spurned using her degree to go teaching or study medicine; instead she talked herself into a job with the *Morning Record*, writing in the women's pages about decoration and fashion. But she really made her mark with graphic reports about the seamier side of Glasgow and hard-hitting interviews with everyone from politicians to football players.

In fact, she married a drunken and querulous sports reporter, Dick Maxwell, by whom she had a son, Stephen, and a daughter, Lois, who was mentally retarded. Maxwell fancied himself as a toper until he met Liz, who had the head to drink even a hardened lush like Maxwell under the table. And she proved not only had she stronger legs but a better liver.

Maxwell was also paranoiac about his wife, thinking everybody who looked twice at her was sleeping with her, or just imagining how she might be in bed. Who could blame them? Liz was well set up; pretty, witty, sexy and unbuttoned about it.

Maxwell fought dozens of fist duels over her at parties, in pubs, even in the street. He would have died prematurely of whisky cirrhosis had he not picked one fight too many and cracked his skull against the rail of Barney McMahon's bar. Liz was there to hold him while he died.

She met Weir when she went to interview him about his powerful novel, *Some City Slum City*, which portrayed life in Glasgow's sordid tenements in Bridgeton and the Gallowgate. She dissected him and the book in an explosive article, which attacked the city and the social system for tolerating slum tenements; she revealed that Weir had to write *Slum City* in the Mitchell Library, not because he needed to research the novel – he had lived it – but because the library was warm and his single end was freezing. They did not hit it off then. Only when he was invited to join the rival *Express* and they had to compete on various assignments did they start by fighting each other and ended by making love then marrying.

Liz first impressed Weir when she scooped him on a gangland murder by palming his mobile phone then drinking with him until he was so drunk he could not have used it or any other phone. That started their feuding. They did each other down and fought like cat and dog until they both decided to call a truce, which they celebrated by booking into a hotel and spending the night making love. Weir moved in with Liz and her two children and after they had lived together for a year they got married.

'Watch Liz, she's as tricky as a jailhouse rat,' Weir had told her. 'She's a hard nut. I'm not giving away trade secrets, but she could outdrink, outwrite, outwit and outperform me in bed.' He had added cryptically, 'Get her to tell you how she screwed me to get a scoop that wasn't worth a bent pin. Just for the hell of it.'

They knew Liz in the restaurant, and the maitre d'hôtel led them to a window table overlooking the pedestrian area in Buchanan Street. When they were installed, she ran a practised eye over the menu. 'Before we start, this treat's on the sheet I give my life's blood to.'

'No, Mrs Maxwell, I can't let you pay. I asked you for the meeting.'

'It's Liz, ducks, and listen – it's my treat and if you don't like it then the chat show ends here. *Compris?*'

Aileen could only nod and watch as Liz called the head waiter over and ordered herself a double whisky and Aileen the martini she wanted as aperitifs. 'It's cold out so save your legs and make it two each,' she ordered the waiter.

When he had gone, she turned to Aileen. 'They're wops here, so I'd suggest we eat wop.' She persuaded Aileen to have the Parma ham and melon, then a scallop of veal done with molten cheese Valdostana style. As she watched Liz placing their order with imperious savoir-faire, Aileen remembered what Weir had confessed he learned from her about the art of living as well as writing.

'Well,' she said, when the waiter had disappeared with their order, 'what do you want to ask me? "Where was I the night Lady Lorna and her lover boy, Kanaday, were murdered in flagrante delicto?"'

'I was saving that question,' Aileen said blandly. She was not going to let Liz write the whole script, asking and answering her own leading questions. Two could play that game. She smiled and said, 'What I really wanted to know was how and when did you stop loving Calum Weir?' She observed that her question tilted the lady.

'Stop loving Cal?' Liz repeated, her voice and her expression suddenly strange. 'Stop loving him? What do you mean by that screwball question?'

'You did love him, didn't you?'

'Love!' Liz said in a what's-that voice which rang false. 'We had mutual interests. We liked the writing game, we liked the newspaper fighting game, we liked drinking and thinking, we liked football and boxing matches, we liked scoring off each other and everybody else and we liked fucking. We shared dislikes, too. Such as Yeh-Yeh and disco noise, the kilt-and-sporran set, hell-fire-and-damnation Presbyterians. If all those likes and dislikes add up to love, OK. Let's say we read and understood each other's life scripts and we were very fond of each other.'

'Were?'

'All things pass.' Liz tilted her blonde head back and blew smoke at the ceiling. 'Though some fondness doesn't.'

'What happened to break it up between you?'

'It couldn't last ... it was too hot to last ... we'd squeezed our orange dry ... if we'd gone on we'd have killed each other.' Liz thought about that statement, then lit another cigarette off the stub she was smoking. 'You know, Cal believes in predestination, but not in the Calvinist sense that we're all pre-selected either for the marble halls and harps, or the fiery, sulphurous devil-ridden pit. He thinks we're all programmed by our DNA and RNA and everything's written in our palm, so to speak. I was scripted into his story. So was Kirstie. So was Lady Lorna and the five bullets his script told him to use on her. Maybe so are you.' She looked at Aileen. 'To answer your do-I-still-love-him question as Cal might, life had decided to write us out of each other's scripts.'

Aileen listened, captivated by Liz's answer. For she knew from meeting Weir and reading his books that he had the notion everything had been somehow pre-ordained in some supreme moment or by some supreme being. That same feeling had hit her when she picked up Meney, heard his confession and made her decision about Weir.

Liz was grinding out her glowing cigarette stub, almost symbolically. Suddenly, she surprised Aileen by saying: 'Let me put the question to you – do you love Cal?'

'I don't know – I hadn't thought.'

'If you haven't thought, which I doubt, and you don't know, which I doubt even more, then he's hooked you. But I can tell that by looking at you.'

'I'd do what I'm doing whatever I feel about Calum Weir,' Aileen said, curtly.

Liz laughed. She had a throaty, burbling, sexy laugh and a way of wrinkling the skin round those blue eyes as she looked at you. It disturbed Aileen. 'I'll take a rain check on that,' she said. 'But I like it. The impartial lady jurist hoping to right a wrong by searching for truth and justice, those two great abstract plati-tudes. When she's really trying to justify falling for a man doing "life" for a double murder. I just hope you'll recognize truth and justice if and when they pop up and hit you between the eyes.'

'You believe he did it, then?'

'I do – though sometimes I just wonder why.' Liz shrugged her shoulders then took an ample gulp of her second whisky. 'He couldn't have done it out of jealousy, for he knew his well-born, well-heeled, well-made and well-laid spouse was having it off with Tom, Dick and Harry. Ross Kanaday was only one of a small multitude.'

'But he and Weir hated each other according to those who knew them and the trial evidence.'

'Well, Ross came by a play Cal had written and was revising. I don't know the whole story but Cal was a six-fingered hand with a typewriter and probably asked somebody to type the play. So they put in a carbon black for Kanaday, and he rewrote it as a screen play and sold it to a film producer for a hundred thousand pounds – more money than Cal had seen in his working life. Cal bided his time until the day Kanaday went on a TV chat show to talk about his screenplay. He walked into the studio, grabbed Kanaday and belted him silly then forced him to confess he had pinched his ideas and most of his play. It made great viewing so they kept the cameras on the action and the confession. Then Cal broke his nose and removed his teeth.'

'Was that the assault he got sixty days in jail for?' Aileen asked.

'Yes, and he thought it was worth every minute of the forty days he did.' Liz gave that contralto chuckle. 'Kanaday wasn't worth it. He was a dismal hack without an atom of Cal's talent, and they were never bosom pals. But after that double bill on TV, it was real hate.'

'But Kanaday, according to the autopsy, was half a head bigger and a stone heavier than Calum.'

'Ah! I can see you've never watched a street-fighter like Cal in action. He had to fight all his life, from the day he could crawl.'

'So, why didn't he fight at the trial and why has he stopped fighting now?'

'Go and ask him.'

'All right, I will.'

Their first course arrived to break up that line of discussion and give Aileen the chance to return to the question that Liz had ducked. 'When did Liz Maxwell stop loving Calum Weir?'

'Was it because Calum Weir ran off with Lady Innesfall?' she asked. 'Was that when you changed your attitude to him? Because your attitude changed. Some people even heard you swear you would have liked to murder him and his rich, blue-blooded bitch of a wife.'

'That was rhetoric out of a whisky bottle,' Liz said. But she still took a long swallow of the white wine they were now drinking and she lit a fourth cigarette off the glowing tip of her third and pulled fiercely on it.

'Well, since you said it yourself and some people thought you meant it, can I come back to the question – where were you on the night Lorna Innesfall and Kanaday were murdered?'

'You have a helluva nerve,' Liz said, loudly enough to turn heads their way. More softly but still vehemently, she said, 'You know bloody well from reading the trial transcript where I was.'

Aileen saw she had needled Liz and kept it up. 'All right, the transcript recorded where you said you were. And where Johnnie Marr said you were. You were having dinner with him in his big house at Milngavie and you watched a film on TV after dinner and then went your separate ways.'

'You're not suggesting we're both lying and I lied on oath.'

'No. You both had an alibi, but what does that mean? Other people can be paid to do the hands-on operation. And you had a motive for putting Calum Weir out of circulation.'

'Oh, what was that?' Liz's voice had a razor edge.

'His money. He would have inherited his wife's fortune if he hadn't been found guilty of murdering her. And he has left a fair part of his money to your daughter and his goddaughter, Lois. He loves Lois, doesn't he?'

'Yes, he does, and we haven't touched a penny of Cal's money.'

'But your son, Stephen, the free-spender, might like to, wouldn't he? And since we're on the subject of motive, where was Stephen that night?' She saw she had touched Liz on the raw. A chill had enveloped them.

'You have a nerve,' Liz said through her teeth. 'They told me something about you!'

'Who told you – Geddes or Jennings or Marr?'

'Take your pick. But they told me enough to make me look you up. Something of a fencer, aren't you?'

'I was until I gave up.'

'Well, I'd give this one up if I were you. Or if you don't, be prepared to use your foil without a tip – for other people will.'

Liz spoke through her teeth and was obviously mastering her temper. She put out her cigarette and drained the Chianti in her glass. 'But I have to admire your gumph,' she murmured. She folded her napkin deliberately then said she had to go and powder her nose.

Aileen watched her disappear towards the toilet room, knowing that the fencing match was over and she could call touché and take the prize for what it was worth. Liz would not return. Quarter of an hour went by before the head waiter approached to say that Mrs Maxwell had been called urgently by her newspaper and she had asked him to transmit her apologies. She had settled the bill.

Aileen could only blame herself for handling the interview badly. Liz had given nothing away, but on the other hand, she had learned something from Aileen about her suspicions. She suddenly realized why Liz had asked if she loved Calum Weir. Her question really was: Would she go all the way to prove him innocent?

Aileen's answer to the direct question would have been: Yes.

From that day, Aileen had the curious but persistent feeling that someone was following her. She warned herself against becoming paranoiac, but she had the impression when she stepped into the street that someone was tailing her. And when she drove around the town she would see someone drop into her wake. She might have been fancying things, but intuition told her otherwise.

chapter nine

A feint simulates an attack in order to lure the adversary into parrying the thrust and therefore leaving himself vulnerable to a real attack.

Aileen might have made an official request to see and examine the exhibits from the Weir trial, which were kept in the archives of the High Court, but she suspected her demand would leak into the court and come to Geddes's ears. That meant everyone would know that she was reviewing the trial evidence in the Weir case. That would bring the media down on her and she might run into trouble with the victims' families. It would also require her to sign the archive register, something she wanted to avoid.

Dorothy McKee, who kept the court records, was a friend so she approached her casually. Through her, Aileen met the assistant archivist, a spry redhead in a denim jacket and jeans called Margo Macgregor, whom she invited to lunch.

Margo was intrigued when she explained she was writing a book about Calum Weir and the Weir case. She had documented and prepared the trial exhibits herself and had followed the case closely. She promised whatever help she could give. Aileen merely said she'd be grateful to have a quick look at the exhibits. It would give her a much better feel of the trial.

'They're all in the archives so it's no trouble to dig them out for you,' Margo said.

'Could I have a look at them without bothering the archivist?'

'Oh, he wouldn't mind,' Margo said. 'We get requests from

writers every other week and we just have to watch they don't walk out with a gun or a knife or other lethal weapon and they put back the written evidence where they found it.'

Margo met her in the basement of the High Court and accompanied her to the section where they kept the criminal archives. A grisly, gruesome place that smelled of decaying files and the cardboard boxes where they kept the exhibits.

For a *cause célèbre* like the Weir case, there weren't many in the box that Margo retrieved from a shelf and placed on the table before her. There was the Beretta pistol which had belonged to Weir. She recognized it from the reproduction in the trial transcript and from having found a description in the firearms maker's website.

Hefting it in her hand, she found the gun surprisingly light when it looked so solid. So this was the Beretta from which Weir was said to have fired all twelve 9mm bullets into his two victims, lodging six of them in the body and head of the man, Ross Kanaday, another five in his wife's head and body and a single bullet into the head of his dog, Appin.

It looked new, the Beretta, and she could see the gun had hardly been used. As she peered at it under the table lamp, something intrigued her. It was one of those with a threaded end to the muzzle to take a silencer, and the thread glinted in the light; it had lost its original black paint, which suggested that someone had used the silencer. When would that be, she wondered, and made a mental note to ask Calum.

All twelve empty cartridge cases were there, lying in the small cardboard box which still bore the Exhibit 5 ticket from the trial. As she gazed at them, it struck her they were not all the same. Three of the metal jackets which had housed the 9mm bullets and their powder looked a different colour from the others. One by one she held up the cartridge cases to the light. Yes, three of them were of a deeper yellow. She peered at the cartridge bases. Most of them had an Italian stamp and had probably been bought with the gun. A glance at the other three shells told her they were Webley 9mm ammunition.

So, Weir must have fired that weapon only three times and replaced the three cartridges? She must verify that with him.

Another fact about this firearm she must determine: Who of his friends knew he had it and knew where he kept it? And when had he last seen it?

In the box were the jack handle which had been used to bludgeon the victims over the head so savagely that their skulls were smashed; and the broken champagne bottle which had disfigured their faces so badly that one of Jennings's detectives threw up.

Something glittered in the bottom of the box. A glass lobe from the chandelier. Aileen remembered wondering where it had gone when she made the rounds of Creggan House. Why was it here, when it had not even merited a mention at the trial? She turned it in her hand. Perhaps that crack and chipped edge had happened when it had dropped from the chandelier on to the floor. It couldn't have been hit by a bullet since they had found all twelve bullets in the three bodies.

She looked at the plan of the two main floors of Creggan House and the layout of the bedroom, showing where the victims lay and where they had found Weir, lying dazed after his brainstorm and his sadistic orgy. At her request, Margo ran off photocopies of the drawings.

Left on her own, Aileen picked up the mobile phone which had belonged to Calum. He had taken two calls on this phone, and it was one of those that logged the last half-dozen calls. So, they'd be in the SIM card, the memory chip of this instrument, as well as leaving a trace somewhere in the network that served this phone.

She slid the back off the phone, meaning to palm the SIM card out of its holder and drop it into her handbag.

But someone had beaten her to it and removed it.

Who and why?

She clipped back the rear panel of the dead phone and stared at it. Of course its battery had run down and the instrument would need to be connected to the mains and charged before going live. She must not alert Margo to the fact that she had examined the phone. Calling the young archivist, she explained she would have liked to take some of the registered numbers from the phone. Did she have a connection to charge her own mobile which Aileen could borrow?

Margo found the flex, plugged in the phone then pressed the main button. Up came the message: Insert SIM card. She removed the back panel.

'But the SIM card's gone,' she said, looking at Aileen, puzzled.

'Was it there when the exhibits came down from the court?'

Margo nodded. 'I checked them myself.' She ran to her office and came back with the register listing the people who had asked to see the Weir trial exhibits.

In the past six years no more than half a dozen people had consulted the papers and mostly in the months following the trial. But two names stood out: R.G. Geddes and Detective Inspector Francis Jennings.

Geddes had seen the exhibits a few months after the trial and given his reasons; he had stated in the register that there was the possibility of an appeal. Yet Aileen had never heard from him or from Weir that an appeal was on the cards.

But why did Superintendent Jennings suddenly betray an interest in this box eighteen months after everybody had forgotten about the Weir case? Police business was his reason for looking again at the exhibits.

Which one of the half-dozen people had stolen the SIM card, and why?

Aileen quickly scribbled the names in her notebook.

She left the High Court wondering exactly what game Geddes and his dubious friend Jennings were playing.

chapter ten

A false attack is never completed but is made to discover an opponent's natural reactions.

Farmacogen Laboratories looked nothing like the headquarters and research centre of a drug firm specializing in creating drugs and vaccines by using advanced technology and the latest discoveries in genetic engineering methods. To Aileen, as she sighted the building from the road just beyond Linwood on the south-west fringes of Paisley, it had the appearance of a early nineteenth-century manor house with its pillared portico and the turrets at its four corners. At the main gate a uniformed security guard announced her name over an intercom system and waved her through, telling her to leave her car in the visitors' car park.

There, another official met her, conducted her to the building and walked through with her to the rear where they had grafted low modern units to the back of the original mansion. He used a smart card to open the heavy door between the main building and the labs, closed it behind them then led her along a corridor to a spacious room where two people, a man and a woman, were working at a lab bench. He was using a multiple pipette to drop a pinkish liquor into a battery of test tubes. His blonde companion was drawing off a blood sample with a deft hand from a guinea pig which looked terrified. She smeared the sample on a slide, slid it under a microscope and peered at it.

Aileen's eye took in the three lab benches with their optical and electron microscopes, test tubes by the score, glass slides, beakers, two autoclaves and a couple of plastic blackboards covered with chemical equations. On one wall were half a dozen cages containing white rats, grey and white mice, rabbits and two cats who looked at her with suspicious and apprehensive eyes. Alley cats, she thought, and probably rounded up by some bounty hunter to sell for medical research.

When the guard whispered something in the man's ear, he signed to the woman and both rose. She picked up the guinea pig by one of its ears and thrust it, kicking and struggling, into a cage containing two others on the bench and banged the door shut. She crossed the room with a heavy stride to greet Aileen.

'So, you're Miss Seaton,' she said in a voice tinged with the faintest Scottish accent. Aileen had noticed the woman peering through the microscope without glasses but she suddenly lifted the tortoiseshell glasses hanging on a thin gold chain from her neck and put them on. Then you're short-sighted, Aileen thought, feeling those dark eyes behind the glasses scanning her face almost line by line. And those dark eyes meant her blonde hair had come out of a tube. So had the eyebrow dye. Evidently a lady with a meticulous eye for detail.

'It's Mrs Seaton,' Aileen said, smiling, 'I'm divorced.'

'Sorry. It seems you're writing a book on the Weir case. Why waste your time and bother with a man like that?'

'There were other people involved as well. You and your husband, for instance. And Lady Innesfall.'

'I still think it's a waste of time.'

Her attitude irritated Aileen, who riposted, 'It's still something of a *cause célèbre* and Calum Weir is, after all, an important novelist and essayist.'

'It seems some people think so,' she said, leaving Aileen to take what she wanted from that statement. After a pause she said, 'Now, what do you want with me?'

At that, the other man looked up from his battery of test tubes and put in, quietly, 'Joan, the lady's only trying to do her job, so if we can help....'

'Thank you,' Aileen said, then turned to the woman and added, 'I've gone about halfway with my research and I realized

I couldn't do the book without consulting one of the people most affected by the terrible tragedy.' She paused. 'Forgive me, but it took me some time to locate you. I searched for Kanaday and didn't know your new name.'

'Perhaps I had better introduce you,' She beckoned the man who was standing by his bench and when he approached, she said, 'This is my husband Alan Kelso.'

'Thank you for sparing the time and effort to see me,' Aileen said. 'It can't be too easy to have someone recall what happened five years ago.'

'No, it isn't, especially when you can't forget what happened,' Joan Kelso said. 'Do you mind if my husband stays for the interview?' When Aileen shook her head, the other woman said, 'The other thing – I don't want anything published unless I can see and agree to it.' She sounded more conciliatory.

'I'll see you get a copy of everything in the book which refers to you directly or indirectly before publication.'

'Can we have that in writing?' Alan Kelso put in, then added, 'We don't want any misunderstandings about what my wife might tell you.'

'Do you have a sheet of paper?' Aileen asked, and when Kelso brought her a pad she wrote, signed and dated an undertaking to let the Kelsos monitor and have their say in what was published about them in her book. She handed it to him. 'That's provisional but I'll confirm it with an official letter when I get back to my office.'

'Now what did you want to ask me?' Joan Kelso said, motioning Aileen to a seat at one of the swivel chairs in front of the lab bench where they had halted. She and her husband sat facing her.

'Did you have any idea that your late husband was Lady Lorna Innesfall's lover?'

'Not the slightest,' Joan Kelso said. 'Until the night that madman, Weir, knocked on our door, then half-killed Ross....' She halted at the memory of the event. 'It was terrible seeing him fell Ross then kick him....' She paused. 'He was kicking him where it hurt most....' Again, she paused. 'Then he was stamping on him and yelling he would kill him if he didn't stay away from his wife.'

While she spoke, Aileen was recollecting reading and lingering over that scene from the trial. Now she had a glimpse of how Joan Kanaday-Kelso had played the scene in court. And watching the lady, she realized those statements and the emphasis she gave them must have had detonated like Semtex in the minds of the jury. If Weir ran amok as she described it, he obviously repeated his frenzy the night he found Kanaday and his wife in bed in his own house. That was how the jury must have reacted, listening to her.

'That was the second time he had attacked your husband, wasn't it?'

'You mean the night he stormed into the TV studio and half-killed my husband in front of millions of viewers. And then he forced him to confess to having stolen his script.' Joan Kelso almost spat the next words. 'Nothing that slum tramp ever had or did was worth stealing.'

'What did you think or do after the second attack at your house?'

'What could I think or do? Ross was badly injured and when he came to his senses I asked him if he had ever had anything to do with that terrible Innesfall creature. He completely denied it. And I believed him.'

'You didn't think of bringing an action against Weir for, say, grievous bodily harm?'

'Ross said that would have played into his hands and given him the sort of muck-raking publicity which was what he relied on to sell those scurrilous and sordid books of his.'

'But as it turned out, he was lying when he denied being Lady Innesfall's lover.'

'I suppose so. He was weak and that blue-blooded bitch seduced him.'

'Joan....' Alan Kelso put in, and raised a finger to signal she should keep calm.

'But it must have come as a shock to you when they were both found murdered,' Aileen said.

Joan Kelso nodded, then said, 'Shock is hardly the word for it. That night changed my life and I still have nightmares thinking of it.' She fell silent for a moment as though recalling something. 'They asked me to come and identify the body in the morgue at the Western Infirmary. They had cleaned up the blood, but oh!, the face, the face.' Again she seemed at a loss for words before going on. 'It wasn't Ross's face ... that face with that smashed skull and all those gashes ... and no eyes, no eyes. Who would do something like that to anyone? ... Only a madman.... Only a madman like that piece of human scum, Weir.'

'Did you know Weir or anything about him before seeing him the night he beat up your husband?'

Joan Kelso nodded. 'I had met him a couple of times at publishers' parties and in a TV studio.' She shrugged. 'He didn't impress me. Nor did his writing. An insignificant man in every way.'

'You had no doubt he was guilty.'

'No doubt whatever. Weir was like the sordid and vile slum he was born in. He has been a thug all his life and he poisoned everything he touched.'

'Joan....' Alan Kelso murmured. 'Don't let it upset you.' He turned to Aileen. 'It took my wife two years to get over what happened, and she still suffers from the after effects; she still has nightmares and she's still on medication.'

He peeled off his latex gloves, put an arm round his wife's shoulder and drew her into him. It gave Aileen a few moments to study him. Her eyes went first to his fingers, which he was running through Joan Kelso's blonde hair. Strong, spatulate fingers with manicured nails. His hands were big and well scrubbed. Alan Kelso she put in his early forties. He was a head taller than his wife, square-faced and solid. As a fencer, Aileen noticed how people moved and this man never seemed to step out of the space he had made for himself; he would never take an undeliberate step, make an undeliberate move. He was slow though not ponderous. He would never need to check that his fly buttons were done up, or go back indoors to see he had turned off the gas taps.

And he obviously thought the sun rose and set on Joan Kelso.

To Aileen he said, 'My wife has been through hell so many times with this Weir business that even referring to it or thinking about it brings everything back. You understand, don't you?'

'Yes, I understand. I just have a couple more questions then I'll leave you in peace.'

She turned again to the lady: 'Where were you when you heard your husband and Lady Innesfall had been found murdered?'

'I was at home.'

'That was Dumbreck Rise on the edge of Bellahouston Park, is that it?' When Joan Kelso nodded Aileen went on, 'Was anyone with you at the time, or were you alone?'

'Is that relevant for your writing?'

Aileen shook her head and said, 'Probably not – but writers ask a lot of foolish and unnecessary questions. Of course, if you don't wish to answer....'

'I was alone.'

'I can confirm that,' Alan Kelso put in. 'I rang Joan at just before eight o'clock from the lab to give her the results of some experiments we were doing.'

'Yes, that's right. I had forgotten,' Joan Kelso said.

'Do you remember who gave you the news?'

'Of course I remember – it was a detective inspector.'

'Was it someone called Jennings?'

'Yes, now when I think, it was Superintendent Jennings. A very nice policeman.'

'That was within an hour of the discovery of the bodies, I believe.'

Joan Kelso thought for a moment, her eyes, with those curious expanded pupils, blinking behind her glasses. 'About eight-thirty, Superintendent Jennings came.' She glanced at her husband to confirm this, but he shrugged as though indifferent to the question.

'Did Superintendent Jennings say how he had identified your husband as one of the victims? I mean, he was difficult to iden-tify physically considering his injuries.'

'No, he didn't say how he had identified Ross.'

'And he didn't suggest that you go with him to the morgue to identify your husband?'

'No, he didn't.' Joan Kelso paused. 'I would have refused anyway, I was in such a state of shock.'

'Of course. I realize that.' Aileen said, closing her notebook.

She thanked them both and Alan Kelso accompanied her to the front door of the manor house and her car. She noticed they had the same Rover model as hers.

As she drove back, she wondered why this man, Jennings, kept cropping up in the case. He and Geddes were thick, and both were friends of Marr. It was just another element in the whole enigma of that night in Creggan House.

chapter eleven

The riposte follows the successful parry. It is carried out by extending the arm and can involve any combined set of movements as an attack.

At the door of the post-mortem room the hospital usher pointed at the bulky man in the green smock and skull cap working at the farthest of three dissecting tables. Leaving Aileen at the door, he pirouetted and disappeared as though scared he would throw up at the grisly sight. Three doctors were working on bodies that had either come down from the surgical or medical wards or had perhaps been brought in by the police after an accident or a questionable death. Around one of the tables where a pathologist was working over the body of a young woman, stood a dozen students, reminding Aileen this was a teaching hospital.

She had tracked the pathologist in the Weir case to the Western Infirmary where he worked as a consultant. Now, she identified Professor Herbert Magee by his craggy Irish horse-face behind thick, horn-rimmed glasses. He was dissecting the body of an elderly man and Aileen noticed he was using his left hand; she remembered reading he had some congenital deformity of his right hand that compelled him to use his left.

When he spotted her, he clumped over in his green, calf-high rubber boots and put out his right hand to grasp hers, though she felt no answering pressure. He had a ruddy face and a smile, though that did nothing to soften his features.

'So, you're interested in the Weir case,' he said in a thick Irish twang so gruff and burring it sounded as though he was spitting out iron filings.

He pointed to the body on his dissecting table. 'This fellow won't mind waiting another half an hour,' he said. 'Anyways, waiting's what every patient does – dead or alive.'

He beckoned to a door that led into a small room which had a knee-hole desk and two chairs and little space for anything else. He kept his smock on but peeled off his skin-tight rubber gloves and removed his green headgear to show a mane of white hair, which again she recognized from his newspaper photos. Files and medical books took up three sides of the room, which had a small window giving on to the rear car park of the hospital. Aileen noticed another Irish trait – copies of the *Sporting Record* and the *Racing Post* and the *Mail* open at the horse-racing pages.

'It's very good of you to give me your time,' Aileen murmured.

'I didn't volunteer it. You twisted my arm, remember?' His tone was neutral.

When she had rung to ask for the appointment, he had refused until Aileen mentioned certain details from his evidence and the questions they had raised in her mind.

'I'm sorry about that, but I needed to know some of the facts behind the case.'

'Oh, I should declare my interest, I suppose.' She waited while he reached into a drawer to produce a pouch which she saw to her surprise was full of shag and papers.

Magee pinched some shag in his vast thumb then stopped. 'You don't mind, do you?' When she shook her head, he took a paper and with practised deftness rolled himself a cigarette one-handed with his left hand.

'Don't worry, they're not joints,' he said.

'I wouldn't worry if they were,' Aileen said.

'I like them strong,' Magee said with a shrug. 'It's one of the five I allow myself – four when I'm cutting up a tobacco death.' Aileen looked at him as he lit his cigarette, puffed on it and inhaled deeply. Why didn't he have the courage to make a full commitment to his craving? She didn't know why, but she disliked this man, especially that oblique way he looked at her. As he was doing now.

'You see, I let you come because the Weir case has always intrigued me.'

'What intrigues you about it?'

'Well, now, in my trade you get a lot of smells, and I don't mean when you're cutting up the stiffs afterwards.' Magee looked almost reprovingly at the smouldering tip of his cigarette. 'I had a smell that Weir wasn't guilty.'

'Even though everything pointed to him as the murderer?'

'Now then, I don't deny he had all the form.'

'You saw him at the scene, didn't you?' She looked at him. 'How did so many people get there so quickly on that night, through teeming rain?'

Magee shook his head. 'For myself, I was called on the phone and as I live half a mile away, I got there as they were taking him off under arrest handcuffs.' Magee shook his head at his recollection of the scene. 'Weir looked kinda dazed, sort of punch-drunk, as though he didn't know where he was.'

'He gave that impression at the trial, too, didn't he?'

'No, there he didn't look doped or confused. But he didn't have much to say for himself, and I even had the notion he was trying to protect somebody. And there's another thing. Bob Geddes, his lawyer, either had no help from him or thought the whole thing an open and shut case.'

'But you obviously didn't. Why?'

'At the trial I had to describe the faces of the victims – you know, the cracked skulls, broken bones, broken teeth, eyes ripped out, the whole gruesome, horrible, pathological picture. While I was being examined and cross-examined, I was looking at Weir in the dock, and I thought he was going to break down or faint. A psychopath who shoots a couple of people then when they're good and dead sets about destroying their identities doesn't react even to the grisly details. But Weir did.'

'Was that your only reason for doubting the verdict?'

Magee shook his mane of white hair, shedding dandruff. 'No,

it read too much like a stage or a film script to my ear – and I've done my bit in quite a few murder trials.'

'What was it like when you got inside the house?'

'Terrible. I see a lot of stiffs, but those two bodies still haunt me. It was the foulest night I ever had – both outside and inside.'

'Apart from examining the bodies, did you notice anything else?'

'Just the smell.'

'Of blood?'

Magee waved away that question. 'No, it was the smell of gunpowder from the shooting.'

'Was it that strong, the smell?'

'Ay, it was and all that.' Magee nodded and pulled on his hand-rolled cigarette.

'What was your impression of how the police handled the inquiry?'

'Now, why would you be asking that, Miss Seaton?'

'I wondered what you thought of Detective Inspector Jennings.'

'Not much. Does that answer your question?'

'What about your own evidence? Did Mr Geddes not ask you the right questions?'

'Ay, in a way. But it's always the questions that aren't asked that count as much as the others.'

'But he must have read your autopsy report and asked you to brief him. Why didn't you explain your findings and your doubts then?'

'Everybody was so sure Weir was guilty.'

'So, nobody seems to have bothered to question his guilt, is that it?'

Magee put the ball of his thumb on his cigarette stub and ground it into the ashtray. Now as he looked at Aileen, his grey-blue eyes had gone hard. They fastened on her fingers, which were zipping open the large leather wallet in which she kept her papers. He shrugged when she produced the photographs, though he had guessed what had really brought her.

'It's a few years since I looked at those,' he murmured.

'But then, you had the originals – in the flesh,' Aileen said. 'They must have been much more interesting for a pathologist.'

'So you spotted there wasn't enough blood,' he said.

'It struck me as soon as I looked at them,' Aileen replied. 'And I wondered why an eminent pathologist, a detective as experienced as Jennings and a lawyer as gifted as Geddes had not spotted it, too.'

'Are you suggesting we plotted to have Weir convicted of those murders?' There was no hint of Irish blarney in Magee's voice as he put his question.

'I'm suggesting that Calum Weir might not have had a fair trial,' Aileen said. She didn't dislike this man any more. She despised him.

They both cleared away the documents, the sporting papers and the ashtray from his small desk and Aileen spread half a dozen of the police photographs on its surface so that they could both study them. Magee took a ballpoint from the jar on his desk and pointed to the bullet wounds in the heads of the two victims, two in Kanaday's head and one in Lady Innesfall's.

'They produced some blood, but not much,' he said. 'So did the bullet wounds on the body.' His pen traced the outline of the pillows where the heads had lain. 'Those should have been soaked in blood from the wounds caused by the broken bottle. So should the mattress.'

'But they weren't,' Aileen put in. 'And Jennings didn't ask why the blood had congealed around those horrific wounds.'

'Why should he? He had his murderer.'

'Didn't he even ask you how long you thought the two victims had been dead?'

'He thought he knew that as well. Anyway, if he had asked me I could only have given him an estimate to the nearest half-hour – and that didn't mean a thing.'

'It didn't mean a thing!' Aileen said, raising her voice and staring at him. 'You at least must have known why they didn't bleed as much as they should and how important it might be.'

Magee had forgotten about his pledge and was rolling himself another of his crude cigarettes, lighting it and sucking in and expelling the acrid smoke. He plucked a fragment of shag from his lips and thought for a good moment before replying. 'What I'm saying now is between ourselves. Is that clear?' Aileen nodded, and the pathologist went on, 'If this case was ever reopened and came up before the appeal court, they can call me and I'll give my opinion, but until then we haven't seen each other. Do you agree?'

'All right,' Aileen said. 'But only if you agree to hold nothing back.' When Magee nodded, she asked, 'How long would you guess they had been dead when you arrived there?'

Magee shrugged. 'It's a guess now, but I'd say a good half-hour and maybe even twice that.'

'Why in God's name didn't you put that in your report to the police or the procurator?'

'Why didn't I? I've often asked myself. It bothered me then and it has bothered me since. But I was told Weir had all but confessed to the crime – that is, he had not defended himself. So, my doubts and my findings seemed academic.'

'But you still did tests?'

'I looked for the clotting agents, fibrin and thrombin, that would have been present had those terrible injuries been done before the victims died, or while they were dying from the bullet wounds. And I didn't find any. I calculated they must have been dead for some time before those injuries were inflicted on them.'

'And you say for half an hour, and maybe twice that?' When he nodded, Aileen fixed her eyes on him. 'I suppose you still have the report you made at the time.'

'I have the full autopsy report and my comments, and those pictures.'

'Well, I should keep them in a safe place,' Aileen said, pointedly. 'You never know who might be interested in them.'

Magee did not ask her to elaborate. Aileen collected the photographs and placed them in the wallet then rose. She thanked Magee, who murmured that he would accompany her to the lift.

She sensed he wanted to say something and as they waited for the lift he looked at her.

'I suppose you think what I did was unprofessional – and even cowardly,' he said.

Aileen shrugged her shoulders. 'Dr Magee, what I think about you is neither here nor there. But you should be grateful that they abolished hanging for murder.' She entered the lift without another word.

But going up in the lift she wondered why Professor Herbert Magee should have smelled something like the acrid, pungent tang of gunpowder smoke.

For those cartridges she had seen in the exhibits box were smokeless and should not have left the sort of powerful odour Magee had observed.

chapter twelve

A corps-à-corps means that the foil guards or the fencers' bodies
clash and prevent either of them from using their weapon freely. It
is penalized for being dangerous in high-grade fencing.

Although a fencer with a sideboard full of trophies, Aileen
had only ever watched one bullfight. It was in the arena at
Valencia during a holiday in Spain and she went to see how
matadors handled the espada. She never repeated the experience, judging it cruel, especially to the horses, which were often
fatally gored; also, the contest was weighted too heavily in favour
of the man and against the bull. But she never forgot the brilliant artistry with which the bull was played with the cape to
come face to face first with the picador then the matador.

That was just the way Geddes played her with the cape then the
scarlet muleta in which he had concealed the estoque or sword.

It began when Geddes rang her with an invitation to have
dinner with him. Knowing what might be on his mind, she talked
herself out of that. But canny lawyer that he was, he wrong-
footed her by insisting she compensate him for her refusal by
coming to his house-warming. Didn't she know he'd bought a
rundown mansion in Milngavie and tarted it up? Wouldn't she
like to see it?

Incredulous that Geddes had dug himself out of his bachelor
flat, and wondering if he had a new wife lined up, Aileen could not
resist; but she wondered after putting down the phone if the
dinner invitation was probably his stalking horse to invite her
and warn her off the Weir case.

For Geddes seemed worried about her inquiries. She wondered if he was scared new evidence or a retrial might reflect badly on him for the way he handled the trial.

Aileen had observed how some of her questions had disturbed him; she had also got under Liz Maxwell's tough epidermis. It seemed several other people might be alarmed. When Weir heard about how Liz had walked out on her he had laughed, saying it was very much in her character. But he became serious when she said that after the interview she thought her phone was tapped and someone was following her both on foot and in a car. He warned her to be careful.

She had accepted Geddes's invitation, but since she did not want to get involved either with Geddes or his lawyer friends, she decided to arrive well after the party had begun. It was a limpid evening at the beginning of May and there was still an hour's light in the sky as she drove to Milngavie. She had no difficulty finding the mansion in a tree-lined street for the garden was floodlit and through the car window she could hear music, which sounded like subdued rock. She drove through the gate of the small, two-storey mansion and parked among the thirty-odd cars along the drive.

Geddes came to meet her and escort her into the house and hand her coat over to a girl, who put her name on it.

'I didn't realize you were a man of property, Bob,' she said. 'But I like it. Very impressive.' Geddes told her he had five large rooms with bathrooms en suite, a tennis court and small swimming pool. She wondered why a bachelor like him needed that much space.

'I've a feeling I've seen something like it before.'

'Oh!'

'You must know where – Creggan House.'

'Creggan House?' Geddes repeated, then snorted his disagreement when he realized she was comparing this with Weir's house in Langside.

Looking at the fifty or so people in the living room, Aileen felt underdressed in her silk frock and flat heels; and she didn't give a damn. She knew most of the women there and had already seen them in their best evening gowns set off with their best trinkets. They were standing or sitting in the living room, drinking and eating from the buffet table, which stretched the length of one wall and was laden with champagne, wine and spirit bottles as well as an astonishing array of food. Obviously criminal law paid well, Aileen thought, looking at the oriental rugs on the parquet floor, the good Impressionist and Post-Impressionist reproductions on the walls and the antiques which had probably come from Ritchie's.

One or two of the men she had worked with, and several of their ladies, made a sign to her as Geddes found her a glass of champagne. He also loaded her plate with canapés of caviar, foie gras and smoked salmon, then slivers of what looked like pheasant in a wine sauce and several heads of asparagus. She managed to stop him there.

As they stood there chit-chatting, Geddes suddenly raised his eyebrows as he looked over her shoulder at someone approaching. He whispered to her, 'Uh, uh. You've seen Liz Maxwell, I believe. You're about to meet her son, Stephen.' And, before Aileen could object, he had introduced her to a tall young man with floppy blond hair, a wan face and pale, sleepy eyes. He held out a hand which Aileen took. It felt clammy.

Stephen Maxwell was like his mother; he didn't believe in small talk. 'I'm told you're trying to prove my ex-stepfather is innocent,' he said. A smoking cigarette protruded from the fingers of the hand holding his champagne glass; in the other hand he had a plate with several tit-bits on it. For an eighteen-year-old he seemed to have little appetite. She wondered what had cut it. Hash or heroin.

'I think your ex-stepfather deserves a new trial,' she said.

'What do you think of that, Bob?' Maxwell said.

'I've already given Miss Seaton my thoughts on that, and this isn't the time or place to discuss it,' Geddes said, curtly.

'Well, I can add mine. Weir's as guilty as hell and he's ruined half a dozen lives and it's only a pity they abolished hanging.'

'Stephen, I said this isn't the time or place to air your thoughts,' Geddes cut in. 'Now excuse us.'

He wheeled Aileen round and whispered, 'It's a fine evening and the air outside isn't so contaminated, so what do you say we get out of here?' She nodded and followed him into the garden and along a path between beds of roses to the swimming pool, where about a score of people were standing talking. Geddes left her there with a group of lawyers, some of whom she knew. He went to greet the latest arrivals.

As she stood there, a face she didn't know emerged from the scrum on the edge of the swimming pool and a voice said, 'Can I introduce myself. I'm Frank Jennings. I hear you're going over the ground I covered in the Weir case.'

'I'm looking for the uncovered ground.'

At that he laughed, but it rang hollow. 'So you think I didn't do my job.'

'I won't go so far as to say that,' Aileen replied. 'But some people believe Calum Weir's innocent.'

'Anybody I know?'

'You might have known him. A man called Dan Meney.'

Jennings laughed. 'As he was one of his cellmates, he would think that.'

'It was a dying confession,' Aileen said. 'So why do you think he kept what he knew to himself until he realized he was dying?'

'What did he tell you?'

'Enough to convince me that Weir might have been wrongly convicted,' Aileen said and let him ponder that statement.

In fact, something about this man turned her up. It wasn't just the soapy, smooth voice and the way he had overlaid his Glasgow accent with a bit of Oxford English. Shifty was the word that came to mind. He had small eyes of a bleached blue that never looked straight at you. His hair was stuck down with some cheap-smelling pomade. That tie and blazer could have been old-school but were off the peg at M&S. Aileen asked herself whether this was the man who was having her followed; she also wondered what he had learned from Geddes, from Magee, the pathologist, and the other calls she had made. She tried vainly not to let her prejudices show.

'As a lawyer, I know that the police and the High Court sometimes overlook things and sometimes they make downright errors.'

'Did I overlook anything?'

'I'm still going the rounds and when I've done that perhaps I can answer your question. But I think everyone was too quick by half to conclude Calum Weir was guilty. And it seems to me they fitted the facts they had to that hypothesis.'

'Are there new facts?'

'A few,' Aileen said. 'But I would have looked for a silencer on that Beretta. And I would have run ballistics tests on all the bullets removed from both bodies.'

She observed that those points had set Jennings reflecting and she had another. 'Calum Weir took the call that lured him back to the house that night on a mobile phone which I looked at. Unfortunately, the High Court has lost the SIM card. But even without it, that call should have been traced.'

'But Weir knew who was calling. Why didn't he say?'

'It was a bad line and the caller didn't make things easy, so he wasn't sure. But even after five years there's a trace somewhere of that call and with the other evidence it might reopen the Weir case. It was a phone like this one,' Aileen said, producing her own mobile which resembled both Weir's and the other she had taken from Meney. Jennings could not take his fishy eyes off it.

At that moment they were interrupted by a clutch of young people who were jiving to the rock music on the boardwalk around the pool. Some of them were obviously high on the champagne or spirits which Geddes hadn't stinted, or perhaps hash or cocaine. It was inevitable that one of the drunken youths would side-step the girl he was jiving with and send her sailing into the pool. That was the signal for another trio, two girls and a man, to land in the pool.

Aileen was standing talking to Jennings when the first youth pulled her away and invited her to jive. Jennings tried to shoo him off, but he insisted and Aileen took up his challenge. She saw he was drunk and for a skilled fencer it was easy to read his intentions. He was gyrating around her and trying to do something between jiving and twisting to get her into position where he would pull her forward, side-step and guffaw when she landed in the water.

He did exactly what she had anticipated. Only when he yanked her forward and side-stepped, she held on to his hand, feinted then pirouetted round him, twisted his arm and sent him flying into the middle of the pool. That scene earned her the biggest cheer and laugh of the evening.

'I liked the way you did that,' said a voice in her ear.

Aileen turned to find herself confronted by Sir John Iverson Marr.

So she was really the person who had been wrong-footed. And this was why Geddes had insisted she come to his party! To play her with the cape then set her up for the estocade!

Aileen had heard so much about Marr from Weir and read everything she could dredge up about him, including his biography and newspaper and TV interviews, that she looked at him with some trepidation. She was grateful for the fluid and subdued light on the terrace in front of the swimming pool, which masked her apprehension.

She still had to adjust her whole idea of him when she came to confront him. It was his face that caught and held her eye. His mouth and chin were framed in a cropped beard, dark but stippled with grey hair. His thatch of dark hair had been cut short and slicked back. He was taller and heavier than she had imagined, but when he took her arm and guided her to the edge of the terrace she saw he was light on his feet. She remembered Kirstie and even Weir saying Marr had cut something of a figure in the city dance halls when they were youths together. He still moved like a dancer.

Now he was standing there in his 300-guinea suit with a Glasgow Academicals tie and a handkerchief flowering in his breast pocket – the perfect gentleman.

His speech, too, impressed her. What must have been his burring, guttural Bridgeton or Shettleston twang had been effaced and replaced with smooth, modulated Edinburgh English; but he seemed to listen to the sound of his own voice as he escorted her across the terrace to a corner where she saw someone had already arranged wicker chairs round a table with a drinks trolley. 'We might as well talk here,' he said.

As he removed the top and poured the tonic water she chose, she saw he was handy around bottles. But for all his charm and sophistication she wondered why he struck her as a well-dressed spiv putting on an act. He handed her the glass of tonic water then poured himself a large whisky from a Chivas Regal bottle and fired an inch of soda water into it as though he were handling a pistol. Like a Beretta, she thought.

Something about this man scared her. He exuded hostility, even menace. She recalled how Weir had warned her to avoid tangling with Marr. And Weir knew him better than anybody; he had been brought up with Marr and people like him. From reading his press cuttings and talking to Weir, she knew he had pushed drugs in his slum days and allied himself with other drug dealers. He had formed a gang, which also ran protection rackets in the city. With the extortion money he took over betting shops and made a fortune, which he invested in buying two local boxers who won or lost on his orders. By betting on the fights he rigged, he doubled his fortune. No point in playing probabilities when you can put your money on dead certs. He now had a string of racehorses and she didn't doubt they ran to his orders.

He applied the same system to councillors and then to politicians who handled public works contracts for schools, hospitals, roads. So, Johnnie Marr became a building contractor and a property millionaire with enough cash to buy what and whom he wanted. Including his knighthood.

But one thing he could not buy: Weir. From what Aileen had learned, Weir might have become Marr's Boswell, handling his publicity and public image and sharing some of his wealth. But he was one of the things Marr could not possess with his money. And it rankled with this man who was standing by her side sipping his whisky and soda.

From what she had learned, Marr's father was a layabout and drunk who beat up both the boy and his mother. According to the press reports on the incident and the inquest, Marr's father was fished out of the Clyde at the Broomielaw Quay. One of many drowned drunks. So many the police hardly bothered to inquire how he got there. Along that stretch of the Clyde at Glasgow Green were several places where a drunk might lose his footing, slip and fall into the river. His autopsy proved he had drunk the equivalent of two bottles of whisky or fifteen pints of Scotch ale. They didn't even question his thirteen-year-old son, who had gone to fetch Marr at his mother's bidding but had failed to find him. Marr was brought home, dead, on the back of a pick-up truck.

Young Marr's mother had the foresight to insure her husband. Not for much, but the £400 they got kept them going. It took them out of Bridgeton and into a better part of the town where the boy had better schooling.

Aileen had asked Weir about the father's death, but he knew little more than local gossip about it and the stories she had culled from newspaper cuttings.

Perhaps her antennae were playing her up, but she had the idea that Marr was as uneasy as herself under that casual attitude. She wondered if he might be scared the murder inquiry would be reopened. But scared for whom or what? How much did this man know about her and what she was doing. Probably almost everything.

He'd know how she pulled Meney out of the water and heard his last words; and how she'd been to see Weir twice in prison. Aileen had no doubt Marr had contacts on both sides of the bars in Weir's prison. He'd know about her interview with Magee, the pathologist, her visit to Creggan House and probably her rummage through the exhibits in the High Court archives. He'd have heard from one of his mistresses, Liz Maxwell, about their meeting, and her visit to Kirstie. From Geddes, he would certainly know all about the negligence case against her father and her young brother's drugs problem. That thought disturbed her.

'They tell me you're a very good lawyer,' Marr said.

'If you mean Bob Geddes told you, I did work for his firm at one time.'

'Bob does some work for me, and he'd very much like you to come back into the firm.'

Aileen shook her head. 'Sorry, I've had enough of criminal law.'

'Oh! But I heard you were trying to get a retrial for Calum Weir.'

'That's not a brief, it's an unpaid job I've given myself.'

'None of my business, but isn't it a lost cause trying to prove Calum Weir is innocent?'

'So, you have no doubt he was guilty?'

'Everybody, including the High Court of Justice, thought so.'

'But some people doubted the verdict.'

'Nobody in their senses. Take my advice, Miss Seaton, save yourself a load of trouble and drop it. Weir did it.'

'Dan Meney didn't think so.'

'Meney was a rattlehead who never knew what he was talking about or what day of the week it was.'

'He knew he was dying that evening he told me Weir was innocent.'

'Did he tell you who did it?' Now Marr's voice had an edge to it.

'No, only who didn't do it.' From the fact that Marr had not asked how she had taken Meney's dying confession, Aileen realized how thoroughly he must have checked her actions.

'So you're trying to prove what a drunk and a hophead like Meney tells you.'

'You were good friends once, Calum Weir and you. But you fell out.' She paused. 'What did you fall out about? His wife?'

Marr canted his head back and laughed out loud. 'Over Liz? Liz couldn't wait to download him. That got under his skin, that did.'

'But you were friendly, if that's the word, with both his wives.'

'Lorna was a bitch, and I can understand why Weir did her in.'

'If he didn't commit those murders, who do you think might have done it?'

'Oh, he did it all right. Look here, Calum Weir's just a wee scribbler who made a bit of a name for himself. But he's still a slum boy with a slum mentality, and that's why he ran wild and murdered his second wife and the man who was having it off with her. And that why he's now getting what he deserves and doing life for it. And I would leave him there if I were you.'

'I don't think you can call him a wee scribbler. He's one of our best writers.'

'I know … what do they call him? The Bard of the Slums?' He reached into an inside pocket to produce a silver cigar case, flip it open and take out a large cigar. He rolled it slowly between the fingers of both hands, watching her. 'I hope you don't mind if I smoke,' he murmured as he notched the end of the cigar. She shook her head.

He went on: 'To tell the truth, I haven't read any of his stuff, but then I don't read much outside the *Herald* and *The Times* and even then I go first to the stocks then the sport. For me, scribblers make their little marks on paper because they believe mankind has a future and they belong to it. Weir's one of them.'

'Weir was one of the few people who knew your whole story, wasn't he?'

'What do you mean, the whole story?'

'How you got from where you were to where you are?'

'Everybody knows that, so it's no secret. What do you mean?'

Something in the upward swerve of that last question and the way he expelled the smoke from his cigar made Aileen think she had touched a trigger spot. So she probed a bit further.

'Weir knew something that hasn't been in the press, didn't he?'

'Is that the yarn he has been spinning you?'

'No, he has mentioned nothing so far. But I'm working on it.'

Marr had stopped acting casually. He picked up the whisky bottle and poured himself half a glass, but this time he didn't dilute it with carbonated water. He swallowed half of it neat. He glowered at her through his thick eyebrows and Aileen thought for a moment he might strike her, even strangle her. His right hand went into such a tight clench round the glass the knuckles showed white; he threw the cigar down and ground it out under his heel, as though it was her neck he was crushing.

'Now look here, Mrs Aileen Seaton, whoever you are and whatever game you're playing, just make sure your own hands are clean before you accuse other people.'

'What are you implying?'

'Not implying, just stating facts. You had a brother – one Roderick Gregor Seaton, or Roddy for short. He was a junkie and he stole a lot of money from his accountancy firm. He'd have done time if he hadn't taken a bit too much heroin. And even though it was hushed up, it would still make quite a splash.'

'My brother, Roddy, only took drugs when my father was wrongly accused of medical negligence, and he had paid for his small crime, which is more than people who accuse him have done for their much bigger crimes. My family and I can take whatever the law hands out to us. I hope you can say the same for yourself.'

'We've nothing more to say to each other,' Marr growled and hoisted himself out of his chair. But as he turned to walk away, he suddenly stopped and looked at her.

'You'd better tell your murderer friend, Weir, to shut up. A lot of accidents happen in prison. Some of them fatal.'

Both the menace and the cold, neutral voice in which it was delivered sent a shiver through Aileen as she watched the tall, burly figure retreat into the crowd around the swimming pool. She rose and went to recover her coat, whispering to the girl to make her apologies to her host and say she had a headache.

chapter thirteen

The stop thrust is a counter-attacking move against an opponent as he is making an attack. It closes the line where he is intending to end his attack.

She had an intuitive feeling as soon as she opened the door that someone had been in her flat during the two and a half hours she had spent at Geddes's party. As she moved cautiously into the living room, she became certain. A slight tang of cigarette smoke. Not an ordinary cigarette but a joint. Someone who went in for cannabis and had left its acrid trace here not so long ago. Aileen would have said less than an hour ago.

Had Geddes invited her to take her out of the flat so that Jennings could send one of his men there to look around? No, he wouldn't have been so stupid. But evidently someone knew where she had been in the last two and a half hours and could take his time to find what he was seeking. And that meant somebody connected with Jennings or Marr or both.

He was obviously a professional. Someone either with a key or the expertise to pick the two complex locks on her front door. Aileen went round checking the door and windows to confirm they had not been forced. Apart from the cannabis odour, he had left his imprint nowhere. He had replaced what he had moved, and he had probably worn gloves.

She knew what he was hunting for – the SIM card. Had he found that and replaced it with another? She located the card where she had stuck it under one of the small drawers of her writing desk. Opening her mobile phone, she removed her card and clicked Meney's card into place and lit the instrument. All the information was still there.

That SIM card evidently held some vital information for someone to risk being caught burgling her flat. She must go through all those stored names and numbers and find out why someone needed to retrieve that card.

She opened her desk drawer to look at the notes, the photographs and other evidence she had collected. Nothing missing, though she wondered if they had been photographed or photocopied.

What worried her and sent a frisson down her spine was the thought that someone had a key to her flat. She deliberated whether she should change the locks, but decided that the man who had already gained entrance knew his locks and keys and there was no point in trying to defy him that way. But she would make certain that everything was bolted while she was at home.

Another thought struck her: had he seized the chance to plant a bug in her apartment? She started with her phone, dismantling it to see if a device had been inserted. Nothing. Methodically she went round the flat, looking at her laptop, her filing cabinet, the furniture.

Aileen went to the spare bedroom to verify nothing there had been touched. She started with the glass cabinet where she kept the trophies she had won fencing for the university, her law school and the Scottish championship. In the cabinet she also kept the half-dozen French and Italian foils she had used in competition and the duelling sword she had used in practice.

Opening the cabinet with her key, she examined the mask and the gloves and took out the French foil with its bell guard and curved handle and silver pommel. All the practice she had done and the tournaments she had won with this weapon were imprinted on the twine bound round the handle and the impressions of her knuckles on the cushion behind the steel bell. Even now, when she had not handled it for more than a year, it felt in her hand like an old friend. She could not resist making several thrusts and lunges and going through half a dozen parries against an imaginary opponent; she then used the floral pattern on her bedroom curtains as a target. Her hand-and-eye co-ordination wasn't what it had been and she told herself to step up her practice sessions.

In the cupboard under the glass cabinet she found her mask, gloves, the 'whites' she wore and the plastron that protected her right side, her leather-soled plimsolls. She went through everything looking and feeling for any listening device. As an afterthought, she even took down the épée or duelling sword from its brackets in the cabinet. She had also fenced with this heavier, stiffer weapon with its triangular blade and button and seen how much damage it could inflict even in competition fencing.

Was she exaggerating the threats from Marr and this burglary and search of her flat, or did she need some form of protection? She had the foil and épée in their sack in the boot of the car, but she wondered whether she should ask the police for a permit to carry a firearm. She continued her search in every corner where someone might have placed a listening device.

When she had satisfied herself that the flat had not been bugged, she went back to her study and picked up her mobile phone with Dan Meney's SIM card in it.

He had logged nine numbers but had used his own code to identify each of his contacts. For instance, there was JAK and MIK and ALLIE. All the numbers but two were in the Glasgow area. She had a telephone code book and consulted it for the two disparate numbers. One was in Renfrewshire and the other in Stirlingshire.

Was the last number the one on which he had called Weir that fateful night?

Aileen thought for a moment. She might call each of those nine numbers to see who answered, but where would that get her unless someone she recognized, like Marr, answered. Another thing: how could she be sure they would not show on the instrument she was calling? She could not take that chance on giving herself away and revealing that she had found Meney's SIM card as well as his mobile.

She felt sure that sooner rather than later, Marr's henchmen would answer some of the questions in her mind.

chapter fourteen

Concentrate on the fact that all the movements prior to the final movement of the attack are made to deceive the opponent's blade and all will be well.

She did not have long to wait. A week after the party she was watching a late-night news programme on TV when her downstairs bell rang. They had a video surveillance system with a wide-angle lens to identify callers and she switched it on and gasped when she saw that a figure was lying on the ground just inside the main entrance.

'Who is it?' she called into the phone.

When the person did not move or answer, she put the phone back, found a flashlight and ran downstairs. Opening the main door, she looked round to check nobody was waiting in ambush then went to the figure on the ground. She caught the moaning, whimpering sound coming from it. Her torch picked out his face.

It was Jamie Gilchrist.

'Jamie, what are you doing here?' she cried.

He looked at her, blinking in the light. 'Who is it?' he croaked.

'Don't you know? Didn't you ring the bell?'

'Naw, they must've rung when they dumped me here. Didn't know where I was.'

Aileen knelt beside him and tried to lift him up. 'Leave me where I am,' he said.

'In your state! I can't do that. I'll help you up.'

'No, just get me a taxi and give them the money to take me home,' Jamie got out.

She ignored him. Putting her hands under his armpits, she hoisted him into a sitting position then to his feet. It was then she noticed the blood running from his face.

'What have they done to you?'

'They nicked me with a razor.'

'I'll get a cab and take you to hospital.'

Jamie grabbed her by the arm. 'No coppers and no quacks and no dressing station. It's not mortal. Get me a cab and I'll get home.'

'Not before you're cleaned up.'

Somehow, she manoeuvred him into the lift and helped him out at the second floor. Jamie managed to stagger to the living room sofa, where he collapsed.

She put a bathroom towel under his head as a pillow and swabbed some of the blood off his face with a cloth.

'They nicked me,' he groaned.

In fact, Aileen saw they had slashed him twice across the cheekbones under both eyes with a razor. Deep gashes, which were bleeding freely.

When Aileen had wiped his face, she found some Betadine and cleaned the wounds with it, then waited until they had stopped bleeding; she drew the edges together with sticking-plaster. Jamie lay with the unflinching stoicism of a pack mule until she had finished. He would bear those gangland scars for life, but she thanked God they had not gone too deep.

'Thanks,' Jamie muttered when she had finished.

'You look as though you could do with some strong coffee,' Aileen said. 'I've just made some if you want to join me.'

Jamie nodded his head. She poured the hot liquor into a cup, sweetened it with four lumps of sugar, spiked it with whisky and handed it to him. He was still so far gone she had to help him hold the cup and transport it to his lips. Whoever had attacked him had really worked him over. His face was a swollen mass of bruises and blood was still oozing from his mouth and lips.

Aileen wanted to ask him who had beaten him up to the point of almost murdering him then left him on her doorstep. But she refrained, knowing that characters like Jamie Gilchrist did not talk. It had something to do with drugs. She had seen her own brother, Roddy, in a similar state and he would never reveal who had manhandled him.

While she held the cup to his lips, Aileen had been watching him. He looked and sounded all in and she even wondered if he'd survive. It wasn't only the beating he had taken, but perhaps the fact that he had not had his fix. What had happened? Had his heroin source failed to show up? Had he quarrelled with his dealer or run out of money to pay? When he had drunk half the coffee, she said, 'Hadn't you better tell me all about it?'

'Nothing to tell,' he mumbled through his swollen lips.

'It's to do with your father, Calum Weir, and the murders, isn't it?' she said.

'I wouldn't know about that.'

'Well, next time they'll kill you to find out what you don't know.'

That sparked some reaction. Jamie lifted his head. Even that movement set him grimacing with pain. She could read in his eyes that he was wondering how much he could tell her.

'Dan Meney's mobile phone. When you found it was there a chip card in it?'

'I didn't look.'

'It wasn't there when you gave it to my old lady.'

How strange to hear somebody as young and pretty as Kirstie described like that!

'Is it important, this card?'

'I don't know. Would it have any record of the calls that were made the night of the murders?'

'Five years after the event!' Aileen shook her head.

'But they could be traced.'

'Yes, they could – but that would take months going through the millions of calls that were made that night.'

'But if they had the time and the number of the mobile that was called....'

'Have you any idea who made that call, Jamie?'

'Maybe Dan, but Dan would never do it unless somebody had forced him.'

'Who do you think that would be?'

'I don't know.'

'If we did know, would it give us the sort of evidence that could mean a retrial for Calum Weir?'

Jamie looked at her, those pale eyes of his narrowing. 'I don't give a tinker's about Weir and whether he rots in jail. He left us in the shit.'

'That's not the story your mother tells.'

'She's still mad about him, that's why.'

To give him time to think about her questions, she made them both more coffee and spiked hers with whisky as well as his. She was sure this boy knew something vital about what happened the night of the murders. But he was scared to talk.

'You know, Jamie, somebody else wants to know about that phone card. They were here a week ago while I was out at a party and had a good look round. Can you think who that might be?'

'Wasn't me.'

'No – but it was somebody who smokes the same sort of reefers you do. Does that mean anything to you?'

'What are you getting at?'

'Nothing. I went over a few names – names like Frank Jennings or another of Mary's gangland errand boys, names like Stephen Maxwell.' She saw that her remarks brought Jamie's head up again, so she gave him another thought to put in his mind. 'Jamie, I've an idea who beat you up and why. They'll be back and next time they might not dump you on my doorstep but where nobody will find you.'

'I can look after myself.'

'In your place I'd be careful who I talked to about your father.' She thought for a moment then said, 'Can you do something for me?'

'Depends.'

'Tell your mother to ring me at my office.' She scribbled the number on a piece of paper and handed it to him. 'But she mustn't use her own phone, either the landline or her mobile. Tell her to ring from a callbox.'

Jamie took the paper and promised to pass on the message.

She left him on the sofa for half an hour to get some of his strength back. She called a cab and she and the driver between them helped him downstairs. She paid the man and gave him Jamie's address. Jamie even muttered a thank you.

Back in the flat, she replayed the conversation in her mind. She felt certain Jamie Gilchrist possessed a key piece of this jigsaw, but Marr or someone else had scared him so much that putting him on the rack wouldn't loosen his tongue.

chapter fifteen

Once a fencer has lost poise he is halfway to being defeated.

As she was walking to her office in Blythwood Street, Aileen saw the headlines on the newsboy's bill outside the Central Station.

BID TO CLEAR CALUM WEIR
Fencing Champion seeks new evidence

She bought the *Sketch*, a tabloid weekly with a big circulation in the Lowlands and found a café in St Vincent Street, where she ordered a coffee and opened the paper.

They had taken up their whole front page with the same headline as on the news bill. But two photos in half-profile faced each other across the front-page text. Calum Weir appeared dressed in a flak jacket and flying helmet, evidently taken during one of his foreign newspaper assignments. They had taken one of their stock photos from her fencing days which showed her in the on guard position, but as though she was saluting Weir rather than her opponent.

She had never heard of Royston Davison, the man whose by-line appeared over a story as tendentious as the pictures. He had scoured his newspaper library cuttings for details about her and Calum and written a sketchy and often inaccurate account of the crime and the trial in crude journalese and with an even cruder attempt at wit.

He began by outlining Weir's background, his literary and

journalistic career in such backbiting and unflattering terms
that they would have cost him a fortune in libel damages had he
not been writing about a man convicted of a double murder and
therefore in no position to challenge his story.

Royston Davison did not spare her. Miss Aileen Seaton might
have made her name as a champion fencer, but she had failed as
a barrister in the criminal courts and had to take refuge in civil
law; her marriage to a prominent psychiatrist had failed; and
when she was called on to defend her own father, a doctor,
against an accusation of medical negligence, she again failed.
And one could only judge her attempt to exonerate Weir as a
piece of rash opportunism designed to put her languishing career
back on course.

Davison continued:

*'There was no doubt in the minds of the detectives who investi-
gated the crime that Weir, who was caught red-handed, had
committed the double murder. The prosecution had no difficulty
proving its case, the more so since Weir and his counsel could
offer no real defence. There was no appeal and no sign of dissent
from Weir in the five years he has since spent in prison....*

*'But now in the shape of Miss Aileen Seaton, we have a latter-
day Pallas Athene, who, sword in hand, rushes to Weir's side and
swears to prove that he is innocent. How, in heaven's name? Is she
going to argue that he wasn't in that bedroom in Creggan House
on the night of the murders? Or if he was in the house, he was in
his bath when the deed was done?*

*'But our Athene, goddess of wisdom that she is, has an ace up
the sleeve of her toga – a confession, no less, from a heroin addict
who knows who did the deed but just didn't have the time to tell
the lady before he died from his addiction, among other things.*

*'In five years, Weir has never once demanded a retrial or
proclaimed his innocence. Nor has he wanted to see his trial
lawyer or any other visitors. Indeed, he has spurned them.*

*'But it seems he has made an exception for Miss Seaton, who
has visited Weir at least three times in his Creeburn Open Prison.
They are now more than just lawyer and client. They are – how
should I put it? – good friends.*

'One can make allowances for a naïve young woman falling under the spell of Weir's undoubted literary talent and perhaps his physical seduction. But she should not allow even close friendship with a convicted double murderer to influence her judgement and make a long and vain crusade to prove him innocent.'

It took Aileen several minutes to regain her composure at such a scurrilous and biased piece of journalism, with all the insinuations it contained.

When she again felt calm she re-read the two-page article then went over it for a third time with an analytical eye. Before and after her meeting with Liz Maxwell, she had read some of that journalist's output in the *Sunday Record*. Some of the phrases in the *Sketch* article had such a strong resonance with the Maxwell articles she had no doubt that Liz Maxwell had inspired much of this attack on her and Calum Weir.

When she looked at the publisher's announcement in an inside page, she realized the *Sketch* and the *Daily News* were printed in the same building. No doubt Royston Davison and Liz drank in the same pub and he had cooked this up at her suggestion.

She had fought several defamation cases and won several. Now, she spent half an hour going through the article word by word, ringing those ideas and statements that constituted libel in her view. It would do no harm to serve a libel writ on Mr Royston Davison and the *Sketch* next day and put out this information through the press agencies.

In the meantime she would demand that the paper print an apology for the dozen or so errors of fact in the article.

chapter sixteen

Disengaging is accomplished by passing the sword point with the smallest possible semi-circular action over or under the adversary's blade, stretching the arm and lunging.

Aileen did not relish the idea of going back to Creggan House. That dank, musty mansion with its gothic atmosphere and its death chamber haunted her and even recalling her previous visit gave her the creeps. But go she must. For her study of the exhibits and her interview with the pathologist had raised several questions in her mind. And she wondered how thorough Jennings's detective work had been and whether in that bedroom and elsewhere he might have overlooked clues about what really had happened that night.

Everything she had gathered was coalescing in her mind into a shape of how Calum Weir had been lured there, trapped and implicated in a double murder.

If indeed he was innocent!

Although Aileen had taken the precaution of having duplicates made of the three estate-agent keys for the front gate, the rear gate and the front door, she dismissed the idea of burgling the house. That nosy Highland woman, McDonald, would certainly see her and inform someone.

So she persuaded the estate agent to lend her the keys for several days, ostensibly to have a second look at the house since she was still interested in acquiring it. She chose a Saturday afternoon thinking that sport on TV and in the nearby stadium might mean she had a clearer and quieter run in that area.

Before entering the grounds and the house, she made her small reconnaissance of the house from the outside, first by driving her car round the building and stopping by the rear gate.

She had not seen Creggan House from this side before but now realized that if someone had baited a trap for Weir that night and wished to enter the grounds and the house unseen from the terrace where Mrs McDonald lived, this is how they would have proceeded. Of course they would have needed keys, but her inquiries had revealed there were at least four sets of keys for Creggan House.

Aileen knew it had rained that night just over five years ago. She wondered if Jennings or his detectives had even bothered to look at the grass verges along this stretch of unused road to see if a vehicle had been parked there. Her question was now academic.

She had opened the rear gate and taken a few steps into the tangled garden when she noticed a glimmer of light through one of the rear windows. Had someone been round the house recently and left the light on? Surely the sole estate agent handling the property would have checked! They would also have warned her if anyone else was looking at Creggan House.

Who could it be? Several names flashed through her mind: Jennings, Marr himself, Jamie Gilchrist, or Liz Maxwell.

Aileen turned on her heel and went back to her car and opened the boot. Her foil and the heavier épée lay in separate bags. She chose the épée. With this weapon she was confident of repelling anyone unless they had a gun. She kept it in its bag but carried it under her armpit.

Before leaving her car and returning to the house, she rang the number of her chambers on her mobile phone and spoke to her secretary, whom she had informed about her movements. She told the secretary she was now entering Creggan House; the girl should give her quarter of an hour then call her with a message that she had an appointment in half an hour at her chambers. If she did not answer the secretary must call the police and send them to the house.

Aileen walked round the drive to the front entrance. Letting herself in softly, she saw the hall light and a corridor light were switched on. For several minutes she stood in the entrance hall listening. Yes, someone was moving around on the first floor and in the bedroom where the crime had taken place. It seemed like no more than one person.

'Is anyone there?' she called upstairs.

That provoked a clatter of feet and a moment later a figure appeared at the head of the stairs. In the half-light, Aileen discerned a man in a leather jacket wearing a peaked cap.

'Are you from the estate agents?' he called.

'Yes, I'm here to look at the house,' Aileen called back.

'That's what I was doing,' the man said. He came slowly downstairs until he stood in the better artificial light. Aileen held the sack covering the duelling sword against her right side, ready to pull it out if this man made a false move.

But he was smiling and held out a hand, which Aileen took with her left hand.

'Bit of a coincidence, isn't it?' he said.

His voice was pleasant, cultured, with a slight Scottish burr. His leather jacket had an Italian cut, obviously from one of the mode shops, and he wore twill trousers and brown ankle-length boots. It was difficult to put a year to that smooth face, but she would have estimated him at between thirty-five and forty. He was half a head taller than herself, thick set with a square face and blond hair protruding from his cap and falling to the nape of his neck and overlaying his ears. He had curious, washy-blue eyes. Colour of stone-washed denims, Aileen thought. A notebook with two pencils clipped to it jutted from one pocket of his leather jacket; in the other was a bulge which might be a mobile phone. Or something more sinister. He was smoking a pipe with a curious chromium stem split in two and a wedge-shaped bowl. He tamped the tobacco with his thumb, made sure it was not burning and put it in a side pocket of his jacket.

'Are you from Briggs and Strachan?' she asked. He shook his head then mentioned the name of an estate agent in Buchanan Street, but so quickly that she failed to catch it.

'I'm a chartered surveyor looking over the place for a

possible client,' he said. 'The estate agent she uses has asked me to survey the place ... you know the sort of thing ... damp, dry rot, wet rot, leaking roof, structural defects, drainage, et cetera.'

'I suppose your client knows what happened here,' Aileen said.

'If you mean the murders, I'm sure she does,' the man said. 'But she's not the type to let a little thing like a *crime passionel* bother her. She's had a look at the place and likes it and she wanted to know how much she'd have to spend to put it into shape, which is why I'm here. So she'll probably make some sort of offer.'

'So you think the house is reasonably sound?' Aileen ventured.

'It's in fairly good lick for a place that hasn't been lived in for more than five years.'

'Is it worth the three-quarters of a million they're asking?'

He hesitated for a moment, then grinned and shook his head. 'I'd have to say no. Maybe a bit above half of that.'

Who was he, this man who was surveying the house and didn't even know what the agency was asking for it? Another thing: he had not asked her why she was interested in a house with such a bad reputation, and if this was her first visit. Did that mean he knew who she was? It might also mean he knew what she had come to look for.

Was he one of Jennings's men? Policemen seemed to dress in any sort of garb these days, though this one looked like some well-dressed Glaswegian on the make. Whoever he was, she wondered what he was looking for in this house. No one came to Creggan House as a potential buyer without going through an estate agent. And so far as she knew, there were no contenders for the house other than herself.

This man was watching her, sizing her up in the way that two fencers do when they take to the piste and are waiting for the signal to start. He knew who she was and by the way his alert eyes had fastened on the bag she was carrying in her right hand, he had probably assumed she had in it the sort of weapon she had fought with.

Aileen did not know why, but an image flashed into her mind.

A face and a build the spitting image of this man standing before her. It was seven years ago when she was acting as a junior counsel to Bob Geddes in a murder trial in the High Court. They were defending a man charged with the cold-blooded murder of a rival drug dealer and two of his henchmen. He was no more than thirty, blond, in a men's-boutique suit, frilled shirt, hand-knitted tie and handmade shoes that must have cost £300. Well spoken with no Glasgow twang and no foul language, he looked anything but a murderer and drug dealer. She remembered interviewing his father, who could not believe it was his own son on a triple murder charge. He testified how shocked he was when he learned of his son's criminal activity; he had given him the best education and assumed he would take over his small electronics business.

Geddes used all his courtroom talent to plead his innocence but the jury did not believe him; the man was convicted (rightly in Aileen's judgment) and was serving a life sentence.

Well, you tossed up to guess which this man was – cop or crook, rozzer or rogue? Didn't they say they were both sides of the same coin!

She had nothing to lose by giving her name. 'I'm Aileen Seaton,' she said. 'I'm a lawyer in Glasgow.'

'I'm Mark Anderson,' the man said. 'What sort of law do you practise?'

'Civil cases, mainly,' Aileen said. 'Where do you work from in case I need a surveyor? At least I know you're serious and you've done most of the work already.'

'I'm a freelance, and I'm sorry I've left my briefcase with my cards in the car. But you'll be in the law list so I can give you a ring with the information.'

At that moment, her mobile phone rang and she heard her secretary's voice saying she had an appointment in a couple of hours.

'All right, Kate, I'm at Creggan House in Langside, but I'll be through here in a couple of hours. Let's say I see my client at six o'clock in the office.' She turned to the man. 'Sorry about that,' she said, 'but nobody's let off the leash these days.'

'Maybe we can go round the house together?' he suggested, but she shook her head emphatically.

'Thank you but no. I prefer to look in all the dark corners on my own.'

'Well, I'll leave you to it,' he said.

Aileen watched him leave by the front door and walk down the drive and out the gate. A moment later his car racketed away. Standing there, she took a dozen deep breaths to expel some of the tension and steady her heart. For she had the strong impression that this man might have attacked her. He obviously knew everything about the Weir case, at least as it concerned the house.

Where did he come by the keys to the gate and the front door of the house? How did he know his way around and where things like the mains switches were? She wrote his name in her notebook although aware it would not figure in the directory of the Institute of Chartered Surveyors, or anywhere else.

Before she started her quest, she bolted both the front and back doors of the house.

Her sole object was the bedroom and when she opened the door she observed from the slight shift of the bed and the bedside tables that he, too, had done a careful search of that room. So, he knew why she was there. Whatever he had found and removed, he would probably not have disturbed what she was seeking. She had brought a torch to augment the buttery light from the chandelier and the one bedside table lamp that functioned. To cover every part of the room, she commenced in the wardrobe, tracking her torch beam over the inside then the floor. In a rear corner, she saw something reflect the beam.

A small round plug of yellow foam rubber the shape and size of a small cartridge case. She turned the stiff foam rubber in her fingers and gazed at it for a good moment before realizing what it was. An ear plug.

Why an ear plug? And why one and not two? She put it in her pocket. In another corner of the wardrobe she found a plastic clip of the sort used on backpack straps.

Meticulously she quartered the room, going round each of the four walls, the inside shutters, then the ceiling. She stood on the double bed to get a better view of the ceiling and the cornices. After this, she began on the floorboards.

She was beginning to think she must have reasoned wrongly, and what she was hunting for just wasn't there. The floorboards yielded nothing. But as a last throw, she moved the bedframe. And there, behind it, she spotted the splintering in the skirting board. Kneeling and bringing her eyes close to it, she saw the round hole and knew that in there was a lead slug. One of the slugs that had not hit either Lady Lorna or Ross Kanaday.

Somewhere in this room, perhaps in a crevice in the cornice, there would be another two holes like this one from random bullets. One of those shots might have nicked and brought down that chandelier lobe that she had seen in the exhibits. But she need look no further. She had proved her theory about those three maverick Webley cartridges in the High Court archives.

That bullet hole in the skirting board told her that not twelve shots but fifteen shots had been fired that night. Two had been fired first, probably into the heads of Lorna and Kanaday to kill them. A third bullet had finished off Appin, Weir's dog. Those three shots nobody had heard since they were fired with the Beretta fitted with a silencer. Three more bullets, but of a different make, were inserted into the pistol magazine and the twelve shots were fired. Nine of those shots were fired into the dead bodies of the two victims.

And to make up the count and convince anyone who heard the shots or knew that both victims had been murdered by twelve shots, the other three shots were fired at random, one in the skirting board, the other two still to be discovered.

Had Jennings and his police team done their work properly they would have found the three random shots which would have told them that Weir had been trapped and framed for the crime. At least that was how she saw it. Perhaps there was another explanation.

When she arrived back in her flat, she wondered if she should ring the estate agent and ask if they had given keys to any other agency or another person to visit Creggan House. But she dropped the idea. If he was one of Jennings's detectives he'd have all the keys. And if he was one of the men who had set up Weir he would have procured keys from someone.

Who had they got them from? That was another unresolved question.

chapter seventeen

To make a direct attack you straighten the arm and lunge when the opponent opens the line.

Before she parked the car in the prison courtyard, she knew something was amiss. Normally, Calum and the dogs were watching and came to greet her by the high fence between the parking lot and the prison. But today somebody else was looking out for her. Ogilvie, the assistant governor. He seemed bleak as he came to whisper that Weir had been ambushed by several other prisoners and was in hospital. Yes, she could see him there, though not for long. He was still sedated for the pain of his injuries and the doctors had forbidden any contact.

During her previous visits she had deepened her acquaintance with Ogilvie and made him an ally. Cut out of Scots pine, straight and solid, his heavy fiddle face always wore a frown. But he was honest. As a quintessential bureaucrat, he was as much a prisoner of his own rigid Presbyterian code as the men in their cells were ruled by prison regulations.

'When did it happen?' she asked, remembering the threat made to her by Marr at the party.

'The day before yesterday. He was out walking with the dogs in the evening and they were waiting for him behind the sports ground.'

'Any idea who did it?'

'Hm!' Ogilvie shrugged. 'We have an idea, but prisoners have their own omerta code. Nobody's going to "grass" on the men who nearly killed Calum.'

'Nearly killed him!' she cried, suddenly scared.

'Oh, he'll survive. He's pretty rugged.'

'Won't there be an inquiry?'

'There has to be – but it won't get anywhere.'

When they led her to his bed in the prison hospital she was shocked. His face was covered with bruises of every colour. His good eye was still almost closed and he had to squint out of the uninjured corner to see her. One of the young medical officers said they had found him in the nick of time. He was choking on the blood in his mouth and had a punctured lung where a splinter from a broken rib had pierced it. He had lost a litre of blood. They had to operate to remove the bone splinters and strut the broken rib. He was still in transfusion.

From the few words he got out through his swollen mouth, Aileen realized her presence was doing more harm than good.

'How long before he'll be able to see me and talk?' she asked the young casualty doctor.

'I don't know. He's pretty strong, or he wouldn't have survived the hammering they gave him,' he said. He thought for a moment. 'Come back tomorrow and see how he is.'

From the prison she rang a hotel she knew in Newton Stewart and booked a room for the four nights that remained of the week.

When she got there, she cancelled her appointments in Glasgow until the following Monday in case Calum took a turn for the worse. When she reported at the prison next day, he was able to hold out a hand and grasp hers and say something which lifted her heart.

'I missed you. Come back tomorrow.'

From the way he said it and the effort it cost him, she knew he had something important to tell her.

But the next day he was still suffering so much pain that the young doctor advised her to say hello and leave it at that.

When she returned on the third day, Ogilvie met her with big, worried eyes and led her into a private room next door to the prison officers' dining-room. From his attitude, her heart jumped, for she assumed something had happened to Calum, that perhaps he had died in the night. But he reassured her that Calum was recovering and she could see him later. He clumped his way into the canteen next door to return with two cups of coffee on a tray. When he dumped himself in a chair, she could almost see his mind toiling, searching for the right words. Finally, he said, 'I want to tell you something. But it's between ourselves and you mustn't whisper a word of it to anyone outside. Do I have your word?'

Aileen thought for a minute, wondering if he was gagging her by pre-empting her from finding for herself the information he was offering. She asked, 'Has it something to do with the attack on Calum Weir?' When Ogilvie nodded, she said, 'All right, you have my word that anything you tell me won't go further, but not anything I find out for myself.'

Ogilvie nodded. He took two sugar lumps and dissolved them one after the other on a spoon in his coffee, still mentally editing what he was going to tell her. When the sugar had disappeared he said, 'We had a suicide in the prison last night. A man killed himself by ripping up a bed-sheet and using it as a rope to hang himself from his locker.'

'But that's nothing unusual in prisons,' Aileen said.

'It's still serious – but this one's more serious.'

'Why more serious?'

'The man who died was one of our suspects.'

'Which means?'

Ogilvie dropped his voice to a whisper. 'It could mean that he might have been helped to commit suicide.'

'That doesn't implicate Calum Weir, does it?'

'Only if it's proved he identified the man to other prisoners, and we don't intend to put that question to him.'

'There were three men, I believe. What about the other two?'

'It so happens two prisoners have applied for a transfer to another open prison in Scotland.' Ogilvie shrugged. 'The governor and the prison authorities will have no objections in my view and their request will probably be granted quickly.'

'You mean the governor will be glad to see the last of them before they're given the same treatment they handed out to Calumi – or even, as you put it, helped to do themselves in like their ringleader.'

'Calum has a lot of loyal friends in this prison.'

'What if I persuade Calum Weir to apply for a full inquiry to the prison authorities and call these two men to give evidence?' She saw that Ogilvie had gone white-faced at the idea and pressed home her advantage. 'I want the names of the dead man and the other two.'

Ogilvie shook his head. She could almost see his Presbyterian hackles rise at the thought of breaking his own principles as well as prison rules. 'What you ask is impossible.'

'Well, I'll tell you why it isn't,' Aileen came back. Briefly she described how she was uncovering enough evidence to justify a retrial of the Weir case and this frightened several prominent people. Then, without naming Sir John Marr or Jennings or their friends, she told of how she had been warned to stop her inquiries and tell Weir to keep his mouth shut or someone would shut it for him. 'That's why I want those names,' Aileen went on. 'And I give you my word again that no one will know where they came from. If you don't name those men, I'll find someone who can, and I shall call for a full hearing of the assault.'

'We don't want any more trouble,' Ogilvie muttered.

'Then write the names down and I'll forget the inquiry.'

Aileen pushed her notebook across the table to Ogilvie, who hesitated then scribbled three names with a trembling hand.

'I've got something else to ask you.'

'What's that?'

Ogilvie sounded so miserable that she felt guilty about putting pressure on him. 'I'd like you to ask the governor on Calum's behalf to give him a couple of weeks' leave from the prison – in my custody.' Observing him hesitate, she turned the screw. 'I think it would be dangerous to discharge him from the hospital and have him ambushed again and perhaps murdered this time. You know, Calum Weir is considered one of our finest writers and I wouldn't like either to see him murdered, or the prison eternally damned for letting it happen.'

That argument had hit him between the eyes. 'I get what you mean. If you can give us the assurances that he will be in your custody and we can put an electronic tag on him, I think I can fix it.'

'Thank you, Charles,' she said, and he flushed with pleasure at hearing his name.

When she arrived in the hospital ward, Calum was sitting up in bed working with what looked like a drawing block and pencil though still grimacing with pain.

He put away the notepad, motioned her to the chair beside his bed and looked at her. 'I'm not much of a sight,' he said.

'You're alive and that's all that means anything.'

'Did Ogilvie tell you about Graham – the man who wanted to do me in?'

Aileen nodded. 'Who do you think gave him orders to beat you up or kill you?'

'Who do you think?'

'At a guess I'd say Johnnie Marr, and maybe I can prove it.'

'If you're thinking of the two others, they don't matter and they're too frightened to talk. Let it drop.'

'Why?'

'Because it's also a warning to you to stop trying to help me.'

'Marr doesn't frighten me,' she said, then told him about the Geddes party and her talk with Jennings and Marr.

'He doesn't like lawyers that he hasn't bought and he doesn't like scribblers like me. He's scared of what they'll find.'

'What did he think you would find?'

'A man like Johnnie Marr has whole cupboards full of skeletons, so he's always running scared of something.'

'Did you know he was sleeping with your third wife?'

'Well, he slept with my second wife, Liz, and he's a man who has certain fixed notions and routines.'

'When did he find out you were writing your own story?'

'You been talking to Kirstie?'

Aileen nodded. 'She told me you'd been asking questions about your father and mother.'

'I was writing a bit about myself for one of the papers that asked me for my story, and I suddenly realized I knew nothing about my old man. I didn't know why and when and where he went. Or whether he was even alive. Kirstie was a bit older than me and had that much more memory.'

'But you remembered your name, your father's name. Were you thinking of trying to trace him? When were you writing that?'

'Oh, about a year before they sent me to Barlinnie.' He looked at her. 'Why the interest?'

'I just wondered how far you had got. Did you discover who he was, your father, and where he went and if he's still alive?'

Weir shook his head. 'No, not a trace. I suppose if I'd had time to try the various records offices and even those people who knew him well and could have run into him after he left home, I might have got somewhere?'

'Does it bother you, not knowing?'

'If you mean do I have an identity crisis, the answer's no.'

'Do you mind if I look it up in the Scottish Records Office?'

'Just watch they don't see you.'

Weir lowered his voice and told her to have a look round and make sure nobody was watching or listening. When she had verified that there were no prison officers or nurses in the ward, he whispered to her to put her hand under his pillow. She complied and came out with the two pages from the *Sketch*.

'Did you see our rave notice?' he said and she nodded, telling him that she had served the paper with a writ and they had printed an apology for getting their facts wrong. Whom did he think had inspired that?

'Probably Liz. It's the sort of thing she'd get a kick out of. But I wouldn't worry about it.'

'It doesn't bother me, only it blows my cover about writing a book on the Weir case. But I came about something else.'

She told him about ringing her ex-husband, the psychiatrist, and explaining to him about the recurrent dreams he had. Her ex thought they might be the key to everything that had happened in the vital half-hour. Exposing and analysing them might unlock that part of his mind which switched off that night. She would go and have a session with him.

'But Calum, you have to tell me exactly what you see in this nightmare that keeps repeating,' she added.

She could see that he had taken everything on board and was nodding. Then he smiled at her and fixed her with his good eye, still black and blue and bruised. 'Aileen, do me a favour. Stand up.'

She stood up then he bid her turn round slowly, first one way then the other.

'What's that for?' she asked when she faced him.

'I just want to see you when you go.'

'Isn't that Irish?'

'I mean, I want to remember how you looked, how you moved, what you were wearing, all the details. I start with your hair, the blonde highlights in it and the way it curls and caresses your face. And those funny little flecks in your irises. And that cleft in your upper lip and—''

'Stop it, Calum....'

'And above all, I wanted to tell you that you're the best-looking woman I've ever seen and am ever likely to see.'

'I know what you're doing, you're trying to stop me from asking questions, then you're going to tell me to drop any idea of getting you released. Is that it?'

To her surprise, he nodded. 'I was coming to that.'

'So all the flattery was just flattery!'

He put out a hand and grasped hers. 'No, Aileen, what I said to you was true for me ... it's the way I see you. And I don't want anything to happen to you on my account.'

He was sincere; she could see that and was moved. She squeezed his hand tight and he answered by strengthening his grip.

'What are you working on?' she asked.

'Bits and pieces,' he said.

He flicked an index finger at her, beckoning her to come nearer. 'I have something to finish which I'll give you to smuggle out,' he whispered, conspiratorially. 'Can you find the dogs and walk them round our usual track? Nobody else will think of doing it, and they know you. Come back in half an hour.'

Aileen picked up the dogs from their cage by the sports ground and walked them round the grounds and through Weir's garden. She noticed that Sami and Rory had taken the hint and kept clear of the aconite among the patch of aromatic herbs. When she returned in half an hour, he passed her a drawing block and a small notebook.

'You wanted to see my dreams, so here they are.' He dropped his voice to a whisper. 'You'll have to go to the doctors' toilets here and hide them in your girdle.'

'I don't wear a girdle.'

'Well, wherever Ogilvie or the screws won't dare to look,' he said with a lop-sided smile. 'Anyway, if they found them they'd think I'd gone round the twist.'

No one thought of searching her as she left the prison with the drawing book and notebook tied round her waist. From the prison she drove home, stopping at New Galloway to have a cup of tea and a bun in a café. She recovered the two books before driving on to Glasgow. There, in her study, she opened the drawing book and the notebooks.

Weir had put together an extraordinary document. He had covered seventeen pages of his sketchblock with fifty-four drawings, some of them linked but others quite random. It was his nightmare in pure Kafkaesque images without any attempt to apply the logic of retrospect to these bizarre dreams or arrange them in any way. He had used his talents as a draughtsman and aquarellist to draw and paint his dreams exactly as he had remembered dreaming them. In their raw, unedited form with no real sequence. He had painted and written his dreams in his own hand.

When she studied some of the vivid pen-and-ink drawings and those in coloured inks and watercolours, it astonished her how much detail had gone into each of the dozens of pictures. He had linked them like a strip cartoon, even though they did not tell a coherent story. None of the pictures was bigger than a passport photo, but they were meticulously drawn with every detail shown. He must have taken her request to heart and worked for weeks on the book.

Calum had added a note to his strip cartoon sequence to say, 'This is the nightmare as I have lived it with minor variations. It wakes me up with such a pain in my chest I think my heart's packing in. It's as I live it, with no logical order. I've tried to reconstruct it with the same shapes and colours that I see. I only wish I could explain why it scares the daylights out of me.'

His strip cartoon begins with dark thunder clouds shot through with lightning. Out of this, a huge crow comes plummeting down to feast on carrion lying on a flower bed on the lawn outside a mansion like Creggan House. A lightning bolt scares the bird away. But it comes back. Now, a collie appears and tries by yapping and snapping to beat off the crow. A fight starts between the crow and the dog, a collie that can be no other than Appin. Now the crow is getting the better of the collie, swooping on him, tearing out great tufts of his fur and then going for his eyes. Appin realizes he is no match for this savage carrion bird and turns and bolts with the bird pursuing him until he finds cover in a thicket of tall, blue flowers.

But the animal that emerges from the thicket is now a wolf who stands by the carrion to beat off the crow with fang and claw.

In the second group of pictures, the crow returns, this time to attack someone who looks like Weir. At first he beats him off but the wolf joins forces with the bird. Weir knows he is losing the battle as the bird dives at his face and aims for his eyes and the wolf tears at his throat. He runs and dives into the thicket.

As both the crow and the wolf seemed to bulk so largely in his dream, Aileen peered at the bird through a magnifying glass. It was a hooded crow, its back and shoulders, rump and underparts grey.

She thought: Crows are death birds and this is a hooded crow?

Why a hooded crow?

And why a grey wolf?

She went back to Weir's strip cartoon.

Suddenly the pictures change. Now a figure dressed as a woman materializes out of the thunder and lightning gliding towards

Weir. Her long tresses of flaming red hair cover her face. On top of her head is a golden helmet. She is dressed in a cloak of dazzling, sparkling, blinding indigo blue with a floral pattern. On her shoulder the crow perches and the wolf pads behind her in the train of her robe. Out of a blue sleeve, like some conjurer, she produces a chalice. But a chalice filled not with liquor but with something like dead, tuberous fingers. And as she proffers this to Weir, her hair parts to reveal a grinning death's-head.

Yet Weir takes her offering as the crow flaps its wings and the wolf bares its teeth. And as he takes a mouthful he feels the poison lapping through his system. The death's-head grows to enormous proportions and battens on Weir, who struggles vainly to free himself.

He now has a knife in one hand and a gun in the other hand and is striking at the hooded figure and shooting. He is even counting the shots. How many? ... seven ... eight ... nine....

There the strip cartoon ended. But on a new page Weir had also done a pen-and-ink portrait and Aileen saw that it was of her.

She wondered first how he had managed to draw her like that. Then looking more closely at the drawing, she asked herself, 'Is that really how he sees me?'

No mirror or photograph had ever reflected or recorded her face like this. It was striking. Weir had managed to portray her face and her bust in no more than three unbroken lines in the way that someone like Matisse or Derain might have drawn it. And they did several dozen dummy runs before attempting the final drawing. How had Calum contrived to work so much of her face and bust into those three lines? He must have puzzled and worked over it for several weeks before distilling her face and half her figure into those three lines. He had drawn her in half-profile, perhaps as he had seen her first as a fencer.

And he had written a caption in calligraphic script:

> *My fair Aileen as no one but me sees her:*
> *And yet to seize her face I had a hundred tries:*
> *No two of them alike or truthful in my eyes*

But this one should not, I hope, displease her
I know – I've lost all your laugh-lines
And mislaid some of your lifelines
And how can I draw the music of your voice?

Beauty is a rare butterfly
But brilliant only on the wing.
To catch it my poor drawing
Is no more to me than a lie

It took her a long time to stop blushing.

chapter eighteen

A parry is used to uncover the opponent's target.

Although she went over Calum's dream sequence picture by picture, it made little sense to her and threw no light at all on that lost half-hour in that bedroom where his life had suddenly tilted and he found himself indicted and convicted of a double murder. And yet she knew that what he had portrayed in those pictures must answer some of the questions in her mind about the crime. She must make a date to see Peter, her ex-husband and a psychiatrist who might resolve Weir's enigmatic dreams.

But at the moment, she needed answers to so many other questions and the more she thought the more she realized many of those answers must lie in the Scottish Record Office in Edinburgh. Other bits of the puzzle might even be buried deep in the criminal records section. How did she get those answers without arousing the suspicions of the men who might have set up Calum Weir? If she made the trip they would find out even if they didn't physically follow her; it would get back to Geddes and from him to Jennings and Marr.

Already she knew most of the questions since they were those Weir had asked himself when he was trying to put together the early part of his own story.

In fact, when Kirstie rang her at Jamie's insistence and they met for the second time, she learned the sort of questions Calum had come asking his first love. Questions about their childhood. Kirstie was two years older and better able to remember Calum's father and mother and their tenement neighbours. Calum had told her he was writing something about himself for one of the Glasgow papers, but he didn't say which. That would be about six years ago.

Did he mention anybody else to her: Marr, for instance?

Kirstie could not remember any specific reference to Marr, but she knew Calum's story was somehow intertwined with Marr's.

That conversation with Kirstie had raised another question in Aileen's mind: When did Marr get his knighthood? Was Calum writing something that might have revealed something in Marr's past that would quash any move to give him his knighthood?

Kirstie had also confessed how worried she was about Jamie's strange behaviour. She said it had something to do with the man who had baited the trap for Calum the night of the murders. It had something to do with Dan Meney. Kirstie had whispered that she thought Jamie knew who had called Calum the night of the murders and that was why he was so interested in the mobile phone she had taken from Meney.

Aileen had asked Kirstie if Jamie might know where Calum kept his gun. She showed the photograph of the Beretta. But Kirstie had never seen such a gun either in Jamie's or Dan's possession.

Aileen filled several pages of her notebook with these questions before seeking out Dorothy McKee, her friend in the law office of the High Court. Yes, Dorothy knew someone in the Scottish Records Office who would help her, a lady called Flora Begley, who ran part of the records office and could trace anyone anywhere.

Aileen rang Miss Begley and arranged to meet her the next Sunday morning in a teashop on the Royal Mile. She chose a weekend knowing that Geddes and Jennings played golf at Killermont and Marr was probably on the Firth of Clyde in his motor cruiser. She found a small hotel just off the west end of Princes Street and booked for three nights.

Flora Begley was just as Dorothy described her. Matronly, with horn-rimmed glasses and greying hair swept back and ending in a chignon. She was no-nonsense and jotted down the names and details Aileen provided, saying she would start work on them next morning. Aileen gave her the names of Weir's father and mother, Alexander Ross Cattanach and Margaret Menzies, and asked her to find out if and when Cattanach died and if she could trace their marriage lines. She wanted any information on Marr and his mother that the records listed. There was no need to warn this lady not to divulge what she was seeking and for whom. Women like Flora Begley did not gossip or give anything away.

On Tuesday morning, Flora rang Aileen in her hotel to say she had traced some of the information in the records but had failed with other inquiries. Aileen had expected something like this.

That evening, they met in Ritchie's, a small restaurant in Corstorphine. Before they sat down, Aileen read in Flora's face a blend of puzzlement and elation.

'I found a birth certificate for Alexander Ross Cattanach,' she said. 'Calum Weir's father was born in 1938 in Maryhill, Glasgow. I also found a copy of his marriage certificate. He and Margaret Brodie Menzies were married in a Glasgow register office in 1961. There's the birth certificate for Calum Ross Cattanach in 1962 and I also found the mother's death certificate dated 15 March 1966.'

Flora handed over the photocopies she had made of the documents, then said apologetically, 'I'm sorry, I couldn't find anything to show Mr Cattanach is dead.'

'No death certificate?' Aileen queried.

'Nothing.' Flora shook her head. 'But that's not to say that he's still alive. He might have died abroad, or died under another name and we have no record.'

'Can we widen the search?' Aileen said.

'I can try some of the missing persons websites on the Internet and places like the Public Record Office at Kew in England.'

'His death certificate could not have been lost – or removed?'

'Very unlikely,' Flora said. 'But if it was we have a chance of tracing it. Most of our files were backed up on computers thirty years ago. I can check on the computerized version, but that might take time.'

'What about Marr?'

'That's a funny story, too. I searched for his birth certificate, but that's not in the records.'

'Isn't that too much of a coincidence, these two lots of missing papers?'

Flora Begley shook her head. 'It happens fairly often. Three years ago we had a fire and last year this basement was flooded and we had to flit with all the papers and sort them out. But I'll run a check on the computerized files when I've found Alexander Ross Cattanach.'

Flora promised to let her know if the computer search yielded anything but suggested that since it might take days or even weeks, Aileen should not waste her time in Edinburgh waiting for it. Flora would ring with any information that she discovered.

For Aileen it was something of an anti-climax; she did not know what she had expected from tracing Weir's father, but it seemed Alexander Cattanach had no relevance to the reason for those two deaths and his son's conviction for them.

chapter nineteen

A barrage is a tie in a fencing bout between two competitors.

She knew Peter was running true to form when his door was opened by a young Indian who was beautiful enough to have been one of the thousand brides of that oversexed god, Krishna. She turned her smile on Aileen and said in English with an unexpected Scottish burr, 'Please enter. Peter is expecting you.' Aileen stepped into the flat, wondering if the girl was aware that Peter and she had been married for four years.

Peter came out of a door giving off the living-room and from what she took for his study. He was dressed in an embroidered kaftan without the girdle. He had sandals on his feet. She guessed that there was only flesh beneath the kaftan. He had an unworldly look which meant he was into Veda or Buddhism or in some other transcendental mode. The Indian girl, she assumed, was the complement of this as well as supplying sexual appeasement.

That notion was confirmed when she heard a high, lilting Indian voice yodelling some florid song presumably in Hindustani, accompanied by a sitar and finger-drum. That sound brought back memories of the hours Aileen had suffered listening to Indian music and Vedic mantras until they almost hypnotized her.

'Ah! Aileen.' Peter came to put his hands on her shoulders and graze both of her cheeks with his. Was that pungent smell off a Boots toilet counter, or incense sticks from Benares?

'You've met Shanta, I see.' He turned to the girl. 'This is

Shanta das Gupta. Shanta, meet Aileen, who found me too difficult to live with and got off the wheel of our life and the eightfold
way. She never attained to more than the second degree of
concentration.' He giggled, but then he was always a giggler.

However, he was right; she had done her best but finally gave
up. She knew Peter was one of those psychiatrists who had
chosen that discipline on the physician-heal-thyself principle. He
was a nutcase himself. But he passed for a brilliant analyst and
Aileen had come to him as a patient when her father lost his
court case and her brother had become a drug addict. She had
done eighteen months of unloading her psyche in his consulting
room while he remained neutral, mute. She didn't know why she
fell in love with him; she could only think she was hooked by the
psychiatric phenomenon of transference and she was projecting
her emotions and fantasies on to his person. When she found he
didn't measure up to those projections, that discovery spelled the
end of their marriage.

She realized later there was another factor: counter-transfer-
ence arising out of his dependence on her. He needed her much
more than she had ever needed him. Indeed, she realized early in
their marriage that he was always as much in need of treatment
as his patients.

He wasn't a unique case. In his hospital and the medical
circles they moved in, she had met limping or peg-legged
orthopaedists, hard-eared, runny-nosed ENT specialists, blue-
nosed, breathless cardiologists, swag-bellied nutritionists,
hop-headed pharmacologists and neurologists who forgot why
they tied knots in their handkerchiefs. To say nothing of neurotic
and nutty psychiatrists by the barrow load.

If Peter was eccentric, he at least had a reputation even among
his colleagues not only as an analyst but for the treatment of the
depressions and schizoid states with drugs.

He hadn't changed. Still the same neck twitch that she found
so hard on his collars; and from the deep yellow stains on his
fingers he still chain-smoked and still called all the statistics on
tobacco cancer and the other smoking-related illnesses damned
lies.

Now he was pointing to a brown plastic sofa like a somnolent hippo which wrapped itself round her when she sat down. Shanta had vanished like one of those goddess-like creatures in Indian films, and Peter had gone to a drinks cabinet and was throwing a question over his shoulder about what she wanted to drink. She opted for mineral water.

He came back with this and a double whisky, saying it was after six o'clock so he felt entitled. He sat down opposite her, wrapping his kaftan round his bare legs and tucking them under him. He looked at her, inching his eyes over her face and head.

'It's your hair ... you never did your hair like that for me,' he said. 'It's fetching ... it's even on-turning, if my drift you get. The way it curves round your face.'

'Peter, my hair's irrelevant.'

'Oh no, it isn't. It's a statement. Who's it for?'

'Nobody.'

'Tut-tut. And you used to have no secrets from your psychiatrist!'

'I came about a problem,' she said, curtly.

'Ah! So you did. It must be a tricky one to bring you here. Hadn't you better start from the beginning and tell me all about it?'

So Aileen carefully explained how she had become involved in the Weir case and some of the inquiries she had made until then. It meant spelling out slowly the whole story, for Peter Farley had little knowledge of the crime and the trial and knew nothing of Weir as a writer. But he listened closely and even switched on his small tape recorder while she outlined the problem and then answered his questions. She omitted the more intimate side of her meetings with Calum Weir, knowing how jealous Peter could be.

But she didn't fool him, good alienist that he was. 'Are you sure when you get him out of jail he isn't going to murder you in your matrimonial bed?' he said with a smile. When she put on a puzzled look and faced him with it, he said, still smiling, 'I'm envy-green that you've found the love of your life. Now, don't tell me you're not in love with him. It's written all over you.'

'Well, if I am....'

'I'm over the moon for you – if you've really found somebody worthy of your steel – someone....'

'Let's leave my love life out of it, Peter,' she cut in. 'Just tell me, is it possible for someone to fire eleven shots into two people then mutilate them and have no recollection of doing it?'

Farley thought for a moment, then nodded. 'It's more than possible,' he said. 'People in a fit of sheer madness or in a brainstorm commit acts that the mind represses to the point that they become completely lost. A sort of defensive oblivion.'

'Would he not even dream about it?'

'He might ... indeed, he probably would ... does this man, Weir, have strange dreams that might be connected to the crime?'

'Yes, he has these odd dreams, but he's not killing people. Though he feels – and I agree – there might be some connection between these dreams and what happened the night of the murders.'

'There almost certainly is,' Farley said. 'But I wouldn't expect the unconscious mind to play back the gory details or even to give this man, Weir, an edited version of them in his dreams. Those dreams you're talking about will have been encrypted by the mind to make them bearable. They have to be decoded for them to be understood.'

Farley rewound the tape recorder and replayed part of their conversation while he went to replenish his drink. Returning to his seat and assuming his yoga posture, he stopped the tape several times to re-run Aileen's description of the crime as it was reconstituted by the police and the prosecution, and the part where Magee, the pathologist, had told her that Weir was dazed and looked either drunk or drugged when they led him away from the murder scene.

'Do you know if Weir had anything to drink that night?'

'No, he didn't,' she said. 'And he swears he has never taken hard or even soft drugs.'

'But you say the pathologist thought he might be drugged. Did the police take some of his blood and analyse it?'

'I don't think so. After all, he confessed. And they had his gun and his prints on the jack handle and champagne bottle he disfigured them with.'

'But you're convinced he's innocent?' When she nodded, he continued, 'Then that means he was the victim of a plot by someone. Any idea who?'

'Yes, I have – one of his oldest friends, Sir John Marr.'

Aileen explained the relationship between the two, both as boys and men; she added that Weir had been trying to find and piece together parts of his own story and might have come up with something that incriminated Marr. In addition, Marr had slept with Weir's first wife, Liz Maxwell, and had also been sleeping with the murdered woman, Lorna.

'This gangland type doesn't strike me as a nice character and he seems to have it in for Weir.'

'That's how it looks.'

'So he kills two birds with one stone,' Farley mused. 'And his policeman friend, Jennings, helps to cover up both crimes, is that it?'

'That's my reading of it,' Aileen said.

'You say he remembers nothing after going into that bedroom and seeing the bodies?' Peter said. 'And you wonder if he could have been knocked out by somebody and given a drug to induce amnesia.'

'That's the theory that would fit all the bits of the puzzle I've gathered up to now.'

Peter had kept another habit. When he was thinking hard, he curled a lock of his lank, streaky-blond hair and twirled his index finger round it as though dialling someone on another planet or getting a line to his own brain. He was musing. 'It's not impossible ... he'd have to be put out.' He dialled once more then said, 'Leave it with me and I'll let it simmer and come back to you.'

Aileen had wondered if she should break Weir's confidence and show him the sequence of drawings he had made of his dreams. She decided he must see them.

Freeing herself from the embrace of his couch, she produced them from her wallet and laid the seventeen pages of the sketchbook out in the order Weir had given his fifty-four drawings. She noticed at once how they had gripped Peter's attention. He picked up the pages and, wide-eyed, scanned each one, murmuring to himself.

'It's amazing. It's Kafka in pictures ... he's remembered the dream as it happened ... and that's remarkable.'

'It isn't when you think he's had something like this dream for five years,' Aileen commented.

'No ... I meant he's got all these symbols – the crow, the wolf, the poison roots in the chalice, the death's-head, the robe with the floral pattern. With these and what you know of the case we should be able to arrive at something like the truth.'

'All right, let's start with the hooded crow feasting on the carrion.'

Farley dialled his lock of hair, teasing his brain for a minute. 'The hooded crow isn't the only animal. There's the wolf, which allies itself with the crow to attack Weir then join the figure representing death and the poison chalice. Is there a link between crows, wolves and poison tubers?'

Aileen shook her head. 'No, I can't see that. The only poison Calum has ever mentioned is aconite, which grows in the garden he created.'

Farley grinned and snapped his fingers. 'But that's it. Wolfsbane's another name for aconite, and its roots are a deadly poison.'

'And it has blue flowers – like the robe on Death.'

'And sometimes yellow – like the pattern.'

'Could the real murderers have used that on him?' she asked.

'I don't see the point. It would have poisoned him, even in small doses.' Farley thought for a moment. 'But there are other things they might have done.'

'Such as?'

He shook his head. 'I'd have to look at the literature and talk to a couple of people. There's a research pharmacologist who's good on amnesiac drugs and a gas-man, an anaesthetist, who might tip my hand. Leave it with me until I see what they say.'

chapter twenty

There is no attack that cannot be parried and no parry that cannot be evaded.

It took two weeks and a mass of paperwork, but she persuaded the board of governors and the Scottish home office to allow Weir two weeks' leave in her care providing he reported to a police station every day. Her hardest task was pleading with Calum to accept the offer. He seemed nervous, apprehensive about leaving the prison. That didn't surprise her, for in a sense prison life was the most stable situation he had ever enjoyed.

However, had he guessed some of the programme she had in mind for him during those two weeks he might never have agreed to leave Creeburn and his dogs.

When she went to pick him up in his cell, she saw him for the first time without his prison denims and wearing the clothes he had when he was arrested and later tried. But he, too, was taken aback when she produced a complete wardrobe and told him to throw away his other clothes. Aileen had gone to the best men's shop in the city centre and ordered trousers, a suede jacket, shirts, a cashmere cardigan, shoes, two ties. Weir looked at them, remarking that he had never seen such clothes let alone worn them. But he did as he was bid and donned his new outfit although he looked uneasy.

'Just don't ask me to look in a mirror,' he said.

His hardest act was saying goodbye to the three dogs, who sensed something bizarre was happening as he picked each of them up and whispered in their ears. Aileen didn't ask what he was telling them, assuming he was reassuring them he would return soon.

Aileen was so relieved to see the prison gate shut in her rear mirror that she pushed the Rover too fast over the hill road until Weir put a hand on her shoulder and called, 'Aileen, you'll kill us both at this rate.'

'At this rate! But I'm not doing sixty.'

'I know, but my biological ticker's on prison time and my watch hands move half as slow again as yours. Anyway, I'd like to smell the heather on these hills, and the pines. Can I ask where you're taking us?'

'There's a hotel just outside Kilmarnock. It's an old manor house and it's quiet and I know the people who run it.' She looked at him. 'How does that suit you?'

'Do they know about me?'

'No, they don't. And if they did it wouldn't make any difference to them.' Her experience with prisoners told her he had to be given time and help to adapt. Like most long-term prisoners, he felt alien, footloose, a stranger to freedom. After all, he had left what had been home to him for five years, he had broken all his routines, he had left his true friends, his dogs. Freedom wasn't a commodity he had used much in five years and he felt lost, disorientated. 'Anyway, you're disguised,' she said.

At that he laughed. 'Ay, that I am,' he said. 'Anyway, your Ayrshire manor sounds fine. I don't think I want to meet your folk just yet. And I want to keep well away from Glasgow.'

In Girvan she parked outside a café, took out her purse and handed him several Scots pound notes.

'What are these for?' he said.

'To buy us some tea and let you get run-in handling money,' she said.

'But it's your money.'

'You can pay me back when you're released and collect your royalties and indemnity from Her Majesty's government.'

'You mean in seven years if I keep my nose clean.'

'I mean when I prove you're not guilty.'

Observing him outside prison for the first time, she noted how he had changed. He ordered and paid for their tea, but tentatively as though feeling his way and having to relearn old habits and gestures. What had happened to the assurance and confidence he had shown in prison? She would have to take things slowly or he might even bolt back to prison, to the only environment he knew.

'How does freedom feel?' she asked.

Weir looked at her. How could he explain that at the moment, it felt like another form of prison, that he felt remote from everything. Like a Martian? Even familiar, remembered things seemed odd, and at times ominous. That short drive had unnerved him as the trees and hedgerows flashed past them in a blur. On these unencumbered roads, cars and the odd truck still came at them so quickly he was ducking them mentally, waiting for the collision. Of course he knew he had to make allowances for his one-eyed vision, which foreshortened and therefore accelerated everything.

Although he knew it was relative, it did seem the dashboard clock was going at full gallop after five years of slow, monotonous prison hours. From time to time he glanced at the attractive woman sitting beside him and couldn't quite believe it, he watched her drive with such careless poise, her silk-sheathed legs shuttling between the accelerator, clutch and brake. Even she seemed different on the outside. He had to get used to her, too. In prison, they had one type of relationship – lawyer and client. He wondered how she viewed him now.

'It feels like getting used to a new planet,' he said.

When they arrived at Cromlin House Hotel, the owners greeted Aileen as an old friend. She had often stayed there when she had difficult briefs to deal with and wanted peace and quiet. It was a mansion in Scots baronial style with no more than seven rooms, which meant they would not meet many people if they used the dining room. It made large inroads into her credit card, but she hired the best rooms in the hotel, a suite with a bedroom and sitting room and a view over twenty miles of open country. A man emerging from a cell measuring four metres by three needed to stretch himself and have the feeling of space.

She had lied to Weir about the hotel, for she had taken the

owners, Jack and Muriel Glencannon, into her confidence, explaining who Calum Weir was and what she was doing with him. He would sign them in as Mr and Mrs Thomas Ochiltree, a good local name.

Weir signed them in without suspecting her stratagem. He carried one of their two suitcases up the curved staircase to their front room, which looked on to rolling and wooded hills and fields where brown and white Ayrshire cattle were grazing.

Weir gazed at the view for a long moment as though it reminded him of something. He turned to Aileen. 'Do you remember Ogilvie's number at the prison?'

'Yes, I have his number, but what for? ... You're not thinking of going back, Cal?' she said, switching on a smile that hardly concealed her disquiet.

'No, Aileen. It sounds crazy, but I wonder if you'd call him and ask about the dogs, if they're all right and they're getting their walk. They may be off their feed.'

When she had rung and assured him they were fine, they'd had their walk and were circling round their feeding bowl like lions round a slain gazelle, he relaxed and stood for a moment, looking at her until she became uncomfortable. Then he said, surprisingly, 'Aileen, this ex of yours, this head-shrink – he must be a nut. He is a nut, isn't he?'

She cocked her head at him, wondering. 'Well, I suppose he is – what trick-cyclist isn't a bit of a nut? But why Peter and why the question?'

'Just that if he wasn't a nut you and I wouldn't be here.' He shook his head slowly, wonderingly. 'And I just can't believe it that I'm here with a woman like you.'

At her suggestion, they went for a stroll in the woods belonging to the hotel, a silver-birch, oak and elm forest which filled with the clatter of wild pigeons' wings and the cawing of rooks as they entered it. A broad stream ran parallel with the track through the forest and when they had walked for half an hour, they sat by the banks under a clump of alders watching the slow water break over boulders and the occasional ripple as a fly-catching trout broke surface.

'Don't move quickly, but look under the trees on the other bank.'

She peered at the grassy hump under the bank and saw a flat-whiskered, cat-like head appear then a rubbery body and long, flailing tail driving him through the water. 'What is he?' she whispered.

'An otter … that's his nest and he's after a fish or a frog for his family supper.'

Sure enough the otter suddenly plunged, surfaced, plunged again before his head reappeared with a small trout clamped in his jaws. He swam bullet-straight and disappeared under the bank.

'He'll polish that off, head, tail and bones, and be back for more.'

'Cal, where did you learn about animals and nature?'

'Oh, one of my newspaper editors tried to turn me into a nature boy and sent me into the Highlands among the bens and glens and lochs to write a weekly birds-and-bees piece. But you can say I picked it up here and there – like everything else.'

As they walked back, she said: 'It's been a wonderful day and the only thing I find hard to believe is that I've persuaded you to swap your dogs for me and come this side of the prison fence.'

'You know why?' She shook her head and he stopped her and looked at her as though to mark what he was going to say. 'It may sound corny, but you brought back my faith in love.' He added with a shrug, 'Only I shall never understand why you bothered with me.'

'I believed you were wrongly convicted, that's why.'

'And if I haven't been....'

'It wouldn't change anything now. I've met you and I love you and whatever you've done I would still feel the same way about you. So if I'm wrong and they're right, I'll come and squat outside that prison until they open the gate for us both – if you want me.'

'Aileen, you don't know what a problem you've taken on – I mean me.'

She reached out and took his hand, which felt cold. 'Nothing's a problem if you care for me as much as I care for you.' She paused for a moment, then said, 'Well, there is a slight problem.'

'What's that?'

'I was wondering when you were going to kiss me. You want to, don't you?'

'Yes, and I want to make love to you. But don't ask me now. My body clock's not set for love-making yet.' He put his arm round her and drew her close to him, kissed her then whispered in her ear, 'Aileen, I wouldn't be here if I didn't love you.'

She decided to take her time from him, to let him find his feet and feel his freedom slowly. He never ceased to impress her with his way of looking at things. That first afternoon they trudged for miles through the woods and over the fields. Weir, the slum boy and city dweller, knew infinitely more about nature than the country girl she was. There was a word that jumped into her mind when she listened to him: anthropomorphism. He identified with animals and plants and saw the hand of a creator in everything that lived and breathed in nature.

In that walk, he followed the flight of two ravens to their treetop nest with young and fascinated her with lore about those birds. He might have only one seeing eye, but had he not spotted them and pointed them out, she'd never have seen the stoat or the red squirrels, or the capercailzie that rose with thrumming wings and flew low along the stream. Men could learn from trees, he said. Like the enormous oak he pointed out, which created its own living space and never thought of moving out of it but wanted nothing other than to enjoy the sun, the rain, the wind and the elements.

'What was it Pascal said? "All the ills of man come from the fact that he cannot sit quietly by his own fireside." '

As they stood on an old hump-backed bridge watching the trout and the minnows in the sunlit stream, her mobile phone went. It was her secretary saying that Geddes wanted to get in touch with her. He made it sound urgent, and asked for her mobile phone number. Should she ring him back and give it to him? No, Aileen told her. Ring and say I'm out of touch for the next few days.

'Do you use that thing much?' Weir asked when she had put the instrument back in a pocket.

'No, not much,' she said. 'Why? Do you think the radiation affects the brain cells and turns us into idiots?'

'Well, it has an effect on the brain rhythms,' he said, seriously, then with his lop-sided grin, 'but most of the idiots who spend their time and money babbling irrelevant rubbish into those things needn't worry – they were idiots before they bought them.'

She wanted to hug him for that remark. For it convinced her that he had not left all of himself in that soulless prison, that he had some of his old spark with him.

But that first night set her wondering about him again. They dined early and retired to their room where they lit up the TV a quarter of an hour before the ten o'clock news. Weir had not seen much television and commented that neither the ads nor the news had changed much in five years.

'Ponchielli would never have written the *Dance of the Hours* if he'd known the TV ad men would use it to sell piss-proof babies' nappies,' he said. 'And Mozart would have left *Eine Kleine Nachtmusik* unwritten had he thought they'd ally it to ads for a chocolate sleeping draught or cat and dog food.'

Aileen thought Weir looked tired and she realized that his first day as a free man after five years had stressed and drained him. She suggested they go to bed and he agreed.

They had a double bed and a single bed in the suite. She quelled Calum's objections and insisted he take the double bed for himself. She let him use the bathroom, undress, don the pyjamas she had bought for him and get into bed. By the time she had finished her toilet, he was sound asleep.

In the middle of the night she woke with the tail-end of a scream echoing in her head. Weir was blundering about in the dark still screaming and moaning. He was having a nightmare. Aileen wondered if she should wake him, but as she rose he suddenly stopped screaming and muttered something. Straining her ears, she listened, and again he mumbled several words.

'They're aconite, you hooded swine ... it's poison ... it's murder.'

When he began moaning she went and led him to the bed

and laid him down and covered him with a sheet and blanket. Within a few minutes, he had quietened down and fallen asleep.

In the morning, when they brought breakfast and they were sharing this at the table by the window, she said, casually, 'Did you sleep well?'

'Well enough – but I had one of my dreams.' He looked at her. 'I didn't wake you, did I? Some of the inmates at Creeburn complained about my yodelling in the wee small hours.'

'No, I heard nothing,' she lied.

When he had the same sleepwalking nightmare for the next two nights she repeated what she had done and led him back to bed. On the last occasion after he went back to sleep, she climbed into her single bed and fell asleep.

Something woke her again. It was still dark and the luminous hands of her watch told her it was four o'clock. She had slept for no more than half an hour. Her eye went to the window where someone had drawn back the curtains. Weir was sitting on a chair, his back to her, staring out the window. She turned on her bedside lamp, rose and went over to him. She could see he was almost rigid with tension so she went to the bathroom and came back with a glass of water and one of the pills her father had given her in case Weir had a nervous crisis. He took the pill without question and swallowed it with a little water.

'What happened, Cal?'

'I don't know. I had that dream. I dreamt it again but there was more to it and it was worse, much worse.' He got up and paced back and forth for a minute then turned to her 'Aileen, I think I should go back to prison and stay there.'

'Calum, why? What is it in that dream that frightens you?'

He sat down and took her hands and pressed them tight. 'I saw myself shooting both of them, firing twelve shots into them, then breaking the bottle ... I lifted it out of the ice bucket....'

'Calum,' she interrupted. 'There wasn't an ice bucket.'

'I broke it over the iron bedhead....'

'It was broken over one of the bedside tables. I'll take you back there and show you the dent and the small incisions it made in the wood.'

'Aileen, there's another thing – the blue flowers.'

Blue flowers! ACONITE: that was the word he had uttered in both his dreams that had woken her. She remembered it had blue flowers and spiky leaves and she had seen it growing in his prison garden; he had even forbidden the dogs to touch the roots. Those tapering roots! Weren't they the poison roots in the chalice that he had drawn and painted as one of the series about his dreams?

She wondered if she should try to explain what she thought his dream might mean; but perhaps it wasn't the moment, when he was as tense as a harp string. Instead, she said: 'Calum, you had a mixed-up dream and you were just projecting yourself into everything you know about the crime. And your guilt feelings completed the picture.'

She sat with him until his pill took effect then persuaded him to try to sleep.

That morning, without letting on to him, Aileen rang her parents who lived in Troon, and asked them to come up and have lunch with her and Weir in the hotel. When they arrived around eleven, to her surprise and chagrin they had brought Roddy with them. And Roddy had brought his dog, a mongrel he had rescued from the final oblivion needle in the local pound. It was a mutt with bits of a cocker spaniel, a wire-haired terrier and other breeds.

'What made you bring them?' she whispered to her father.

'I couldn't keep Roddy away when he heard Calum Weir was only ten miles away. And Mandolin's all right ... she goes everywhere with him.'

'It's a girl! And he calls her Mandolin!'

'She has a high-pitched falsetto chuckle, that's why.'

She gave up. What could anyone do about Roddy, but like him for his zany attitude to life?

Yet Roddy and Mandolin saved the day for her.

Mandolin gazed at you with her piebald head and lollopy ears cocked to one side and eyes like a doe's with affection shining out of them. She took to Weir at once, obviously scenting Sami, Rory and Meg and his love for animals. She laid her soft muzzle in his hand and gave a funny soprano gurgle and he was hooked.

Roddy, who had recovered from his drug episode, was working as a hospital orderly; but he was toiling just as hard in his spare time trying to write a novel. Aileen knew he had been inspired by hearing her talk about Weir and warned him about bothering the writer. 'Calum's got more on his mind than listening to you going on about your writing,' she said.

But Roddy ignored her. Even she was impressed that he had read most of Weir's books and could talk about them with some insight. She was more surprised when Weir explained how he had started writing and gave him points about how to read and dissect good writers, how to construct a story and acquire a writing routine.

He and Roddy walked off into the woods with Mandolin quartering the ground before and behind them. When they returned just before lunch, Aileen noted the change in Weir. He was bright-eyed and more alert than at any time since she had known him.

'Roddy, what did you do to him?'

'I just got him to talk about books and bookmen and bookwomen. He's fantastic. He's a whole history of literature on the hoof. I never knew that a storyline was like two and two. It means only what's on paper. Like music, it defies analysis. What you and I feel about a piece of writing are different things. Even words have a different resonance for every one of us.' Roddy was really excited. 'Calum makes you see things in a new way, don't you think?'

She nodded, then asked: 'Was that all you talked about?'

Roddy gave her that arch look which she knew covered up something.

'Well?'

'I suppose you could say literature was his second choice. He really wanted to talk about you, all about you.' He shrugged. 'So, I filled him in.'

'What did you tell him?'

'Just your whole curriculum vitae, your exemplary school and university days, your fencing exploits. And of course the downside which interested him.'

'What downside?' she asked, irritated.

'How you had a four-year ride with a sick-tricyclist until you found the tandem act hard to sustain. That and your other peccadilloes amused him.'

Aileen punched him on the shoulder, though not too hard. 'If I had a foil or an épée handy I'd run you through and let you bleed to death.'

'He thinks you brought us up here for him to run the rule over us and decide if we were suitable in-laws.'

'Roddy, stop it. You know well enough Calum Weir is serving a life sentence.'

'Are you going to marry him?'

'He goes back to prison next week.'

'They have special licences, and they also have padres in prisons, didn't you know?'

They had lunch on the terrace of the hotel. Weir kept them in thrall with his stories of Glasgow slum life and his reporting days in places like the Gorbals, Bridgeton, the Gallowgate and the dozens of foreign assignments he had undertaken for newspapers and magazines. He had watched H-bomb tests and space rockets lift off in America and Russia and had followed several African wars. And for half the meal, Mandolin commandeered his lap, she devoured at least half his smoked salmon and ate more of his steak than he did.

When she saw her parents and Roddy to their car, she noticed her father wanted a word. 'Aileen, darling, I know how you feel about Calum and anybody with half an eye can see he's in love with you. And I'm sure you'll prove he's innocent. But by doing that you might put your own life at risk, you know that?'

'You mean I'll have to prove who did those murders.'

'Ay, and since they've done two, another one won't frighten them.'

It was a sobering thought on which to end a memorable day.

But something else put it out of her mind and more than made up for all the risk she might run.

For the first time since he left prison, Calum slept soundly all night without so much as a whimper.

chapter twenty-one

A counter riposte follows the parry of a riposte.

Weir was gradually winding down and finding his feet outside prison. She realized he was making progress when he ceased to be scared of the traffic during their excursions, when he moved among the guests and staff in the hotel without the look of the odd man out, when he could also go to sleep without turning his face to the wall as he did in his prison cell.

Aileen had given him heavily edited accounts of the inquiries she had made and the people she had met in the past four months. She omitted any reference to her search for his father. They walked a lot and made car trips to various places in Ayrshire and Lanarkshire. Slowly they were discovering each other.

At the end of the first week, when they had both dressed and Weir asked what her programme for the day was, Aileen went and fetched the leather wallet in which she kept the fifty-four drawings he had made of his nightmares, though she didn't open it.

She said: 'I remember you remarked once that the Apostle John and the Bible had got things round their necks when they said, "In the beginning was the Word and the Word was with God, and the Word was God." You said that scientifically and philosophically this was baloney – the image came before the word.'

'Aileen, *chérie*, don't take everything I say as gospel.'

'But you still think so, don't you?'

'Well, yes – if that's the answer you're fencing for.'

Aileen opened the leather wallet and produced the seventeen pages he had covered with his fifty-four drawings of his nightmare. Weir drew a deep breath and it was obvious that he had the shivers at the mere sight of his work and what it signified for him. She sensed that he knew where she was heading.

'Perhaps we'd better sit down and I'll tell you everything I've done – well, almost everything – and what's in my mind to do now.'

'But I know most of the story,' he protested.

'Just sit down,' Aileen ordered and Weir threw his hands up but obeyed.

Aileen began at the beginning with the day she fished Meney out of the reservoir and picked up his mobile phone and took him through the whole story: how she had quizzed Geddes, gone to Creggan House and seen Kirstie and their son, Jamie. When she described how Liz Maxwell walked out of the restaurant, Weir interrupted.

'I'd like to have seen that wild-cat contest,' he said.

It was news to him that she had seen and handled the exhibits in the High Court archives and met and accused Magee of failing to do his job as a forensic pathologist properly – before and during the trial.

'What could you expect from an Irish drunk? I heard him and thought he'd been got at by Jennings, another fraud and a crook besides.'

Weir listened impassively as she described her night at Geddes's party and her face-off with Marr. 'You were lucky he didn't try to rape you,' he said. 'That man's a copper-plated bastard. He was a bastard as a boy, he was a bastard as a street-corner boy and even his fancy get-up, his big house and his title haven't changed him.'

When she came to the night her flat was burgled, she omitted any mention of finding Jamie almost beaten to death on her doorstep as she did not want to disturb him or provoke him into seeking the gang responsible and avenging the assault. From a pocket of the leather wallet, she produced the SIM card from Dan Meney's phone. 'This is what they were looking for in my flat,' she said.

Weir took the small rectangle of plastic and gazed at the amber chip it contained as though searching for its secret in the geometrical tracing on its surface. Aileen retrieved it, broke open her own mobile phone and substituted the chip from Meney's for her own. One by one, she went through the nine numbers Meney had logged on the phone stopping at the crude code-names he had given for three people – JAK, MIK and ALLIE.

'Do any of these names or numbers mean anything to you?' she asked.

Weir nodded. 'Only one – the Stirling number. It's the number of the golf club I was staying at that weekend.'

'But whoever it was called you on your mobile phone to ask you to return to your sick wife's bedside.'

'Ay, and it was probably Meney, who'd have had that number – though I can't be sure.'

'But you thought it might be somebody else – Jamie, for instance.'

'Ay, I did.'

'And that's why you said nothing.'

Weir nodded, then pointed to the other odd number that Meney had logged. 'Have you tried that number?'

'No. I was scared they would log the call and trace it back to me.'

'What about trying it now? If you think they'll register the number that's calling them we can use a callbox.'

Aileen shook her head. 'I'm not sure that's the number of the people who were behind the burglary and probably had something to do with the murders at Creggan House. But if it is, we'd only alert them before I have enough evidence to face them.'

'Why would Meney have it and log it into his mobile phone?'

'That's a question I've been puzzling over for weeks. Another thing: Where was Meney coming from and where was he going the night he chose to end his life?'

'Dan was a bit of a rattle-brain and he never knew where he was from one minute to the next.'

'He knew when and where to phone you and bait the trap,' Aileen said.

'I suspect somebody got at him, either through drugs or by threatening him.'

'You mean Marr.'

'Could be.'

She told him about going back to Creggan House and finding where one of the missing bullets had landed and being surprised by a man calling himself a surveyor by the name of Mark Anderson; he was obviously looking for something in the house. She described the man, but it meant nothing to Weir, who also had no idea of what he might be seeking there.

Aileen picked up the drawings. 'I've something to ask you,' she said.

Weir shrugged. 'I knew it the minute you produced those hallucinations. You want me to give you playback, is that it?'

'Worse than that. I want you to go back to Creggan House to see if it helps you to supply the key to the puzzle.'

Weir got up and paced the room and she could see the agitation working in his face. Aileen went to put an arm round his shoulder and whisper in his ear. 'It's only for an hour and if your nightmares are true they may suggest what really happened in that bedroom.' She paused. 'Peter, my ex, thinks you have almost the whole picture in your sketches, but now they are just symbols. We have to try to translate them into facts. After all, they made enough impression deep down in your mind to surface as your nightmares so they're important. Now, I have a rough idea of how the events happened that night, but perhaps you can help me fill things out.'

'All right. It scares the hell out of me, but I'll do it – for you.'

Aileen had planned not a reconstruction of the crime since she was convinced that someone other than Weir had committed the murders; she had decided to pilot Weir through the actions he must have been aware of taking.

That night she drove them to the outskirts of Glasgow, turning off the Kilmarnock Road at Langside. There, she handed over the Rover to Weir. 'I know you came in that night along the

Edinburgh Road so we can go round Queen's Park and come in along Langside Road and that way to Creggan House.'

'I haven't handled a car for more than five years,' Weir grumbled, but he took the wheel and drove well in the dark, following her navigation orders which brought them in sight of the mansion at about 7.30, the time he had arrived on the fatal night. Weir drove up to the gate and halted but kept the engine running.

'It's not raining, but that doesn't matter,' Aileen said. 'What did you do at the gate?'

'I didn't stop, but opened it with the remote control and honked the horn twice.'

'The signal for Appin to come running.'

'Ay, and I wondered that he didn't, for the first time ever.' Weir turned his head fully to look at her with his good eye. 'That should have alerted me that something was wrong.'

Aileen dismounted and went to open the gate with her key and they drove up to the house where Weir stopped in the exact spot where he had parked the car that night, outside the garage with its three cars.

'I let myself in with my key,' he said.

'Here you are.' Aileen handed him the three keys she had for the house, and he opened the door and stepped inside.

'Was there a light in the hall?' she asked then crossed the hall to find and push the mains button. 'A light like that?

'Ay, there was. But no noise. Not a sound. I thought that funny. No dog. No servants and no one noticing that I had opened the gate and the front door.'

'What did you think?'

'I thought they might have taken Lorna to hospital. Meney had told me on the phone that she was desperately ill.'

'So you went upstairs.'

'I did. Like this.' Weir stepped softly to the curved staircase and mounted two steps then stopped abruptly. 'I heard a noise here,' he said. 'A clacking sound, like a door closing. Not a bedroom door. Something lighter. Like a cupboard door. It came from upstairs.'

'The wardrobe in the bedroom, maybe?'

'Maybe.' Weir resumed climbing the stairs to the landing and the corridor leading to the bedrooms. He had approached the door of the main bedroom and was about to open it when Aileen called out: 'Wait.'

He turned and looked askance at her.

'Was the door shut? I mean, did you have to turn the handle?' she asked. When he nodded, she had another question. 'Did you open it fully and was there a light on in the bedroom?'

'I opened it wide and there was no light.' He opened the door and stepped inside with Aileen behind him. For a moment he paused and ran a hand over his head. 'No, no light. Not even the light from the streetlamp that we see now. But there was a glimmer from the chandelier behind me. I saw the bed dimly but didn't have time to see if there was anybody on it.'

'So, the windows were shuttered.' Aileen went and closed the shutters on both windows.'

'They must have been.'

'Now you're standing there in semi-darkness. Did you try the light switch by the door?'

'I didn't have time.' A long pause while he stood there scanning his mind before he said, 'I remember there were several knocking sounds then a flash and a tremendous bang and I don't remember anything more.'

'The knocking sounds?' Aileen groped over to the wardrobe, took an object from her pocket and threw it on the floor in Weir's direction. 'Did they sound like this?'

'Ay, and I think there was a clacking sound.'

Aileen opened and shut the wardrobe door. 'Something like that?'

'Just like that.'

'Think of the flash before the bang. Did it light up anything? The bodies on the bed? A figure?'

Still standing just inside the door in the dark room, Weir tried to recall that precise moment, but it would not come. Finally, Aileen felt her way across the floor and switched on the chandelier light. Weir glanced round the room, his eye halting on the double bed, the bedside tables, the table, the wardrobe, the patterned wallpaper. They were familiar since he had used this bedroom for several years. But now he could find no inspiration from them.

'Think hard, Cal,' Aileen said. 'That flash lit up your mind. Somebody must have caused it. You saw nobody.'

Weir shook his head. He sat down on the edge of the bed for a short while and shut his eyes to let his mind concentrate on that moment. Aileen retrieved the cricket ball she had thrown on the floor. She did not attempt to prompt him, but let him sit there.

Finally he said: 'I don't know if this happened, but I'm almost certain I didn't fall straight away. Something hit me in the chest and knocked me back against the door. Then I fell.'

'Was it a blow?' Aileen asked. 'I mean, did you have a bruise there after your arrest.'

'No, nothing.'

'And you never saw the bodies of Lorna and Kanaday?'

'I only saw them when I came to and the police were smashing their way into the house. And I couldn't think that I hadn't murdered them then mutilated them. I felt as though I was breaking surface after an anaesthetic.'

'But you told me you never took any drugs.'

Weir nodded his confirmation.

Aileen sat down beside him and produced the strip-cartoon series of sketches he had done showing the crow, wolf, the death's-head with the poison chalice. 'Something that happened here in those moments must have given rise to these dreams and the nightmares you still have. They must mean something. For instance, did you see a helmeted figure?'

Weir pointed to the sketches. 'Those dreams say I did, but there's nothing like that in my conscious memory.'

Aileen gave up that line. She described how one witness at the trial, Mrs McDonald, had described seeing him go back to his car, presumably for the gun and the jack handle. Did he have any recollection of doing this? Weir shook his head and said emphatically that he could not have even thought of it. A mechanical illiterate, he did not even know where the jack handle was kept in his Rover. And as for the gun, he knew that was not in the car, for he had put it in his desk drawer in his study. As he had already told her, it was something he carried when he was on newspaper assignments in unfriendly countries, but he had never once used it, even in practice. Firearms made him nervous.

'How do you think your prints were on it when the police found it beside you?'

'They'd probably been there a long time.'

'So, somebody could have used the gun wearing rubber gloves,' Aileen mused. 'How did they get your gun?'

'Money knew where it was. So did Jamie and probably the servants and Lorna.'

Aileen looked round that sinister room with its double bed and bedside tables, its table and chair. She gazed at the huge wardrobe and knew what her mind was searching for.

To Weir she said: 'Calum, when you came round and they found you, could you make out what they were asking you?'

He shook his head. 'I didn't really know where I was. And I couldn't hear a thing. I was deaf.'

That was what she was trying to remember. From her handbag where she had kept it, she produced the small yellow cylinder of plastic foam – the earplug that she had picked up in the wardrobe. She held it up for Weir to examine. 'Did anyone in this house ever wear earplugs like this – for the noise, or to sleep?' He shook his head, and she went on. 'Then whoever was waiting for you in this room was wearing this and probably another like it.'

'So you think he threw a stun grenade and that knocked me out and deafened me.'

'I'm sure of it,' she said.

She could see that her crude replay of the murders had shaken him. But she had one more question for him.

'Everybody I've met says you looked dazed or drugged – anyway disorientated – when the police found and arrested you. How did you feel the next day?'

'I felt bloody awful,' he said. 'As though I'd mislaid a bit of myself. I was light-headed and as though I was walking on air.'

It was the answer she had expected.

'Calum, somebody carried out those murders and pinned them on you. Who do you think might have plotted to murder Lorna and Kanaday and incriminate you?'

'I've turned that over in my head for more than five years – maybe Johnnie Marr, though I wouldn't know why he'd want kill Lorna and put me away.'

'Could it have been Liz, your ex? Or Jennings, the bent policeman? Or Jamie? Or even Dan Meney?'

Weir shook his head at these suggestions saying that if Liz Maxwell and he weren't the best of friends and she could be something of a Lady Macbeth, he didn't see her going this far. Jamie wasn't involved, he was sure.

But on the drive back to the hotel he was silent and she could see he was trying out on his mind each of the characters she had mentioned as the sort who hated him enough to frame him for two murders.

They had supper in their room. She suggested watching the TV news but he shook his head and said he wanted to go for a walk in the woods. It was a limpid evening and the low hills to the east were lit and silhouetted by the silver-blue aura of a rising moon. They took the track along the stream and found a bank with a stand of elms and birches behind it. Calum took off the suede jacket she had bought him and placed it on the ground for them to sit on. Now, a reddish half-moon and the more brilliant stars were visible through the tall birches and elms. Night sounds echoed through the forest air. They heard the soft calling of wood pigeons and the raucous voices of rooks in the treetops and nearby a rabbit or a squirrel scuttled and rustled through the undergrowth. They sat silent for some time, until the yellow patina of the waxing half of the moon settled on the stream and the scrub on the other bank. It was a warm and still autumn night, breathtakingly beautiful, and they sat side-by-side silent, watching the moonlight tracking in the slow water.

Weir felt for her hand and held it in both of his. He said, 'It's a funny thing, a life. I've never known whether it's already scripted for us, or we script it ourselves. Who'd have thought up the sort of script I've had?'

'You were given some terrible lines and terrible scenes, Cal.'

'Ay, but some good ones, too.' She felt the pressure on her hand grow, and he turned to look at her, then said, solemnly, 'You're one of the good ones, Aileen Seaton. Know something? I've never said this to any woman, even to the two I married. But I have to and want to say it to you. I love you.'

'Cal, you know I love you.'

'I know that, and I know how lucky I am.' He fell silent. She had never seen or heard him in this meditative phase before, but she waited for him to break his silence. 'We all have the right to love, but most of us never express our love fully, for we never find the person who will accept it all and give everything in return.'

'Cal, I've wanted you to make love to me since the first day we met.'

'There's only one thing,' he said. 'For the first time in my life, I'm scared ... just scared I won't measure up to your idea of me.'

She did not reply but put an arm round him and buried her head in his shoulder. With her other hand, she explored his face, brushing the healed scars round his blind eye with her fingers then running them through his hair.

Calum lifted her face and kissed her, feeling her mouth open to let his tongue play with hers. His hand went gently under her blouse to her breasts and she reached behind her to unclip the halter of her bra and let him caress the ruched flesh round her nipples and feel them harden under his touch.

She was running her nails over his chest and feeling downwards when he tensed and she felt his hands go still.

He breathed into her ear: 'Aileen, darling, it's too quick for me, it's swamping me ... I'll have to stop for a minute.'

'Cal, darling, there's no hurry and don't worry.'

They pulled apart and relaxed for several moments but neither of them could stop what they had begun. Aileen took off her leather jacket and placed it on the ground. They lay down and began to fondle each other, Aileen taking the initiative and leading his hand to her breasts, then to her pubis and the cleft of her sex. She, too, was having to clamp down on the emotions that were surging through her. She groped for his penis, which expanded in her hand.

'Cal, oh Cal, I can't wait, I can't wait,' she whispered as she pulled him over her and opened everything to him.

'Slowly and we'll come together,' he said as their bodies locked. She clung to him, wrapping her legs round him as he guided himself into her and began to thrust. And each thrust sent shock waves of emotion through her, picking her up until she knew he was reaching his climax. 'Cal, I'm coming,' she cried, and felt as if her whole body had been drained of all her energy. But it was a relaxed, wonderful feeling.

He was still clinging to her as though he never wanted their bodies to separate. So she lay there under him and whispered, 'Cal, I know now that nobody has ever made love to me before.'

'It was just how I thought the first time would feel,' he said. 'And it never did, then or any time until now.'

They lay in each other's arms without speaking, watching the moon and the stars through the tracery of leaves, listening to the forest; they heard the chucking of magpies, the piping sound of a young pheasant and the splat of something landing in the stream before them. And Aileen played each sound back so that she would remember them and associate them with every other emotion of this night. She did not want to break the spell.'

When Calum stirred and made to rise, she checked him, whispering that she had blankets in her car and would fetch them. He insisted on going with her and they brought back enough blankets to keep them warm and a bottle of drinking water.

They slept, they made love again and woke with the rising sun in their eyes and regained their rooms in the hotel before the kitchen staff had started.

Calum had another week before he was due back in prison. They decided to make the most of it so they forgot about their inquiries. No one but her parents knew where they were so she switched off her mobile phone, put the inquiry to the back of her mind and said they were going to enjoy their last week. They drove for miles through the hills of the Southern Uplands and found picnic spots by burns among the purple heather where they spent the day and made love; they toured the countryside around Kilmarnock and Ayr, they walked hand in hand along the sugar-sand beaches of the Firth of Clyde at Saltcoats, Fairlie and Largs. They went hand in hand to Burns's cottage and birthplace at Alloway where he recited 'Tam o' Shanter' word for word and a dozen others of Burns's poems in Ayrshire speech and accent like the poet's own and filled her head with Burns lore in a way that she could never have found in books or imagined herself.

His two weeks ended all too soon. She wondered what he was thinking and feeling as she drove him back to Creeburn. He stopped her on a hill to look down at the prison with its high walls and barbed wire. 'Drop me at the gate and don't come in with me,' he said as he kissed her.

She was relieved, for she did not want to go inside with him. As she sat in the car outside the prison, he kissed her and held her tight, then pulled apart and looked at her.

'Aileen, watch yourself with people like Marr and Jennings.' She nodded, and he went on, 'If anything were to happen to you, or if anybody lays a finger on you, I swear I'll break out of this place and this time really commit murder.

chapter twenty-two

A fencer is covered when her sword-hand and sword are positioned to prevent the adversary making a thrust.

When she returned to her flat on the Sunday evening, Aileen had a dozen messages on her answering machine including one from Peter asking her to call him or come round. But she was much more interested in a week-old message from her secretary telling her that a lady called Begley had called to say she had found some of the documents that had gone missing and she was sending them by registered post to her office.

Aileen could not wait until she returned to her office the next day or even unpack her things to discover what those papers revealed. She had Flora Begley's home number and rang her, apologizing for disturbing her on Sunday, and explaining that she had just returned from two weeks' holiday and could not open her office until the next day.

Flora waved away her excuses.

'We've started an inquiry to find out how those papers we discussed went missing,' she said. 'But fortunately we had backed everything up on our main computer and we found the details there. I've printed them out for you. And just in case they get lost again, copies of everything have also been restored to the archives.'

'Did you find out what happened to Alexander Ross Cattanach?' Aileen asked.

'We did, and there's two pages of police report and a summary of the inquest verdict which was "accidental death by drowning".'

'What about Marr?'

'I found his birth certificate and that's with the other papers. Were you aware that he is illegitimate?'

'No.' Aileen managed to contain her surprise.

Although she was burning to find out who Marr was, she could hardly ask Flora to try to recall the details when the lady handled hundreds of birth certificates each day. She thanked her and said she would ring back if she had any queries about the papers.

So Marr was a bastard in every sense. Wait till Calum heard of this! He could not have known or he would have told her.

She called Peter's number and a breathless, tongue-clicking, sing-song voice said Dr Farley was busy and would madam call back when he was free. What had happened to Shanta? Had she finished her treatment sessions or had she merely been usurped on Peter's couch by a Chinese? Peter, she knew, was colour-blind but he always contended it affected only the reds and not brown and yellow.

She waited a few minutes and thought perhaps he did have a patient on his couch, so she unpacked and put away her clothes and tidied the flat. She had just made herself some coffee and was sipping this and sifting through her mail with half an eye on a TV news bulletin when someone rang her bell. Her videophone brought up Peter's face and she opened the street door for him.

'Sorry, I had to come round and tell you face to face,' he said.

'Why? – Didn't you want Suzy Wong to hear?'

'Her name's Mei-lu and she's doing a bit of secretarial work,' Peter said.

'Oh, I thought from her short-winded answer on the phone you were doing Falun Gong exercises together.'

'That's something I miss, Ailie – your sense of humour.'

Aileen offered him coffee, which he accepted on his feet. Spooning sugar into it, he lit a cigarette one-handed then sat down on the sofa next to her. He whispered into her ear: 'If you want to know, two things brought me round. One, I wondered how you were getting on and I had a yen to see you. And it may be paranoia, but I thought somebody was tapping my phone calls.'

'Why would they tap your phone?' she asked, though remembering how they had burgled her flat and she had her suspicions about phone-tapping as well.

'How do I know how many enemies you and your demon lover have?'

'That's what I'm trying to find out and why I came to you.' She realized he was uncomfortably close to her and managed to put a few inches of distance between them. 'You were going to see a pharmacologist about Calum Weir's amnesia the night of the crime.'

'That's really what brought me round. I did consult our needle-and-pill man, Philip Higgins.' He was twirling a lock round his finger, dialling outer space or his inner mind with his cigarette hand, and she wondered if his hair lotion was inflammable. 'Phil Higgins has more savvy than anybody I've ever met about drugs and their effects on the mind and body. And he has also read a whole archive of whodunits and knows a dozen perfect murder scenarios. Trouble is he hasn't the guts to try one on his wife.'

'Peter, I'm not interested in Dr Higgins or his domestic scene. Stick to the point and tell me what he thought about Calum Weir.'

'I told him the tale and he has an idea of how Weir might have come to murder two people without knowing where he was or what he had done.'

Aileen stopped him as he made to continue; she reached into her handbag for the notebook in which she had recorded the facts about the Weir case.

'OK,' she said, 'fire ahead.'

'Higgins thinks that if he was set up for the crime, he might have been hit either with a stun grenade which would have blinded and dazed him. Or a stun gun which might have knocked him out for several minutes. Then whoever was waiting for him used a short-acting barbiturate anaesthetic like thiopentone sodium or methahexitone sodium to keep him unconscious. You can time these anaesthetics to the minute and they leave hardly any trace in the cells....'

'But surely they wouldn't completely rub out his memory,' Aileen commented as she wrote down the chemical terms for the anaesthetics as he spelled them out.

'No, perhaps not everything. But Phil says there's a whole range of hypnotics and anxiolytics called benzodiazepine which can cause transient amnesia in the right dosage. And this effect is heightened if they're used with barbiturates. It could be that someone might have learned how to use them to erase that half-hour.'

'But they'd be difficult to give, these anaesthetics and drugs.'

'Are you joking?' Farley said stabbing a finger at the crook of his left arm to mimic injecting himself. 'Any heroin or coke addict can find a vein and use a syringe even in a dark alley.'

'Would the police have found those drugs if they had done their job properly that night and taken blood samples?'

'Hmm. If they'd taken blood samples quickly they might have found traces of the anaesthetic. And they'd have found the benzodazepine drug for a day or two afterwards. But from what you say they weren't bothered about the finer points of proving his guilt.'

When Aileen described how Weir had felt light-headed and disorientated for days after his arrest, it confirmed in the psychiatrist's mind that someone had indeed planned and carried out an ingenious crime and pinned it on Weir. When she had made all her notes, she looked at him. 'I don't know how to thank you, Peter,' she said.

'You only had to ask,' Farley said. He looked round the living room then at her. 'You know, I never found a flat I liked as much as this one. But that's because it has so many great memories for me. And tonight felt just like old times, *chérie*.'

'Old times are old times.'

'But we had some good times, some great times.'

'Those are the ones to store in the memory.'

'Ailie, darling, it was the saddest day in my life the day I packed up here and we parted company. I've always thought we'd somehow get back together.' His arm had gone round her shoulder and he edged nearer her and whispered in her ear, 'I always thought you were the prettiest woman I ever had on my couch – and the sexiest.'

She realized that he was becoming amorous and reached up and removed his arm. What happened next took her completely by surprise. He turned and pinioned her body against his with his right hand and put his left hand behind her head and thrust his face against hers and kissed her brutally. Still confused by the speed and violence of the attack, Aileen felt herself being forced back on the sofa and a moment later he was on top of her, hoisting her skirt and grappling with her underpants. She felt his excitement in the quick rise and fall of his body. He had loosened and opened his trousers and had caught the band of her pants and was pulling them over her thighs when she realized he meant to rape her.

'Peter, you bloody fool, stop it!' she yelled. But he paid no heed.

Aileen tried to wriggle free and roll off the couch, but he had her pinned with his weight. She did the only thing left to her. Making a blade of her right hand she swung her arm and brought the edge of her palm down on his neck just below his left ear. Even that did not stop him, so she chopped and chopped again at his neck until finally she hit an artery or a nerve. His head lolled and he slumped over her. She kicked and pushed his inert body off the couch and got to her feet.

When she had pulled up her pants and fastened her skirt, she stood looking at him. She was still shaking and bewildered from that assault by her ex-husband who had never before laid an angry finger on her.

Farley was coming round, shaking his head like a spaniel emerging from the water.

'What happened?' he got out, still on the floor.

'You tried to rape me,' Aileen said. She pointed to the door. 'Now get up and get out before I call the police and have you charged with attempted rape.'

'Aileen, let's be adult.'

Aileen walked to the hall phone and picked it up. 'You have ten seconds,' she said, her finger on a button.

Farley saw she meant it. He got to his feet and made, shakily, for the door and banged it behind him.

Aileen watched until he had left the building and was walking along the quiet street before she went and poured herself a sizable whisky and gulped it down.

She was still trembling.

chapter twenty-three

Compound attacks are so called when the actual attacking move-ment is preceded by one or more feints, these being made with the sole aim of drawing the opponent's weapon into one line and thus making it possible to hit him in another.

Next morning Sheila, her secretary, produced the registered packet containing the Edinburgh papers and handed them to her. Aileen was about to step into her office and open them in private when the girl stopped her. 'Mr Geddes rang for you a dozen times in the past ten days. He seemed so anxious to contact you I had a job stalling him.'

'Did he say what he wanted?'

'No, but he seemed to know you'd been in Edinburgh at the record office.'

'How did that come up?'

'He asked if you were back from Edinburgh, and I said I didn't know you had gone there and you were now on holiday.'

'And of course he asked where?'

'No, I think he realized he wouldn't get anything from me, and from what he let drop I think he knew you were with Calum Weir.'

'Our friend, Geddes, obviously has good sources.' Her mind went back a few weeks to the sight of Calum lying on a hospital bed, disfigured and bruised after being beaten up.

At her desk, Aileen opened the packet and saw Flora had done the papers up in a file, each one of them tabulated.

She recognized the copy of Marr's birth certificate. Flora was right. There it was in some bureaucrat's broad-nibbed copper-plate: John Iverson Marr, born at 56 Braemar Street, Bridgeton, on 15 June 1963. His mother, Margaret Iverson Marr, was listed as a spinster, aged thirty-two. And in the column giving details of the male parent were two words only: Father Unknown.

So Marr had taken his mother's family name. And Father Unknown meant that the father refused to acknowledge the child. Or alternatively, Margaret Marr did not know who had fathered him.

Aileen turned to the death certificate of Alexander Ross Cattanach, which was dated 14 November 1974. It gave the details she already knew from the marriage lines and gave the cause of death as accidental drowning.

But one entry in the certificate hit her between the eyes. She read it three times before believing her own mind. Cattanach's address was given as 56 Braemar Street, Bridgeton.

She stared at the address for several moments, confused. It was hard to believe Cattanach was living with Marr's mother. How long had he been living with her? She knew that he had walked out on his own wife and son in 1962 and had disappeared without trace.

Calum's mother had never divorced and had died two years after Cattanach left them. So, he had most probably changed his name to Marr and no one in Bridgeton would bother whether they were legally man and wife. But when it came to acknowledging his child, Cattanach might have refused to have his own name on the certificate. Probably because he feared being discovered by his wife or later, his son.

And if he had fathered Margaret Marr's son....

That meant Calum Weir and John Iverson Marr were half-brothers.

Did it also mean that Marr took fright when he knew Calum Weir was writing his own story and was searching for his missing father?

She had another shock on reading the police report on Cattanach's death.

For the policeman called to the scene when they fished

Cattanach out of the Clyde at the Broomielaw Quay that night was none other than Police Constable Francis Jennings. He had signed the report dated 19 November 1974.

Jennings had taken a statement from Margaret Marr who said she had sent her thirteen-year-old son to look for his father, who had gone for a drink somewhere in the area of the Saltmarket, the other side of Glasgow Green.

That confirmed the evidence of the birth certificate. Cattanach was the father. So Calum Weir and Marr were half-brothers!

But according to that interview with the mother, the son had come home two and a half hours later, around eleven o'clock, without having found his father. He insisted he had looked in half a dozen public houses.

Yet Jennings had interviewed witnesses who claimed to have seen young Marr leaving one of the Gallowgate pubs with Cattanach around nine o'clock. Others saw them take the gate into Glasgow Green and head along the Clyde in the Bridgeton direction.

But the boy denied this and the constable could not find anyone willing or able to identify him.

Aileen wondered how hard Jennings had tried. She saw the ambiguity of the report and its omissions were as important as the facts it cited. Why did he not ask young Johnnie Marr where he had gone in the two and a half hours he was looking for his father? Which public houses did he visit in that time? And why no sworn statement from the boy?

Jennings had written that Alexander Ross Cattanach was the boy's natural father and had described how the mother sent the boy to fetch him.

His report contained details of the post-mortem findings, which proved that Cattanach had drunk the alcoholic equivalent of a half-bottle of Scotch whisky or ten pints of beer. According to the pathologist he had been in the water that bitter late-autumn night for just over two hours.

But what really gripped Aileen's attention was the fact that Alexander Cattanach had received two blows on the head from either a blunt instrument or a collision with something on the river bank or some floating object. Professor Maitland, the pathologist at the Western Infirmary in 1974, also found Cattanach had little water in his lungs, which suggested to him that he was unconscious at or just before the time he fell into the water.

However, his findings were ambiguous enough for the police to conclude it was accidental death. And for the coroner to agree.

So, Jennings's report was filed and the case closed almost as soon as it had been opened, for it was in no way rare to find drunks ending their days in the Clyde, either accidentally like Cattanach or voluntarily.

But why, Aileen asked herself, were Marr and Jennings so worried about the facts in that report and birth certificate that they had arranged for them to vanish from the Scottish Record Office archives? Did it give them a motive for setting up Calum Weir for the murder of his wife and her lover?

She must not forget Marr had been Lorna Innesfall's lover himself and might have been angry or jealous enough to order or commit the crime.

Those papers left such a host of questions in Aileen's mind that she realized only Marr and Jennings could supply the answers.

chapter twenty-four

*A warning line is a mark drawn near the edge of the piste to indi-
cate the competitor is in danger of overstepping the boundary.*

But Aileen had no intention of making a frontal lunge at
either of those two men. Instead, she rang Magee at the
Western Infirmary and said she wanted his advice about
something, to do with the Weir case, and could he give her no
more than five minutes of his time? Magee told her to drop in at
any time, straight away if it suited her. Evidently, he wondered
what she had found, and if it affected Professor Herbert Magee
adversely.

When she called at his small cubicle of an office she caught
him with a red marking pen ringing his selections for
Newmarket and Sandown in the margin of the *Sporting Life*. He
stuffed the paper in his drawer and held out a ham fist as she
entered.

'Now then, mavournin, what brings you here?' He had
produced his invariable packet of shag and was rolling himself a
cigarette.

'Before I tell you, professor, I want you to swear that this is
strictly between ourselves.'

'On the head of St Patrick himself.'

Aileen outlined the substance of the report on Cattanach's
death without revealing the name of the dead man. What she
wanted to know was whether after nearly thirty years a forensic
examination might tell whether a blow to the head was inflicted
before or after death.

'What sort of death was this?'

'Drowning. The body had been in the water for two hours, and there was little or no water in the lungs.'

'Who did the PM?'

'Professor Malcolm Symes Maitland. Did you know him?'

'Ay, I did that – though near the end of his run. A good pathologist. A bit nit-picking, a bit inclined to – how'd I put it? – hedge his bets.'

'So you would say it's possible perhaps to revise what he said, even this far removed?'

'We're none of us, thank God, like the Holy Father in the Vatican – infallible.'

'Thanks, professor. That's all I wanted to know.'

When Aileen looked back, his long, horse face and Irish eyes had an expression of sheer mystification written all over them. Her own bet was that he couldn't wait to unload their confidential talk to the person or persons whom it might concern.

She had to wait three days before her secretary buzzed to say Mr Geddes was with her and wanted a word. Aileen kept him waiting for five minutes before allowing him to enter. He crossed the room and grazed both her cheeks with his lips, leaving her wreathed in his tobacco breath. They had not met since the night of his party. She waved him to the seat facing her across her desk.

'How're tricks, Aileen?' he said.

'So-so.'

'I hear you got my client out of prison. For a couple of weeks.' His voice had acquired a slight edge, which meant he might still consider Calum Weir his client, not to be poached.

'Sorry, I should have informed you. I did suggest to Calum that he ring you but he said your lines were still crossed.'

Geddes asked politely if his smoking would bother her and when she shook her head he lit a cigarette. His eyes had already fastened on the envelope she had left prominently on the desk with the Scottish Record Office stamp on it. Finally, he broke his silence. 'Are you getting anywhere with your crusade for Weir?'

'Yes, I am.'

'Would you like to talk about it?'

'Last time the name Weir came up you weren't all that keen to talk. Why now?'

'Just interested in my client.'

'What does that mean – you're looking for appeal work?'

They were like a couple of fencers measuring each other then feinting, thrusting and riposting, seeking the weakness in the opponent's defence before the lunge, the hit and the cry of touché. Aileen was drawing him forward along the piste to the point where she could mount and carry through an attack. And Geddes was probing at her defence, though wondering how and where she would strike.

'Appeal! He has a snowflake in hell's chance of getting an appeal hearing let alone winning an acquittal or a lesser sentence.'

'That's your opinion and I don't share it,' Aileen mused. 'I had thought of trying on the grounds of new evidence and the with-holding of prosecution evidence.'

That scored a hit.

Geddes snorted smoke and said, 'New evidence! What new evidence? And what didn't the prosecution disclose?'

'Quite a few things. For instance there were fifteen shots fired that night in Creggan House. Your friend Jennings didn't look hard enough. He missed a couple of other things, too.' She pointed her pen at him. 'Though not as much as Calum Weir's lawyer – you.'

'What did I miss?'

'You missed taking blood samples from your client and having them analysed. They might have revealed how the crime was committed by someone else. Without bothering to do your own homework, you swallowed everything your friend, Jennings, told you and concluded that Calum Weir was guilty. So you put up hardly any defence, and everybody knows that. Including you.'

'I told you that if you take that line I'll have you up before the Bar Council,' Geddes snapped.

'That could be interesting, too, since it would give me the chance to cross-examine you,' Aileen murmured. 'Anyway, who sent you here to pry or spy?' Aileen said. 'Was it the devious Superintendent Jennings? Or his boss, Sir John Marr?'

'Don't be insulting!'

'Bob, you're getting very thin-skinned for somebody who likes to throw the law book at other people. As you know, sometimes it boomerangs and knocks the thrower out.' Geddes was on his second cigarette and trying vainly to suppress the fury which had twisted his features into a tight clench. To break the tension, Aileen rose, found an ashtray and pushed it across the desk for Geddes's spent stub. She kept her voice light as she said, 'As a matter of fact, I was going to ring Sir John myself and ask if he'd see me and answer a few questions.'

'Not a hope,' Geddes said, making a backhand gesture to emphasize his statement. 'He thinks you're obsessed with Calum Weir.'

'That's my business,' Aileen said. 'But all I wanted to do was whisper one word in Sir John's ear – and ask him to try it on your mutual friend, Jennings. Perhaps you can pass the word on for me.'

'What is this word?'

'Cattanach. Try it on both of them. They'll get the message.'

'Who or what is Cattanach?'

'Go and ask them.'

'I'd just like to know what game you're playing,' Geddes muttered.

'Bob, believe me I'm glad you don't know.' Aileen looked at her watch and said, 'Sorry, but I have an important appointment and have to go. Let me know where and when Marr and Jennings would like to have a chat with me. It's in their interest and I think you should be there, for there might be things that concern you.'

She escorted Geddes through her office and out the front door. Bewilderment was written all over him, from the hunched shoulders to his slow-footed stride as he walked off.

Sir John Iverson Marr had a big house with a high wall round its fifteen acres on the borders of Bearsden and Milngavie. He had bought the mansion and its dependencies, including a swimming pool and a nine-hole golf course, as a job lot from a shipping millionaire who had gone bust.

Geddes had fixed the appointment within a day of their chat, although he obviously remained unaware of why Marr had agreed so quickly. He drove her to their rendezvous at six o'clock in the evening. He surprised her with the awkward and uncertain way he handled his Jaguar. This wasn't the self-assured man she had witnessed in court dealing with gangland toughs and drug dealers without a tremor; now he was as twitchy as a badly-strung puppet and she wondered if he'd get them there in one piece through the rush-hour traffic.

He knew the routine, taking them past the gate guard with his Alsatian and along the rhododendron drive that was certainly under surveillance by other bodyguards. Marr did not meet them himself. A manservant led them through the entrance hall and a vast living room with mixed furnishings – modern Swedish-style chairs, table and sideboard, several other pieces in chrome and glass and a few oriental rugs scattered here and there on the polished marble floor. They followed the servant on to a terrace where Marr and Jennings were sitting drinking champagne. Both had smoked cigars to the halfway mark, which meant they had spent time discussing her visit.

Even then, Marr did not rise, but nodded at Geddes, fixed his pale eyes on Aileen, and waved them to seats. They had placed Aileen with the sunlight in her eyes, whether purposely or not she could not guess. She had only seen Marr in dim light at Geddes's party but now she had a close-up. He was dressed in a white, open-necked shirt, a cashmere sweater and light slacks with sandals on his feet. With his cropped beard he might have looked to some like a latter-day buccaneer. But to her he never seemed other than a spiv or a yuppie.

But Marr obviously felt he fitted into the high life as he sat by the drinks trolley with its champagne in an ice bucket and looked over his blue-water swimming pool and golf course, his tennis courts and regimented gardens. From having met him she knew he was intelligent; from reading his background she realized he was a ruthless thug.

He had already made it clear tonight that this was not going to be a friendly get-together. That suited Aileen, who was determined not to let this man or his police lackey scare her.

Jennings was sitting to Marr's right. He gave her a dry nod and helped himself to one of the canapés on the drinks trolley. Geddes had sat down beside Aileen.

Marr glanced at the manservant, still standing by the trolley, and the man turned to Aileen, inclining his head. 'What would madam like to drink?' he said.

'Nothing.'

'Not even water?' Marr said with heavy sarcasm.

'I'm not thirsty, and I didn't come here to drink,' Aileen said to match the tone they were setting.

Marr signalled to the manservant that he was no longer required and the man retreated into the house.

'Well, hadn't you better tell us what you came for?'

'Would you mind answering a few questions which bother me about the murders at Creggan House five years ago?'

Marr glared at her. 'Would I mind! You have a damned cheek to come here and question me about a crime which has been judged and doesn't concern me.' He emptied his champagne glass and half-filled it from the bottle. 'But since you're here....'

'Well, let's start by asking this: Why didn't you and your policeman friend, Superintendent Jennings, do anything to help your half-brother?'

From the way that Jennings's glass stopped halfway to his mouth and Geddes was pulling on his cigarette, she could sense that neither knew the full story. Nor, it seemed, did Marr.

'My half-brother?' he said.

'Maybe you didn't know, Sir John, but Alexander Ross Cattanach was Calum Weir's father.

Marr's pale blue eyes widened and his face was a study in confusion and bewilderment. He and the other two men watched as Aileen produced the birth certificate of Alexander Ross Cattanach, then the certificate of his register-office marriage to Margaret Brodie Menzies dated 1961. She followed this with Calum Ross Cattanach's birth certificate just over a year later.

Each of the men in turn studied the three papers before Geddes handed them back to her and looked at Marr, who was shrugging his shoulders and laughing openly, evidently relieved at what he had read.

'These documents are interesting as proof of the existence of Calum Ross Cattanach alias Weir. But what have they got to do with me and your absurd allegation that he is my half-brother?'

'Do you remember where you lived in Bridgeton, Sir John – the address where you were born?' When Marr hesitated, she went on, 'Wasn't it 56 Braemar Street, and weren't you born there on 15 June 1963?' As she spoke, she produced Marr's birth certificate showing that John Iverson Marr was born to an unknown father and had been given his mother's maiden name. She passed the certificate first to Geddes, who stared at the column with Father Unknown written on it.

Marr and Jennings were looking askance at each other, wondering how to react. Aileen guessed they had never thought to see that piece of official paper again. She caught the superintendent looking at the leather wallet in which she carried her papers, no doubt asking himself what other shocks she was going to produce.

Marr, too, had lost some of his poise, but he glared at her and said, 'All right, if my father was unknown how are you going to prove he fathered that scribbler and murderer, Weir?'

From her wallet, Aileen had conjured another document which she handed to Geddes who in turn passed it to Marr.

She said, 'It helps to know that Alexander Ross Cattanach had lived at 56 Braemar Road, Bridgeton, and was buried from there on 21 November 1974.'

Geddes put up a finger to halt her. 'You say he was buried from there. Didn't he die there, or in hospital?'

'Neither,' Aileen said. 'He died by drowning in the River Clyde on 19 November but the circumstances of his death are curious. You see....'

'Now wait a minute, Miss Seaton,' Marr interrupted. 'Before you start making wild allegations, remember there are two witnesses here who can repeat anything you say before a libel judge and jury.'

Aileen turned to him, surprise and amazement on her face. 'Who said I was going to make allegations? How Alexander Ross Cattanach died is all here in black and white, conceived, written and edited by one of the company here, Superintendent Jennings, who was then Police Constable Jennings.'

It was the coup de grâce. Marr and Jennings could hardly credit their sight when they saw the police report that the policeman had written nearly thirty years before. Before they could act to stop her, she passed it to Geddes, who ran his eye quickly over the two-page official document then handed it to Jennings, who had gone white in the face.

'Where did you get that?' Marr said, pointing to the file.

'Not in the Scottish Record Office archive,' Aileen said. 'Somehow that document and your birth certificate had vanished from the paper records, though fortunately they had been backed up on the computer files. Edinburgh is holding an inquiry into the whys and wherefores of the disappearance of the originals.'

'Are you implying that someone stole them?'

'Not just someone,' Aileen murmured. 'It may be the same person who took the SIM card from Weir's mobile phone after it had been consigned like other exhibits to the High Court archives.'

A chill had descended on the terrace. Although he had not uttered, Aileen sensed that Geddes was beginning to understand that the Weir case was not as simple and straightforward as it had appeared to him when he was defending the accused man in court. He had already burned half a dozen cigarettes and was looking queasy and even more twitchy than usual. Jennings had turned pale. And Marr? Aileen had noticed that under his spiky eyebrows his curious pale eyes had turned blue-green; and from the way they were sparking and the glowering set of his face, she had the impression that he would rape her without taking any pleasure from it and then get his real kick by strangling her. Or the other way round. She was glad she had invited Geddes to monitor the proceedings.

Geddes finally broke his silence by turning to Aileen and asking, 'So, you think there was something odd about the way Alexander Cattanach died, is that it?'

'One of the things,' she replied. 'I think Jennings did thirty years ago in the Cattanach case what he did five years ago in the Weir case – he very conveniently failed to ask the right questions.'

'Why are we listening to this crap?' Jennings said, looking at Marr who motioned him to shut up.

'What are the right questions?' he asked.

'Well, imagine a mother sends her son to fetch his natural father whom he meets and who then disappears into the Clyde and drowns. The boy also disappears for more than two hours. Constable Jennings doesn't ask where the boy has been and if he met his father. He does not take statements from witnesses who saw them together on Glasgow Green. He doesn't go into the relationship between the boy and his drunken father, whom he hated and who beat him. Or the boy's attitude to his mother, whom he worshipped. A classic Oedipus Complex. But nobody expected a constable to know the story of how Oedipus murdered his father and married his mother or how it might apply to a sordid situation on a chill November evening in Glasgow. He never even mentioned that Cattanach refused to acknowledge his son. Or why he did not marry Margaret Marr. He did not wonder if he was already married and had a son. Calum Ross Cattanach alias Weir. So he did not discover that Cattanach had walked out on his wife and one-year-old son, moved a couple of miles south-east and lived for more than thirteen years with Margaret Marr using her name until an official death certificate had to be filed. It would be interesting to have a look at the notebook in which Constable Jennings recorded the data which he edited for his report.'

She could see that Marr was suppressing his rage, but his face mirrored something else: fear and anxiety.

'She's crazy,' he said through his teeth to Jennings and Geddes.

'That's what they'd say if she took that story to the procurator's office,' Jennings said. 'They'd ask for proof, not a fairy tale.'

But even with Marr looking askance at him, Geddes remained silent.

'Do you agree, Bob?' Marr asked.

'It would be hard to prove – or disprove,' Geddes said, defensively. 'But I'd like to hear what else Aileen Seaton has to say.'

'It might suggest grounds for an appeal,' Aileen said, then turned to Marr and Jennings. 'You're both probably wondering why I went to the bother of getting these papers. It was because Calum Weir had been making inquiries about his father for a memoir he was writing about his own career.'

'What has that got to do with me?' Marr said.

'Just this. You or someone close to you has gone to a lot of trouble to suppress details of your birth and your father's death. You might have wondered what Weir might come up with when he started probing his own background. How many skeletons might fall out of your cupboard. You dismiss Weir as a scribbler, but you realize scribblers are dangerous. So, why shouldn't you try to suppress Weir as well by setting him up for two murders.'

Marr sprang to his feet and pointed at her, his face livid with fury. 'Get out of here with your bits of paper and your crazy notions. Get out.' He bent down and pressed an electronic buzzer on the trolley, which brought the manservant to the terrace. 'Show this woman out now,' Marr shouted at the man.

But before the man had taken two steps, Geddes had risen and gripped Marr by the arm. 'Wait a second, Johnnie,' he said and drew Marr to one side and beckoned Jennings to join them. He whispered, 'We've got to hear her out.'

'Why? To listen to a lot more slander from this nit-picking legal twit who has all but called me a murderer?'

'We've got to learn what she's found and why she thinks you and Frank are involved. There may be things we don't know ourselves. What if she has found grounds for an appeal and we're caught wrong-footed?'

Jennings backed his argument, they returned to their seats and Marr waved his manservant back into the house.

'All right, Aileen, you have a stay of execution,' Geddes said, with half a smile. 'Maybe you'd like to tell us what you really think happened the night of the crime at Creggan House.'

Aileen realized what arguments he had used to convince Marr.

However, she had not counted on having to relate the story of the Creggan House murders almost like a prosecuting counsel. But having lived and breathed the Weir case for four months, she knew more about its background than Jennings and Geddes, the two men confronting her, who had handled the investigation and the trial and now had doubts about their performance.

She started by saying, 'For me, the Weir case began with Dan Meney, who confessed with his dying breath that Calum Weir was innocent.

'This same Meney was the man who rang Weir on the evening of the murders to tell him, falsely, that his wife was seriously ill and he should return at once. We do not know who persuaded or forced Meney to betray Weir, one of his friends.'

As she spoke, Aileen opened her purse and extracted a SIM card and saw every eye riveted on the stamp-sized object with its electronic chip. 'This is the SIM card from Meney's mobile phone and in it he logged the numbers he used most.'

'Where did you steal that?' Marr snapped.

'I picked up his phone by mistake when I pulled him out of his waterlogged car.' She glanced at Marr. 'It has your fixed and mobile numbers, Sir John, but then Meney did errands for you and probably got his fix of heroin or coke through you.'

'That's a damned lie.'

'Never mind. Meney did what he was bid and we have Weir on the road that wet night returning to Creggan House. But when he got there around seven-thirty both his wife, Lorna, and her lover, Kanaday, were already dead. They were dead but not yet mutilated as the post-mortem evidence showed – though nobody ever mentioned this at the trial. They had been shot in the head at point-blank range.'

'Now how the hell can you prove that?' This time it was Jennings who put the question.

'Because fifteen and not twelve shots were fired in that bedroom. If you and your detectives had looked they'd have discovered three bullets in the skirting and the cornice. The first three lethal shots were probably fired with a silencer—'

'The first three shots....' Geddes prompted.

'Two for Lorna and Kanaday and the third for Weir's dog, Appin,' Aileen explained, then went on, 'The other twelve were fired after Weir was in the bedroom. Nine of them were fired into the dead bodies, the three others at random so that anyone hearing them would say there were twelve shots.'

None of her audience of three said anything; she did not know whether it was because they were gripped by her account or afraid they might give something away. But anyway, they were listening intently.

'So we have Calum Weir coming into the bedroom expecting to see his wife lying there, seriously ill. But he had only a fractional glimpse of the bodies before he was knocked out by a tremendous flash and bang, most probably of a stun grenade but perhaps an electric stun gun.'

'That's pure supposition,' Geddes put in.

'I said probably,' Aileen conceded, fumbling in her wallet for a small plastic bag in which she kept the earplug and the clip. 'This is an earplug which I found in the wardrobe. I think it was left by the murderers who were waiting for Weir. I don't know what the clip was for.'

'All right,' Geddes said. 'They've stunned him. What do you suggest they did next?'

'They needed half an hour to fire the shots, mutilate the bodies, alert the police and make their getaway. So they kept Calum Weir unconscious with a short-acting barbiturate anaesthetic.' She paused to let them digest those facts then said, 'I'm told that if the anaesthetic had been mixed with one of the benzodiazepine drugs the combination would produce amnesia. That is what I think happened, and why Calum Weir had no recollection of what happened in that half-hour and even persuaded himself he might have murdered his wife and her lover. Unfortunately, no one thought of analysing his blood to see if he had been drugged.'

'If that's your case it doesn't really amount to much,' Geddes said.

'That's ripe, coming from somebody who didn't make much of a defence at Calum Weir's trial,' Aileen came back. 'You missed vital post-mortem evidence and Jennings did not follow up important leads which I won't go into. I'm as sure of Calum Weir's innocence as I am of tomorrow. And Meney was also sure of it.'

'So you think I was behind the people who trapped him and set him up, is that it?' Marr said.

'You had the motive and the means,' Aileen said. 'Calum Weir might have raised an old skeleton in the shape of his father and yours. You had slept with his wife.'

'So had Tom, Dick and Harry.'

'You're a jealous man and here was Kanaday, one of your detested scribblers, pushing you out of Lady Lorna's bed and jumping in. And she had betrayed you.'

'Neither of them was worth a damn in my book.'

'And of course there's Jennings. Always around, always the handyman to clear things up and see that you're in the clear.'

Marr hoisted himself out of his chair and for a moment Aileen thought he might advance on her and strike her. Instead, he pointed a finger at her and then at the main door into the house. He did not raise his voice but it carried all the more menace for that.

'Bob, I don't give a tinker's cuss what you do with this crazy, obsessed creature, but get her out of my sight and keep her that way.'

Aileen had the last word. As Geddes took her arm and motioned her towards the house, she turned and said to Marr, 'Just in case you have any perverse ideas about having Calum Weir beaten up by your prison thugs as you did several weeks ago or trying to intimidate me, copies of all these papers have been lodged with my solicitor, who has instructions to send them to several journalist friends of mine and to contact the procurator if anything happens to Calum Weir or myself.'

Geddes pulled her away before she had time to savour the expression of pure rage on Marr's face.

chapter twenty-five

The target is the body area, divided into eight imaginary parts, in which hits are accounted as good.

Aileen was now more aware than ever that her every move was watched. Three days after confronting Marr, when she drove down to Kircudbright and Creeburn to see Calum, a Rover dropped in behind her and followed her as far as Kilbirnie before disappearing. As it was a brilliant autumn day and the trees were turning, she decided to take the coast road to Ayr and branch off there. Only when she was in sight of the Firth of Clyde did it strike her that it was in these hills that she had met Meney. And with him perhaps her fate.

Where was he going that day? Where had he been?

At first she had assumed he had fled from Glasgow in some sort of panic, maybe to escape from someone like Marr. But he had obviously stopped somewhere to take on such a load of drink. And heroin. It seemed he had just met his dealer. And why did he choose to reveal that Calum Weir was innocent? She'd probably never find the answer to those questions.

Calum was waiting for her in the same area where she had first seen him. He had the dogs with him and was throwing a stick for them and playing games with them. When they saw her crossing the patch of lawn with Ogilvie, Sami and Rory ran to greet her.

'I'll leave you here and pick you up in an hour or so,' Ogilvie said. He had still not completely forgiven her for twisting his arm about the men who had assaulted Calum, but he had backed her request for the two weeks' parole leave.

Calum came to meet her and took her hands in his. 'They don't like kissing in public here,' he whispered. 'It upsets the long-term men and it certainly would do that the way I want to kiss you.'

Meg still hadn't said hello to her and when she bent down to caress her, the whisky dog looked first at Weir and only then allowed Aileen to stroke her white head and muzzle.

'What's wrong with Meg?'

'Ah! Dogs, you know, are telepathically streets ahead of us. Meg knows you're trying to suborn me, to break up our partnership. So she sees you as a rival.'

'But you've put her right.'

'I've told her and the others that we leave together or not at all. But only Rory believes that.' He picked up Meg and fondled her and she responded by washing his face with her tongue. 'You know Meg had a hospital bed all to herself while I was away. She went on hunger strike and they had to feed her with a drip for two weeks. She's back to normal now.'

'And Sami – what did he do?'

'Sami was tunnelling in classic prison-escape style. He was halfway through a hole under the fence by the sports ground when one of my mates saw him and reported him to the authorities. They had to keep him locked up or on a lead for the fortnight.'

Aileen had a lot to tell him. She started by telling him what Peter Farley had said about the way the murderers had produced his transient amnesia by using barbiturate anaesthetics mixed with drugs. But Farley had also said his dreams proved he had remembered some things during that period.

Aileen had debated with herself whether to reveal how she had traced his father and found out how, when and where he died and the mystery surrounding his death. Finally, she had decided to withhold nothing.

Calum listened in silence as she narrated the details and how she had confronted Marr and Jennings with them in the presence of his lawyer, Geddes.

'So, like me, Johnnie Marr didn't know we were half-brothers,' Calum said.

'I don't think he did. What worried him more was the fact that you might reopen the inquest on your father's death and incriminate him. That worried Jennings, too.'

'It would make a big splash in the tabloids,' Weir said. 'Even if they didn't prove it.'

'I thought of that,' Aileen said. 'And wouldn't it be ironic if a certain Liz Maxwell broke the story?'

Calum laughed. 'She'd love to score one against Marr, but I would like to see her face if somebody on the *Record* scooped her with a story like that.' He thought for a moment then shook his head and made a backhand gesture as though to dismiss the whole thing. 'Aileen, honey, it's all water under Glasgow Bridge. My old man wasn't worth a light and I'm going to leave his obituary as it is.'

'I just wonder what Marr will do now, knowing we have the papers,' she said. 'I hope they give themselves away.'

They had an hour and it was a blue, limpid day with the hills seemingly pasted against the sky and their heather glowing purple. So she took his hand and they went on their favourite walk round his small kingdom of flowers, shrubs and vegetables. When they were moving through the flower beds, Calum suddenly stopped her.

'I've got something to tell you,' he said. 'They were wearing hoods or cowls,' he said. 'Like monks.'

'Who?' she asked, though aware of what was coming.

'The men in the bedroom.'

'How many were there?'

'Three.'

'Can you say anything else about how they looked?'

'I saw them in that flash.' He paused. 'It looked like flak jackets or anoraks, and their faces were covered. Maybe they wore goggles.'

'Goggles! Of course.' That clip she had found. 'Anything else?'

Calum shook his head, then looked at her with a new light in his face. 'I don't dream any more – but I'm beginning to remember. And that's due to you and your faith in me – and your love.'

'But there was something else,' Aileen said. She took a few steps to where tall, spiky stems were growing among a bed of trollius, delphiniums and other flowers. She broke off one of the stems, which were now topped by clutches of blue flowers, and brought it to Calum. 'That's why you were dreaming about aconite and wondering why it gave you nightmares and headaches.' She pointed to the cluster of brilliant blue flowers in the form of helmets. 'They look like monks' hoods,' she said. 'And that's what your subconscious mind was trying to tell you all the time.'

He stared at her. 'That's its common name,' he breathed. 'Monkshood.' He shook his head. 'Why didn't I twig it sooner?'

'Because you thought you might have been guilty of those murders, that's why.'

'Where do we go from here?' he asked.

'I go back to where the action is – Glasgow. And I hope I can put a name to those hooded villains.'

When her hour was up, they walked to the prison gate and she said goodbye to the dogs. Meg still seemed dubious about her but Rory planted his paws on her shoulders and gave her a lick.

Calum kissed her and whispered in her ear that she must watch every step she took, for the people who had planned and carried out the crime would not hesitate to kill again for they had nothing to lose.

chapter twenty-six

An attack can be made with a firm strong beat on the blade with the object of deflecting the opponent's weapon and so opening the line for a direct attack.

Three days after her visit to Creeburn Prison, Aileen returned to her flat after working late on a brief she had been persuaded to take by a firm of solicitors who knew her well. While she was working alone in the office, she had received two calls, the first a wrong number and the second from someone who had hung up as soon as she answered. She wondered if someone was verifying if the office was empty with the intention of burgling it.

She was already alert as she steered her Rover through the underground garage at her flat to her bay in the corner or she might never have looked twice at a strange car in a flat owner's place across the garage from her own; yet she did not feel unduly concerned since some flats were rented or the owners allowed their visitors to park in their space. This car, a BMW, lay empty and that reassured Aileen.

She shut her car door, opened the boot and picked up some shopping she had done earlier. As she was closing the hatchback she caught a reflection in its window and heard a click. She did not turn round, but her rear window showed two people opening the boot of the strange car and taking something out of it. They left the hatch raised as they turned round.

They were wearing hoods and even in the dim garage lighting she saw their faces were covered.

Fighting down her panic and moving deliberately, Aileen dropped her shopping bag and pulled her duelling sword out of its bag, drew on a glove and held the blade behind her leg as she closed the boot quietly.

As she turned slowly, she realized there were three men, not two. Emerging from the shadow of the car, the third man had something in his hand. And as he bowled it towards her along the concrete floor of the garage, a flash of insight told her what it was. There was no time to avoid the object or even escape by running.

All she could do was turn, run between her car and the wall and wrench open one of the rear doors of the Rover to close part of the gap. Shielding her body behind the door, she shut her eyes and clapped her hands to her ears.

Even then, the flash when it came partially blinded her through her closed eyelids. And the bang pierced her hands cupped over her ears and deafened her. It resonated in her head and set the air in the garage thrumming. So powerful was the blast that it thrust the car door against her, knocking her over on her back.

Aileen got on to her knees, dazed and groggy. She was still wedged behind the car door. Had she not had an inkling of what was coming she would have been knocked out cold.

Her duelling sword had fallen from her hand and she felt for it and grasped it round the handle. Somehow, that steeled her and gave her courage. She lifted her head slowly to peer through the car window.

One of the three men had climbed behind the wheel of their BMW and started the engine. Both the others were coming towards her, treading cautiously. One was making for her side of the car while the other went to cover the off side.

Their car had now backed out of its space and sat, its engine running and its boot raised.

Aileen stifled her nerves and her fear. They won't kill me here, she thought. They'll knock me out as they knocked out Calum. They'll dump me in the boot and murder me well away from here then dispose of my body.

Now as they approached, even in the poor light she saw the full significance of Calum's dreams: they had cowls like a monk's. And these, with masks and dark goggles, turned their faces into something like the death's-head in Calum's dream.

She thought: They'll think the stun grenade knocked me out. So, stay quiet, play possum.

Just the intimate feel of that sword in her right hand gave her the courage to wait for them. She felt tense, taut and nervous, as she did when waiting for the start of a bout. Only this time she'd be fighting for her life.

She watched the man on her side. His goggles were now dangling from his neck. She counted his steps. He could only reach her by coming between the car and the wall.

Aileen waited until he had advanced into the tight space then threw the car door forward, hitting him on the chest. As he fell backwards, she banged the door shut and bounded after him.

But before she could strike with her sword, she had to turn and confront the other man. He had witnessed what had happened and came running full tilt at Aileen.

She jumped over the fallen man and turned and brought the triangular blade of her sword down, giving everything she had, on the attacker's neck where it joined the shoulder. He staggered back with a yell, but before he could turn and run Aileen had hit him twice with the button of her sword. First she aimed at his breast bone and thrust hard as though she meant it to come out the other side.

That brought another bellow from him which hadn't died away before Aileen hit him again with the button of her sword under his rib cage just below the heart. That forced him back, his head down, grunting with pain and falling on his haunches.

At that moment, she heard a scuffling sound and looked round to see the man who had fallen was back on his feet and coming towards her. He was reaching for something inside his anorak when she struck him with the sword blade on his gloved wrist. Before he felt that blow and dropped his arm, she belted him again with the sword edge, this time on his neck just below the ear. That drew a tortured gasp from him and he stumbled backwards, his hand on his head. To cripple him and prevent him coming at her again, she cracked his hand with the sword blade. A cry came from the driver of the car. It sounded like, 'Run for it.'

But nobody ran. And in those few seconds, her first assailant had got his wind back. She realized his thick leather jacket had absorbed some of the blows. Now he was boring in on her. He had something in his hand and meant to use it. And she could guess what it was.

Aileen could no longer take a chance with these two thugs. This man was coming at her, intending to kill her. It was him or her. As he rushed at her she knew what she must do. Throwing her weight forward on to her right foot and straightening her right arm, she aimed the blade at the man's breast bone and lunged with enough force to go through his clothing and stop him in his tracks or knock him cold.

But as he closed on her, he suddenly lowered his head and exposed his neck to the sword. Aileen held her lunging position and the man's own impetus and Aileen's rigid set did the rest. Even with a button on the end of her sword, it went through the goggles hanging from his neck, splintering them; it pierced his mask then struck his Adam's apple and pierced his throat before she could do anything to stop it. She felt it hit and splinter bone at the back of his throat.

A gasp burst from the man. He stopped in his tracks then keeled over on his face and hit the floor without another sound. Aileen knew he was dead before she withdrew the sword blade from his neck.

A yell came from the driver of the car, who had taken no part in the fight. He had kept the engine running and the boot open as though waiting to make a quick getaway. He had also seen what had happened to his two companions.

'Run for it before she kills you, Allie,' came the cry, high and piercing. 'It's no use, run for it.' One of the rear doors of the BMW was flung open for him.

Aileen had turned to ward off another attack; but the masked and hooded man had witnessed his accomplice die. He answered the cry. Turning on his heel, he half-ran, half-limped towards the car. He threw himself into the back and the driver gunned the engine and took off with squealing tyres and the boot lid still flapping open.

Aileen ran after the car, hoping that the ramp door would stop it. But it opened and the BMW scraped under with an inch to spare.

For several moments Aileen stood, still shaking from having to fight for her life. She went back to her own car. She could hardly believe she had killed this man who was spilling blood all over the concrete floor.

When she had taken several deep breaths and regained some of her composure, she pulled out her mobile phone and dialled Geddes's home number. She groaned when she heard his voice on the answering machine but as she was leaving a message he broke in and asked why she was ringing.

'Bob, I've just killed somebody,' she said.

'Aileen, I don't appreciate jokes at this time of night.'

'It's no joke.' She explained what had happened and he heard her out.

'Do you know who the dead man is?'

'I haven't looked and I haven't touched anything.'

'Have you rung the police?'

'Not yet. That's why I'm ringing you. I want to know if you could give me the name of a CID superintendent I could call.'

Geddes got her message. She did not want to ring the police and find Superintendent Frank Jennings on the scene. He said: 'Ring the central police station and ask for Detective Inspector Alec McLennan. If he's not there ring him at home and mention my name.' Geddes gave her the home number. 'And don't touch a thing.'

She ran McLennan to earth at home and he said he would be with her in quarter of an hour. Before he arrived Geddes rang her on his mobile phone from the entrance to the flats. She climbed the stairs to the front hall, let him in and led him downstairs into the garage.

'Good God!' he said, staring at the dead man then at the sword lying on the floor. 'You killed him with that!'

'There were three of them – and they meant to kill me, so I defended myself with the only thing I had.' She looked at him. 'Bob, I may need a lawyer. Would you take it on?'

'Of course. But wait and see what McLennan says.'

Detective Inspector McLennan was in his forties, tall with a Highland face and reddish hair and a voice with the accents of the Western Isles. He was a thorough professional, noting everything. Aileen described what had happened and Geddes informed the detective that she would make a full statement later.

Beside the man's body, they found a small, curved plastic device with two electrodes which McLennan picked up with a gloved hand. 'A stun gun,' he said, replacing it where he had found it. They found the remains of the stun grenade by the side of Aileen's car.

They had to wait until the police squad arrived with a pathologist to examine the body, a photographer to record the scene and two more detectives to search the premises. They put out a general alert for the other car.

Aileen was with McLennan when they came to remove the smashed goggles, the cowl and the mask from the man's head.

'Do you know him, or have you seen him before?' he asked Aileen.

She stared at the face. It was square. Its dead eyes were blue, washy-blue. Blond eyebrows and eyelashes. Long blond hair released from the cowl and covering his ears.

'Yes, I've seen him before,' she said, describing how she had met him at Creggan House on her second visit there. 'He gave his name as Mark Anderson.'

chapter twenty-seven

Closing in means the foil guards or fencers' bodies clash and prevent free use of the weapons. Closing in is penalized as dangerous and also makes good fencing impossible.

Aileen made a full statement to the police, who made no charge against her for the death of the man who had called himself Anderson. His real name was Richard Bryce Torrance and he had two convictions for burglary and assault. Since Torrance was legally an intruder with criminal intent, she had no other course than to defend herself. But Geddes warned her against making statements or trying to convince the police there was a link between an assault on her person and the Weir case.

'You still have to prove it,' he said.

'What more proof do you want? They tried to kill me. They were hooded and masked as Calum said they were at Creggan House. They used the same method – the stun grenade and stun gun. And I met Anderson on the crime scene. What more do you want?'

Geddes shrugged. 'You're a lawyer and you must know. Proof that'll stand up in court, that's what.'

Somehow she had to find the link between Anderson, the bogus surveyor, and the Creggan House murderers. In fact, she had to track down the two people who had escaped from the basement car park.

It was when she was sitting in front of her computer scrolling and scanning every note and comment she had made on the Weir case that Jamie Gilchrist's name flashed on the screen. And then on her mental screen as an inspiration. She rang Kirstie and asked if Jamie was at home.

'Ay, Jamie's here, but he's in bed.' Kirstie lowered her voice as though afraid someone was eavesdropping on her. 'He'll no' let on to me but his cocaine dealer's let him down and he's got the shakes real bad.'

That fitted Aileen's suspicion. She rang her father and told him to send Roddy on the next train with several doses of cocaine to be used both as a snuff and intravenously. If he did not have it in his surgery, Roddy should bring a prescription. An hour and a half later she met her brother at the Glasgow Central Station and with his prescription obtained the drugs from the pharmacy at the station. From there, she drove straight to Kirstie's housing estate and was shown up to Jamie's bedroom.

He was lying under a mass of blankets, visibly shivering and so agitated he could hardly speak. She handed him one of the phials of cocaine and they waited downstairs until he had injected it. Aileen gave him quarter of an hour until the drug had taken effect then produced one of the police 'mug shots' of Torrance and one of the photographs taken of him, dead, in the basement car park.

'Jamie, do you recognize this man?' she asked.

Jamie looked at both photographs then at her, quizzically. 'What's he done?' he asked.

'He's dead. He tried to kill me and his two mates will try again unless you tell me what you know.'

'Jamie, if you don't tell Aileen you'll no' live here a minute longer,' Kirstie put in.

Jamie looked at them then at the photographs. 'It's a man called Bryce,' he said.

Aileen nodded. 'His real name is Torrance,' she said. 'Richard Bryce Torrance. He was the pusher who supplied you with heroin and cocaine, wasn't he?' Jamie nodded. 'And Dan Meney? He supplied him as well, didn't he?'

'It was Dan put me on to him. Said he'd access to any amount of coke and horse and it was dead cheap.'

'But not so cheap when he blackmailed you and Dan by refusing to supply you until you both got him what he wanted.'

'What was that, Jamie?' Kirstie put in. 'What did you give him?'

Jamie hesitated and hung his head. 'How was I to know what he was gonna do?'

'So you gave him the gun – or was it the keys of Creggan House?' Aileen said.

'I let him have the keys for a day and told him the layout, that's all. It was Dan pinched the gun and handed it over.'

'And Dan who phoned Calum Weir the night of the murders?'

'Dan was never the same after that; he couldn't live with what he'd done,' Jamie said. He was now weeping openly. 'Nor me.'

'But when he thought you were going to talk to me he beat you up and left you at my door. It was Torrance that night, wasn't it?'

'He said he was gonna do you, too,' Jamie said through his sobs.

Aileen turned to Kirstie. 'Don't be too hard on him,' she said. 'I'll try to keep his name out of it, but if the police come asking questions, then it was Dan who gave the gun and the keys.' Aileen handed Kirstie the cocaine she had bought with the prescription. She also wrote Dr Peter Farley's name and hospital on her business card and handed this to her. 'If Jamie takes that card to Dr Farley on my behalf, he might help him break his addiction before it's too late. He was my husband and he owes me several favours.'

Driving back into the town centre, she replayed mentally the whole of that conversation with Jamie. Everything fitted, the keys, the gun, the plans, the phone call. But there was something else he'd said that had triggered her interest. Bryce had access to any amount of cocaine and heroin. Where would he get that? A pharmacy? Or a lab?

Then an image lit up her mind. A dark-eyed blonde woman, very handy with a hypo, doing a blood tap on a frightened guinea pig then picking it up by the ears and throwing it back into its cage with callous indifference. Then her voice with that faint Scottish burr, saying, 'Oh, the face ... the face.... It wasn't Ross's face … that face with all those gashes … and no eyes, no eyes. Who would do something like that to anyone? … Only a madman … only a madman like that piece of human scum, Weir.'

And Aileen's mind went back to those big, well-scrubbed hands of Alan Kelso's with their spatulate fingers and manicured nails. He slotted into the jigsaw, too. Hadn't Meney logged the code word ALLIE into his mobile phone with his other contacts?

Those images were suddenly heightened by the memory of a sharp cry echoing through a basement. 'Run for it, before she kills you, Allie.'

She had solved the riddle of Creggan House. With the help of Richard Bryce Torrance and her husband, Joan Kanaday had killed not only two birds with one stone, but three. She had killed her treacherous and lecherous husband and the blue-blooded whore who had stolen him from her. And in everything but name she had killed that piece of human scum, Calum Weir.

But it was one thing knowing, a very different thing proving guilt.

Since Geddes was keeping a watching brief on the case, she informed him of what Jamie had said and the conclusions she had drawn. Canny lawyer that he was, he warned her not to attempt to face two murder suspects on her own. They had nothing to lose by murdering her. Without incriminating Jamie Gilchrist, she must give certain details to Detective Inspector McLennan and carry out the investigation with him.

In plain clothes and in his own car, McLennan drove them down to Linwood and the Farmacogen Laboratories. When they asked the receptionist if they might see Dr Joan Kelso and Dr Alan Kelso, the girl rang the virology lab then the main office and lifted her head to say that both those research workers had taken a few days off.

McLennan had to produce his police card before she would give them the Kelsos' home address, which lay in the Whitehaugh district of Paisley. When the superintendent asked, she also confirmed that the Kelsos had not left an address where they could be contacted if on holiday. Which meant they were probably at home.

They found the house a few miles away and just off the Glasgow Road. It was a two-storey grey sandstone building with bay windows. It sat back from the road in its own small grounds and overlooked a golf course. A wall nearly two metres high surrounded it but Aileen and the inspector were able to study the house through the iron entrance gate.

Aileen pointed to the car sitting in the drive before the front door. 'I'm sure that's the BMW they were driving that night,' she said.

'Looks as though they've shut everything up,' McLennan remarked.

But on the side of the house they spotted another garage with a swing door and two slits of windows above the door for light and ventilation. McLennan peered at these and evidently saw something that intrigued him. 'Both those windows are shut,' he murmured then turned to her. 'We have to get in,' he said.

'But for that we need a magistrate's search warrant.'

'That means losing another day.' McLennan turned and grinned at her. 'You'll have to forget you're a lawyer and say we smelled gas and had to investigate if anybody gets inquisitive.'

As though he had foreseen this problem, McLennan had a bunch of several dozen keys in his car. He tried them one after another until one opened the gate. He did the same with both the mortice and Yale locks on the front door of the house and they were inside.

Even standing in the living room, they both caught the cloying, choking smell of carbon monoxide. McLennan unlocked and opened both the bay windows and beckoned her to follow him through the small passage into the kitchen at the back. There, the odour was stronger, almost overpowering. McLennan pointed to a door, which he opened. It led through a passage to another door connecting the garage to the house.

'We have to open all the windows,' he said.

They went round opening windows in the kitchen, the back bedroom and its bathroom, then the living room and even those upstairs.

'You stay by one of the bedroom windows,' the superintendent ordered her.

Aileen had thought he was exaggerating until he opened the door. A solid mass of monoxide gas filled the kitchen and the back bedroom where McLennan joined her with a handkerchief over his mouth. 'Hang outside and breathe until I say stop.'

They both hung over the windows sill for quarter of an hour before McLennan ventured into the garage and opened the slit windows to release the gas trapped near the ceiling. Again, he kept them waiting until he was certain that the garage was free from carbon monoxide.

'I've seen too many people die from this stuff,' he said. 'Monoxide sticks to the blood and suffocates you and it's a helluva job to get rid of it.'

In the garage, Aileen saw the Rover she had noticed when she interviewed the Kelsos at the Farmacogen Laboratories. A thick rubber tube had been tied round the exhaust pipe and led through a back window open about an inch and a half.

By the buttery light from the overhead bulb and the torch that McLennan had brought, she saw the Kelsos lying as though asleep on the back seat, their arms around each other. Joan Kelso's head lay on her husband's shoulder. With that practical mind and those practical hands, Alan Kelso would have seen they had enough petrol in the tank before he fixed their death line, started the engine then climbed into the back seat with his wife.

Both their faces looked anything but dead. They were bright pink, carnation-pink, and had she seen them in different circumstances, she would have sworn they were alive and just sleeping. But she remembered reading that the effect of monoxide on blood haemoglobin was to turn it pink.

McLennan was using his mobile phone to ring the central police station and ask them to dispatch the homicide team and a pathologist to the house immediately. While they waited, he made a quick check on the whole house as though hunting for something, but came back to the garage shaking his head.

'Were you looking for a suicide note?' Aileen asked, and he nodded. She pointed at Joan Kelso's body. 'Having met her, I don't think she would have left a note, but Kelso might.'

McLennan took the hint. With his usual meticulous care, he prised the bodies apart then methodically searched Alan Kelso's pockets, finding a wallet, car papers and a purse with notes and coins. It was in one of the zipped inner pockets of his anorak that he came across the unsealed envelope with H.M. CORONER printed across it in flaring letters.

Inside, there was a sheet of notepaper bearing the heading of Farmacogen Laboratories. It was dated two days before, the day after they attacked Aileen.

They both read his bold, cursive script by the light of McLennan's torch.

He had written:

To her Majesty's Coroner:
My wife, Joan Margaret Kelso, and myself, Alan Simson Kelso, have decided to take our own lives to atone for the crimes we have committed.

With an accomplice, Richard Bryce Torrance, we were responsible for murdering Lady Lorna Innesfall, and Ross Kanaday at Creggan House. They were planned and premeditated murders.

Not only did we premeditate and perpetrate the two murders, we also executed a plan to lay the guilt for this crime on the author, Mr Calum Weir.

We were also responsible for the murderous attack on Miss Aileen Seaton in which Torrance was killed.

It will be difficult for those who read this confession to realize that these crimes were planned and committed by two of the three people for the love of each other. Love perverted perhaps. But love just the same.

I beg the forgiveness of Mr Weir. I beg God's forgiveness and mercy for the untold harm we have caused innocent persons.
Signed: Alan Simson Kelso

Aileen could have shouted her joy at reading this note. It meant that a judge or the Home Office could free Calum immediately; that there was no need to go through the appeal procedure.

In the next two days, the police found ample evidence in the house to confirm what Kelso had confessed. They discovered the Creggan House plans and two sets of keys. In a locked steel box they found supplies of cocaine and heroin which explained some of the thefts from Farmacogen and the drugs that had gone to Meney and Jamie. There, too, were the phials of thiopentone and benzodiazepine drugs they had used on Calum Weir. In another trunk were the long, hooded anoraks, masks, gloves and goggles they had worn; and the stun grenades and a stun gun which they had also used. There were cheques showing payments of several thousand pounds to Torrance.

chapter twenty-eight

At the end of the contest, the on guard movements are reversed and the fencers salute each other and shake hands.

After the discovery of Kelso's suicide note, Calum Weir was granted immediate release from prison by a High Court judge. But he did not leave prison for another two weeks. Aileen and he had decided this, knowing if they gave a date they would have been mobbed by an army from the world media. Already the hotels from Ayr to Stranraer and along the Solway to Dumfries were full and dozens of reporters and camera crews were holding a round-the-clock vigil outside the prison.

But the man in question refused all interviews and rejected all the written propositions that were made for his story. He also declined to be transferred to another prison because that meant disturbing and moving Rory, Sami and Meg. He had requested that on his release the dogs leave with him and their owners, Ogilvie, the governor and the head warder had agreed.

Anyway, the media had already enjoyed their field day when the news broke that the real murderers of Lady Lorna Innesfall and Ross Kanaday had been unmasked. And, even more sensational, one of them had been killed in the act of trying to murder the woman lawyer who was fighting to prove Weir's innocence. It added bite to their story that the lawyer was also a champion fencer who had used her competition sword to defend herself and involuntarily kill her assailant.

For a whole week the Weir case was dissected by the media, with TV stations running whole programmes about it and featuring it in news bulletins; national newspapers carried pages about the original crime and trial and latest outcome. In their firing line was Superintendent Frank Jennings, who had no answers to the questions put by reporters and TV interviewers about his mishandling of the criminal investigation. Although he refused to resign, it became apparent that his career was finished.

Geddes also had to ship much criticism for his failure to exploit the weaknesses of the prosecution case and follow up obvious leads like the call Meney had made which set the trap for Weir. Why had he not called Meney as a witness for the defence? Geddes rode out the storm by finding himself an out-of-town legal case and going to ground.

Sir John Iverson Marr's luck held, for nobody thought of asking his opinion about the exoneration of his erstwhile friend, Calum Weir, let alone suggesting he had any involvement. But now he lived with the constant threat that the Cattanach case might be reopened.

During the days following the Kelso revelations, Aileen found herself under siege in her flat and had to change her number and remove it from the book to prevent her phone ringing day and night.

One of the people who rang her was Liz Maxwell, who was full of apologies for her high-handed behaviour, her doubts about Weir's innocence and dismissal of Aileen's crusade. Could Aileen see her way to arranging an exclusive interview with Calum? Could the *News* have his story when he came to write it? Aileen accepted her apologies but politely told her to contact Calum Weir herself; she had no authority to act for him. Wisely, Liz did not try to get in touch with her former husband.

Finally, in exasperation, Aileen went into hiding at Cromlin House Hotel with the Glencannons. But she still had to visit Calum. And although no secret agent ever took such elaborate precautions to cover his tracks as Aileen did on these prison trips, some reporters still caught her out.

Each time when she left the prison she was followed until she stopped and let them search her car to confirm that Calum Weir wasn't hiding in it. Every vehicle that left the prison was tailed to its destination by the whole media army. And every move she and others made was reported on TV, radio and in the press.

Yet there were things that not even the media uncovered.

That evening when she and McLennan found the bodies and the suicide note and were back in Glasgow, she rang the prison governor and told him she must come down to see him and Calum Weir. She had important news for them. At that moment, no one outside Geddes and a few police officers knew of the attack in the basement car park or the discovery of the dead Kelsos. Nothing had leaked from police headquarters and McLennan had imposed a news blackout.

When she got to the prison, Calum was waiting in the governor's office. Aileen described to both of them what had happened in the past two days. She then produced a photocopy of the note Alan Kelso had left and let the governor read it before handing it to Calum.

When he read it, tears brimmed over and ran down his cheeks. He sat down in one of the two chairs facing the governor's desk as though his legs had given way under him. Aileen went to comfort him and he put his arms round her, hugged and then kissed her.

Aileen told them she had already applied for the immediate release of her client from the prison and this would probably be granted the next day.

As she made to leave, the governor suggested she stay in the prison that night to save her the drive back to Glasgow over the hill roads in the dark. Although she had brought an overnight bag in case she had to stay in Dumfries, she accepted. They had an empty cell in the same block as Calum's and she moved into that.

Nobody could stop them making love. Or talking through the night. And it was while they were lying embracing each other on the single bed in Calum's cell that he whispered, 'Aileen, were you serious when you said you would sit here until I'd done my time?'

'Never more.'

'They have a chaplain here,' he said. 'He's a Heelanman, one of the Macleans of Mull.'

'Are you scared you'll change your mind?' she asked.

'Haven't you got that the wrong way round?' he said, running a hand though her long hair and over her face.

'Calum, I'm like Sami and Meg and Rory and you know how they feel about you.'

So, next day they were married in the prison chapel with the governor and his wife as witnesses. They celebrated their wedding in the governor's office with Ogilvie and his wife and three of the prison officers who had befriended Calum and whom they could trust not to leak the information. From somewhere, the governor had procured a bottle of Macallan whisky which Calum had not seen for years.

She knew that if the media had missed their marriage, it would not miss Calum's departure from prison whatever subterfuge they tried – ambulances, hearses, catering vans, helicopters. Their only hope lay in making a pact with the media.

So, they stipulated that if Calum Weir gave a press conference outside the prison gates on his release he would be allowed to go his own way unmolested.

Everyone agreed and two days later, Calum sat at a table outside the prison gates with Sami on his knee and Meg and Rory at his feet and answered questions about his side of the story of the Creggan House crime; he talked calmly, eloquently and without rancour about his five years in three prisons.

'What did you feel about those lost years?' someone asked.

'Those years weren't lost. I made some good friends on every side. I met the four creatures in this world that I love the most.' He held up Sami then Meg and lastly Rory, then pointed to Aileen. 'What more do I want?'

When he had answered all their questions and called a halt to the press conference, the hundred or so case-hardened media men burst into applause and several of them shouted their praise and wished him luck.

They had already packed Aileen's Rover and now they fitted the dogs into the rear seat, buckled themselves in and drove off towards the road for New Galloway. There, they turned off and made for the Kilmarnock Road but several miles along it she drew up by a burn. She let the dogs out and they scampered up the hill, Sami losing himself in the thick heather and Rory and Meg frisking with each other.

Calum and Aileen followed them and found a grassy patch to sit with their arms round each other and watch the dogs enjoying their free run.

'Aileen, my love, you haven't said where we're going.'

'You like Cromlin House, don't you?'

'It's the place I've dreamt about most for the past three weeks. Especially one corner of the woods there which is hallowed for me.'

'Well, I thought we'd have our honeymoon there.'

'I couldn't have chosen better. So, what have you in mind after that?'

'The Glencannons have a house near Strathyre, and I've rented it.'

'Bonnie Strathyre, among the lochs and the bens – it sounds great.'

'You can write your story there.'

'Story? What story?'

'The one you've been writing for the past three months. I've had a peep at your papers and your computer. I should confess something to you. I have received film offers varying between half a million and a million for your story and a dozen publishers are fighting like sharks for the book rights.'

'Aileen, honey, I've never given a damn about money. Tell them no.'

'Well then, you'll still write it – just for us.'

Calum went silent for a moment then turned and took her in his arms, kissed her, held her at arm's length and looked at her.

'What do you think I've been doing?' he said.

'You mean it's a love story?'

'That's what it was and is and always will be – a love story.'